G000153766

Return

Rosemary Gemmell

Opal Scot Books

First published in 2016 as a Kindle edition
Second Edition Paperback 2019

© Rosemary Gemmell 2019
Opal Scot Books

www.rosemarygemmell.co.uk

Return to Kilcraig is a work of fiction. Names, characters, places and incidents are the product of the author's imagination or are used fictitiously. Any resemblance to actual events, locales, or persons, living or dead, is purely coincidental.

ISBN: 978-1-9162577-2-6

Dedicated to my friends and fellow authors
Myra Duffy and Joan Fleming,
for all their encouragement, support
and conversation!

Return to Kilcraig

Chapter One

Christy Morrison stepped down from the train at Glasgow Central Station and took a deep breath. Almost home. Loading her two cases and bag on to a trolley with difficulty, she pushed them along the busy platform, searching for a familiar friendly face.

The wood-fronted shops and cafés on the concourse were a welcome sight as was the famous Victorian clock suspended from the ceiling; a meeting place for countless rail travellers over the years.

Cameron had offered to meet her and she couldn't wait to see him again. As she glanced around, Christy stood still. Making his way towards her was a familiar face all right, but it wasn't Cameron. She watched as Ross McKinley noticed her and continued towards her without increasing his pace.

She had time to note how he towered above most men, how his dark brown hair flopped slightly on to his high forehead, then she was staring into dark grey eyes that examined her solemnly.

"Hello Christy, welcome back."

He held out a hand and Christy hesitated. Then she let her small hand rest in his for a moment before she withdrew it.

"Hello Ross. I didn't expect to see you here."

"I had business in Glasgow yesterday and stayed over so I could meet you. Save Cameron a journey."

Christy smiled briefly and indicated her luggage. She wished his brother had come instead so she could chat without restraint. Although she was glad to have been met at all, she reminded herself. But there was still constraint between her and Ross that they'd never had a chance to resolve.

"The car's in the adjacent street." He lifted the luggage easily, leaving the trolley for someone needier and Christy followed with only her bag to carry, determined to keep up with his long strides.

Not exactly welcoming, but she didn't expect anything else of Ross McKinley where she was concerned. Their earlier friendship through childhood and teens had changed one year after a foolish New Year's kiss that she had treated too seriously and he had laughed off in embarrassment. She had been glad to spend her next few years studying and living in London with only fleeting visits back home to her beloved grandmother. And she didn't need Ross McKinley's unspoken disapproval to remind her how much she had let Gran down when she became ill. The guilt still followed her around at not being with the elderly woman in her final days.

Pushing such memories aside, she slipped into the passenger seat of Ross's BMW. She wasn't going to speak first, lest she be accused of distracting him from concentrating on driving out of the busy streets of Glasgow.

Sure enough, silence hovered between them until they were heading down the motorway.

"So, you'll be up on a quick visit again." The grave voice broke into her thoughts. "I expect you'll want to settle your grandmother's affairs and get back to London as soon as possible."

Christy remained silent while she absorbed his tone. So many assumptions and not a single question. Truth to tell, she hadn't come to any firm decision and hoped coming back here would give her the inspiration she sought. It would be unbearably sad returning to an empty cottage, but she longed for the peace of the hills and soothing of the river. She also had need of some solitude to finally come to terms with the trauma of her recent accident and devastating loss.

"I don't know how long I'm staying." That was all he was getting for now on the subject. "It was good of you to pick me up. Thank you."

It was his turn to be silent. Then she felt his shrug. "No trouble. As I said, I was in town anyway."

This time, the silence was more comfortable, as though both were content with their thoughts. Christy watched the passing scenery, struck again by the vivid shades of green and brown. The west coast might be one of the wettest parts of Scotland, but she reckoned it was also one of the most beautiful, with the hills and mountains reaching towards the sky, a glorious backdrop to the broad expanse of sea. The River Clyde accompanied them for part of the motorway drive, before the car turned off towards the countryside and Kilcraig where Christy had spent so many happy summers.

They arrived in the small village within the hour. She was surprised how quick the journey had seemed considering the lack of conversation, but was glad to escape Ross's enforced company before it became too strained.

"There's bread and milk and some basic provisions in the kitchen. We thought you might not have brought any with you."

The words were carelessly thrown at Christy as she closed the passenger door. At least he had the courtesy to get out of the car, she allowed.

"That was kind. Thank you." He could interpret the 'you' as singular or plural, for he probably wouldn't have thought of such kindness by himself.

"Well, I'm sure you'll want to get settled in." Did she imagine his voice softening for a moment? "I'll leave the cases inside the door for you, unless you want me to carry them upstairs."

"No, that's fine, thanks, I'll manage." She certainly wasn't going to let him haul her cases upstairs, no matter how difficult it would be for her. "But I really do appreciate the lift from the station." She received the merest flicker of a smile in response.

As soon as he had deposited the two cases in the hall, Ross turned and left with the briefest of waves. Christy closed the door behind him and suddenly felt like weeping. Coming back to her gran's empty cottage almost defeated her.

The whole place was filled with echoes of the happy laughter they had shared, the warmth of her gran's love and care for her only granddaughter. And, among it all, the terrible guilt Christy couldn't shake at not being there when Gran most needed her. It had not been her fault, but she still carried the self-blame around with her, and Ross McKinley's disapproval didn't help.

Pushing her negative thoughts aside for the moment, she inhaled the soothing scent of the cottage. Time enough to address her problems and make decisions about staying on, or not, once she'd been here a few days. Meanwhile, she was grateful for the few supplies in the kitchen. The first thing she needed was a good cup of hot tea. She made some comforting toast and sat at the old scrubbed kitchen table where she had helped her gran make scones during the school holidays. The cottage would be filled with such sweet memories and she welcomed them, hoping they would eventually dull the pain of loss.

Once she had placed the plate and cup in the sink, she turned her attention to moving the cases upstairs to unpack. She had managed to get everything into one medium case and one small; enough to last her for as long it took to make decisions about her future. Additional necessities would be available in Glasgow, or Edinburgh, or any of the smaller towns within reasonable distance.

Although narrow, the stairs were straight until the turn to the landing at the top and she took the largest, heaviest case first, to get it over with. Balancing it on the bottom stair, she gradually manoeuvred it to the top, using her knees to support it on the way. Her left arm still didn't have enough strength to take too much pressure.

She paused to catch her breath on the landing. At least she could pull the case along on its castors to the room and leave it on the floor to unpack. Now for the other one. She had reached the small entrance hall when she heard a knock at the door. Although she didn't feel much like company at the moment, the silhouette was visible through the glass. She had to open the door.

"Oh, Cameron! Come in, it's so good to see you." Christy was surprised at her rush of pleasure.

"Thought I'd welcome you back officially, Christy, love." He pulled her into his arms in a warm hug, planting a kiss on her cheek.

Christy returned his hug, reflecting briefly on the difference between this McKinley and his taciturn brother.

"So, have you unpacked yet?" he asked.

"Give me time, Cameron, I've not long arrived. In

fact I'm just about to take this other case upstairs."

"Show me the way, and I'll bring it up."

Christy wished he'd been there in time to carry the bigger one, but was grateful for his help. She led the way to the pretty back bedroom she had used since childhood. She couldn't bring herself to take over Gran's large front room.

"Do you want both cases on the bed, to save you bending up and down?"

"That would be great, if it's not too much bother."

"For a strong man like me? Ach, it's nothing at all."

Christy's spirits rose with Cameron's good-natured banter. He always could put her in a happy mood and it helped to dispel some of the sadness at being alone in the cottage.

That done, they went back downstairs.

"Would you like a cup of tea, or I think there's coffee too if you prefer."

"No, I won't hold you up, thanks. As well as welcoming you back, I'm here to issue an invitation. My mother would like you to come up to the house for a bite to eat this evening. Drinks at six o'clock, if that's okay. It'll be mostly the family."

"That's very kind. Please thank her, Cameron. It'll be good to eat out this evening." Christy meant it, as it would save having only her own company on her first night back. She wasn't exactly thrilled at the thought of having Ross's disapproval thrown in her face again, but Cameron would more than make up for his brother's ill grace.

"Well, I'll leave you to it for now. I'm sure you're dying to unpack and have a rest. See you tonight." With that he was gone, taking all the warmth with him.

Christy shivered. It was a dreich autumn day, grey and dull, and the cottage had that unlived-in feeling after lying empty for a while. First the unpacking, then she would set to and make the old place more like a home again.

Afterwards, she would enjoy a leisurely bath and make herself presentable for going up to the Big House, as it was known throughout the village. Although Mrs McKinley was kind to invite her, Christy knew it wasn't only Ross who often made her feel uncomfortable. His mother was more subtle, but something in her apparent friendliness had never rung true. And Christy had no idea why.

Ross McKinley watched Cameron return to the house and knew his brother couldn't wait to welcome Christy back to Kilcraig. No doubt she'd been pleased to see him too. He continued staring at the long drive that led to the village, wishing he could rewind their meeting.

He should have offered his sympathies for her gran's death right away. But his own grief at his elderly friend's passing had fuelled his disappointment and reminded him how much old Mrs Morrison had longed to see her granddaughter again. And Christy had left it too late. In all fairness, it seemed out of character in the girl he'd known for so many years. And today, he'd given her little chance for confidences or excuses. Cameron had been the only one to speak to her by phone about the funeral but he couldn't remember him passing on any valid reason for Christy's absence.

As soon as Ross had noticed her standing so small and forlorn at the station, his conscience twisted this way and that until his cursed obstinacy rendered him silent in the hope she would fill in the gaps. But Christy Morrison had her own share of determination and he recalled again the stubborn little chin and cool blue-green eyes that gave nothing away. But something in her manner niggled at him and he was sure a strong reason must have kept her absent so long from the grandmother she undoubtedly loved.

It didn't help that he remembered the unexpectedly pleasant kiss they had shared one Hogmanay when he, Cameron, Fiona and Christy had brought in the New Year. He knew it had meant more to Christy at the time but he'd been embarrassed in front of his brother and their friend and had laughed it off. Nothing had ever been the same again, especially when Fiona had then snogged him thoroughly and he hadn't pulled away. He had recognised the fleeting hurt in Christy's eyes and hadn't known how to apologise, so he'd ignored her for the rest of the evening and no doubt had hurt her even more. Yet, he'd never forgotten it, or her, even when he had eventually started dating someone he'd imagined marrying one day.

Not wanting to dwell on yet another mistake, he turned at the sound of Cameron entering the room. Ross suspected his brother would have provided the kind of welcome the girl probably needed, and the thought caused a sharper prick of guilt.

"Wow, isn't wee Christy a looker?"

Cameron's greeting made him smile. No doubt he'd conveyed such sentiments to the girl in a slightly more subtle manner.

"I suppose she's pretty enough," Ross agreed, "although I don't think she's the kind of girl to care much about what men think."

"Don't be so stuffy, brother. Bet you enjoyed

hugging her even more than I did. I'm glad she's back, although I don't know how long she intends staying."

Ross winced at his brother's openness, although he had never seen him with a girlfriend so far. He hadn't even thought of giving Christy a welcome hug, and was quite sure she neither expected it nor wished it from him. His conscience twisted again, along with the unexpected thought that it might have been a very pleasant feeling.

"I expect we shall find out soon enough what Christy's plans are for the future," Ross said. "I've no idea whether or not she'll go back to London. Maybe someone is waiting for her in the city. But you'll get the chance to talk to her again this evening."

As Ross glanced at his brother's expression, he knew it had never occurred to Cameron that Christy might have someone special in her life. And until this moment, it hadn't occurred to him either.

Chapter Two

The final approach to the house was by way of a long winding path through a sparse wood and Christy was relieved she had worn sensible low-heeled shoes with her wrap-over dress. She felt smart yet comfortable and had topped the dress with a chunky-knit cardigan that kept the autumn chill from her shoulders.

She wished she'd been able to bring a bottle of wine to the table but hadn't had a chance to buy any. Instead, she was thankful for the box of after dinner mints she'd pushed into her bag when leaving the flat in London. They would have to do.

At six on the dot, she rang the doorbell, trying to muster the confidence she didn't feel. Only the thought of Cameron's cheerful welcome stopped her from making an excuse not to stay. Besides, she had to admit she was hungry after her journey north.

"Hello, Christy dear, welcome back to these parts. Och, it's lovely to see you again, lass!"

Christy stared at the large homely woman who opened the door, wondering for a moment if she'd come to the wrong house. Then she remembered.

"Mrs MacPherson, isn't it? I haven't seen you for a long time." Christy had almost forgotten about the housekeeper who usually helped out at the McKinley's and she was glad of another friendly face.

"Come away in. They're waiting for you in the lounge."

It was like stepping back a century, entering the large hall with the black and white patterned tiles and grand sweeping staircase. She suspected the mistress of the big house liked to keep up the illusion of grandeur. Then Christy pushed such uncharitable thoughts aside as the lounge door suddenly opened and Cameron hurried to greet her.

"Thought I heard the doorbell." He kissed her cheek then led her into the room. "You look wonderful, Christy, love."

She smiled gratefully at him as they entered the large room, before she glanced at the four people gathered there. She hadn't realised that Fiona would be a guest, and Christy was surprised to see a less than friendly look on the girl's face when she smiled at her. Then she noticed a tall, distinguished looking man in his late thirties or early forties who regarded her with obvious interest. She had no time to wonder who he might be, since Mrs McKinley was approaching her with a glass of sherry in her hand.

"Hello, Christina, my dear, welcome back to the village. Here's a small sherry before dinner." She held out the tiny glass.

Christy took it, glad to have something to hold, although she wasn't keen on the taste. She could pretend to sip it out of politeness. She hadn't exactly expected a kiss from the older woman but a handshake would have been a welcoming touch. It was funny how the word 'dear' suggested more than one meaning when it came from two very different women. Mrs MacPherson had sounded as though she really meant it, while Mrs McKinley still called her by the full name no one else used.

She noticed Ross observing them all from the side of the room where the drinks tray was arranged. He nodded as he poured a drink for his mother.

"Fiona often eats with us in the evening and I'm sure you'll have a lot to catch up on." Mrs McKinley smiled fondly at the young woman sitting on one of the armchairs.

"And this is Nick Anderson, a former business associate of Ross, although he's as much a friend to the family nowadays." Christy heard the admiration in the older woman's voice as she introduced him.

"It's a pleasure to meet you, Miss Morrison. I've heard a lot about you."

"Christy, please." She wondered who had been talking about her and why, as her small hand disappeared inside his firm grip.

"Nick had some business here today so I persuaded him to stay on for dinner before driving back to the city." Mrs McKinley spoke with the kind of warmth she'd never shown her.

As they sat down again, Christy found herself beside Fiona and was glad of the chance to speak to her.

"Hello again, Fiona. It's such a long time since we've seen each other. That's a pretty dress." Christy meant it, for the soft blue accentuated the girl's fair hair and complexion.

The young girl who had shadowed their play on long summer days had blossomed and she was obviously still a close friend of the family. She had never quite forgotten the way Fiona had thoroughly kissed Ross that embarrassing New Year and wondered how close a friend she had become. She vaguely remembered Fiona as Mrs MacPherson's niece or some such and had always seemed to be hanging around the family.

"Thank you. You don't look so bad yourself,"

Fiona said but didn't carry on the conversation.

Christy was thankful she had brought at least one decent dress with her. She'd been told the green and black wrap-over was flattering to her chestnut colouring and curvy figure and she needed every aid to confidence she could muster. Mrs McKinley was always well turned out, even in her own home.

It wasn't until they had sat down to dinner that Ross made the effort to speak to her when he unexpectedly took the chair beside her.

"Are you settling into the cottage okay?" The question sounded pleasant with no sarcastic undertones, Christy noted.

"Yes, thanks. It's very sad, of course, without Gran. But the thoughtful provisions made me feel welcome. It was kind of your mother to think of it."

"Oh, you'll have to thank Ross, not my mother," Cameron said, as he caught her words. "Don't know I'd have thought of that myself!"

The revelation raised her eyebrows. She had never imagined Ross would be so concerned for her comfort.

"Then I sincerely thank you," Christy said, smiling at the solemn man beside her.

"It's really not necessary. I was used to looking in on your grandmother and it was force of habit, I suppose."

Why did he have to spoil the moment? Christy sighed inwardly. He had to mention the fact that he was the one who regularly called in on Gran. Was he still casting it up to her, the fact that she hadn't been there in the final months?

Then she noticed the slight smile that warmed the cold grey eyes and decided she was being unfair. Obviously her own guilty conscience made her imagine his every word was barbed. She would simply relax and enjoy what was left of the dinner then make her escape to the solitude of the cottage.

"Quite the caring sort is our Ross, isn't he?"

Christy glanced across at Nick Anderson, surprised to hear the words delivered with undeniable sarcasm. Ross carried on eating as though he hadn't heard, and she saw the other man smile as though aware he'd rankled the elder brother.

Still wondering at the unexpected undertones between the two men as the main course was served, Christy unthinkingly took the heavy tureen of potatoes from Ross with her left hand.

Next minute, the potatoes landed upside down on the embroidered tablecloth as Christy tried to prevent her gasp of pain.

"Oh, I'm so sorry… it slipped right out of my hand. Please let me clear it up." She stood up, mortified she had made such a fool of herself on the very first night.

"Of course you'll do no such thing," Mrs McKinley ordered. "I shall get Effie to take it away. Fortunately, most of us have been served, so there's no harm done."

The tone of voice made Christy squirm even more and she promptly sat down again. Then Cameron jumped up and brought his spoon over to the scattered potatoes.

"No point in letting these go to waste, I'll have a few more."

Fiona laughed and agreed she would too and the moment passed.

Christy felt a gentle hand on her arm. "Are you okay? You seemed to be in a bit of pain. Is that why the tureen fell?"

Trust him to notice, was her first thought. Then she saw real concern in Ross's eyes and again felt churlish. Oh, how she liked to think the worst of this enigmatic man.

"I'm fine, honestly. I have a bit of weakness in this arm and I should never have tried to lift it like that, especially at such an angle." She was relieved to see everyone else talking amongst themselves again, once Mrs MacPherson had cleared away the remainder of the fallen potatoes.

"Please don't say anything, it was just a stupid accident," Christy said quietly.

"The dropped tureen, or the reason for the weakness?"

This time, Christy was overawed by his astuteness but was saved from replying when Cameron stood up.

"This seems like a good time to toast our guest. Long may you stay in these parts, Christy." And Cameron drank from his glass.

Now Christy felt well and truly embarrassed, even more so when the others also raised their glasses. Did Cameron not realise it wasn't exactly the best idea while she was trying to divert attention from herself after the potato fiasco? Then she noticed Fiona's unsmiling stare as the girl held her glass to lips that didn't drink. And Nick Anderson seemed to be observing everything far too closely.

As soon as they reached the coffee stage, Christy decided she'd had enough of them all for one evening. She waited until they moved back into the lounge then made her apologies.

"Thank you so much for inviting me here this evening, Mrs McKinley. I'm sorry for spoiling the lovely dinner. If you will all excuse me, I think I must be more tired from the journey than I realised."

"Think nothing of it, my dear. Get a good night's rest for I'm sure you must have many things to sort out at the cottage," Mrs McKinley answered kindly enough.

Cameron planted another kiss on her cheek and hugged her tightly. Christy saw Fiona watching with a frown on her face but smiled warmly at the girl as she pecked her cheek.

"We must have a proper girly day to catch up, Fiona," Christy said and was rewarded with a reluctant smile.

Then her hand was gripped in a firm handshake again. "It was a pleasure to meet you, Christy, and I look forward to the next time." Nick Anderson seemed to be quite sure there would be one.

She replied with a fleeting smile. There was something she didn't quite trust about this too self-assured guest.

She had turned to lift her cardigan, when she was surprised to hear Ross's voice.

"Let me walk you back to the cottage, Christy, since it's dark outside now."

Much as she appreciated the gesture, she wanted to get away from them all and wasn't sure she could cope with Ross.

"That's kind of you, but there's really no need. I know the way well enough, and it's not that far."

He seemed about to protest when his mother intervened. On purpose perhaps? Christy wondered later.

"I'm sure Christina is perfectly able to find her way to the cottage. Besides, I have matters to discuss with you all." And Christy was effectively dismissed.

Ross gave in without making a fuss, but she thought his mouth tightened at his mother's blatant interference. He saw Christy to the door and she was aware that he watched for a while as she made her way down the path, before the door closed, cutting off the glimmer of light.

The almost full moon partly illuminated the path which was barely lit with one or two dim lampposts, so the trees appeared less menacing. One small stretch of shadow loomed near the end, and she was beginning to relax when she heard a slight sound behind her. Thinking Ross might have followed discreetly after all, she half turned.

Next minute, the ground was rising to meet her. Someone had given her a hard push. Frightened now, Christy waited for another blow. Instead, she heard the distinct sound of footsteps running off into the night but couldn't make out anything more definite.

Shaken, but able to hobble the rest of the way to the cottage, she unlocked the door with trembling fingers, making sure no one was near. She thought of going back up to the house but couldn't face the questions. Besides, she'd caused enough drama for one night. She locked the door behind her and quickly made sure everything else was secure.

Then she went straight upstairs. Tiredness, delayed grief, fear and confusion combined to make any further decisions impossible. She couldn't even be bothered to make a cup of tea.

Eventually snuggling between the cool cotton sheets and cosy old-fashioned blankets, she tried unsuccessfully to blank out her thoughts. Why on earth would anyone do such a thing to her in this small place? Maybe it was a random thief. Then she remembered the sound had come from the direction of the big house. As though someone had followed and waited until the shadows to strike. But that didn't make sense.

As sleep gradually took over, Christy had to the face the horrible thought that perhaps someone didn't want her back in the cottage or in Kilcraig.

Chapter Three

Next morning, Christy felt even more confused, but also more rested than expected. Maybe she had imagined the hard push on her back? Perhaps she was overtired, and had caught her foot on a tree root. Yet, she did hear a sound, never mind the impact of the blow to her back and the running feet afterwards.

Surely no one from the house would have followed her, although she sensed the person had come from that direction. Mrs McKinley and Fiona didn't seem overjoyed about her return to the cottage, and Ross hadn't bothered to hide his disappointment over her neglect of Gran. He at least had cared a little about her comfort. Even Nick Anderson had made her feel uneasy in an indefinable way. The only person genuinely delighted to see her was Cameron, and perhaps Mrs MacPherson. It was more than likely that some village youth had rushed past, knocking her out of the way.

As she showered, Christy discovered her arm was now even weaker, between lifting the heavy tureen and banging herself as she fell. No other obvious damage, but she'd have to content herself around the village for a while until her arm was strong enough to drive again, though she'd need to do something about a car.

The bright morning beckoned and she was glad to see none of the seeping dampness that so often accompanied autumn on the west coast. Pulling on her comfortable fleece and jeans, she was determined to retrace her steps of the previous night. Not that she expected to find any clues, but she needed a walk before making a start on the cottage. After being on a train for much of the previous day, she was eager to stretch her legs and didn't want to waste such lovely weather.

The track was devoid of people as Christy began to walk in the direction of the McKinley's. From her cottage, a road stretched in both directions: to the village square on the right, and a narrower road towards the house on the left. Once she had left the cottage behind, she soon reached the path.

She paid close attention to the ground as she walked, examining the dirt path and grassy verge. But what exactly did she hope to find?

"Looking for clues?"

The words, as much as the sudden appearance of Ross McKinley, made Christy stumble.

"Sorry? Clues to what?"

"My feeble attempt at a joke, Christy. You seemed to be absorbed with the pathway as you walked."

"Oh, now I do feel foolish. I was deep in thought." She could hardly tell him she was indeed looking for clues of a kind.

"I was on my way to ask if there's anything you need, or maybe you'll be taking the Mini out later."

She had forgotten about Gran's car, which she supposed was now in the garage awaiting its new owner.

"Thanks, I have all I need at the moment. I don't think I'll be driving for a while but I can easily walk down to the village. Please don't feel you need to check up on me."

When she noticed his frown, Christy realised she sounded ungrateful. But she couldn't help wondering why Ross was suddenly being so helpful when he clearly didn't approve of her.

"At risk of sounding like I'm checking up on you, is it something to do with your arm? The not driving, I mean. I wouldn't like to think of you stuck around the cottage for months. If you decide to stay, of course."

The last sentence goaded Christy into answering truthfully.

"Yes, it is because of my arm. And I imagine I'll be here for quite some time. Now, if you'll excuse me, I'm going back to make a start on sorting out the cottage."

Christy said goodbye and walked away without turning round to see if Ross had gone or not. She couldn't face any more of his questions, or his suspect concern.

Ross watched in bemusement as the small figure walked away in seeming haste and resentment at his questions. Surely he hadn't been that insensitive and she could recognise his concern? Or had his lack of warm welcome destroyed any chance of being friends? The thought depressed him.

Her unexpected vulnerability had caught him unawares at dinner the night before, especially after the potato incident. For the first time in his life, he had wanted to hold a woman to offer only comfort without expectation or desire. Not that Christy Morrison was unattractive, as Cameron had already appreciated. But Ross was surprised to find that an unexpected protective side had suddenly kicked into gear and he had genuinely wanted to walk Christy back to the cottage.

But it was evident the slim, yet curvy frame hid a stubborn determination and he smiled as he walked on to the village. Whatever he'd expected to feel when Christy returned to the cottage, it was not this sudden preoccupation with her wellbeing. Yet something had damaged her arm and caused those dark shadows under her eyes and he knew it was more than her grandmother's death. Perhaps it was the same reason that had prevented Christy from being here during her beloved gran's final days, and he felt even guiltier at his lack of sympathy on her arrival. At least now he might be able to redeem himself, if she allowed him the opportunity.

As he neared the village, Ross pushed aside all thoughts of Christy Morrison. Right now, other matters were causing him enough trouble. When he severed the business partnership with Nick Anderson, he had hoped their paths would now completely diverge. He had long disapproved of the other man's ruthlessness and had no wish to be tarred with his reputation. But he'd reckoned without his own mother's interference and her determination to back Anderson's proposed plans for the village, and his ancestral home.

Recalling the man's comments at dinner, he knew Anderson would be a formidable enemy. And he hadn't mistaken the way in which his predatory glance had lingered a little too long on Christy. Given Anderson's past behaviour with Ross's ex-girlfriend, that might be an added complication he hadn't expected and could never welcome.

Once inside the cottage, Christy changed into looser, more comfortable jeans and sweatshirt and tied her hair back from her face. Time to start going through Gran's effects and sort out what to do with them. She was tempted to put it off for longer, knowing it would tear at her heart. But it would also stop her thinking about Ross McKinley, and her prickly responses to his conversation.

She found surprisingly few clothes and suspected the elderly lady had whittled her wardrobe down to the necessities. She had never been one for owning too many outfits that she would never wear. The private papers and books were more difficult to deal with as those were the items that defined her gran's life and personality.

Most of the books were well-loved novels: romantic suspense by Phyllis Whitney and Mary Stewart and such like, or cosy crime by Agatha Christie and Ngaio Marsh. Gran had been a huge fan of *Midsomer Murders* and *Morse* on television.

The other books were an interesting mix of poetry and treasured classics. She had introduced Christy to Jane Austen, Charlotte Bronte and Dickens. She would keep the novels she didn't already have and take the rest to a charity shop along with the clothes.

She picked up an unusual looking slim volume from amongst the poetry books: a beautifully bound copy of the *The Rubaiyat of Omar Khayyam*. She had never seen it before in the cottage. Then she remembered she hadn't seen Gran for far too long.

Opening the front page, Christy was dumbfounded. She stared at the sloping writing and strong signature.

To my dearest Marian
With fondest love
Ross

Marian was her grandmother's name, although she hadn't heard anyone use it for a very long time. She was usually referred to as Mrs Morrison. It seemed that Ross McKinley was even more of a friend to her lovely gran than she had realised, although the words seemed a little formal, even for him. No wonder he was so disappointed in Christy when she failed to be with the old lady in those final days.

She opened the slim red and gold book. It obviously had been read time and again. Many people quoted from it, but she had never properly read it herself. She would look through the whole volume this evening. If Gran had liked this book so well, then no doubt she would too as they had shared a love of poetic writing.

She glanced at one or two random verses and was immediately struck by some of the sentiments. The first two lines of verse twenty made her pause.

'Ah, my Beloved, fill the cup that clears
Today of past Regrets and future Fears.'

Quite without warning, tears filled her eyes and blinded her to any more words. Too many regrets indeed. Regret for her absence from this place when the woman she loved best in the whole world needed her most, regret for the terrible accident that had robbed her of that time, and of the man she once thought she would marry, and even regret for her parents who had died too young and too suddenly all those years ago.

Even *'future fears'* spoke to that uncertain part of her that didn't quite know where she should settle. The events of the evening before had added new fears, when so roughly pushed to the ground for no apparent reason.

It seemed as though all the sadness and tears she'd

suppressed for so long were finding expression through these ancient words in a small book. Christy put the volume down and, hands to her face, she wept as she sat on the floor beside the sofa. She missed Gran so much and longed to have her sitting beside her as before, setting both their worlds to right through their conversation and shared opinions. More than anything, she wanted to tell her the real reason she couldn't make the long journey to be with her in her final days, to assure her she had never stopped loving and thinking of her for a single one of those days.

Gradually, the tears lessened and Christy hiccupped as she took deep breaths, reaching for a tissue to wipe her eyes and nose. There was nothing she could do to change the past and, in her heart, she knew Gran had understood. It was always the living that carried the guilt of lost time after bereavement.

Feeling mildly better for having grieved, Christy rubbed her eyes and was just standing up when a knock sounded at the door. Sighing, she contemplated ignoring it but the knock came again. Hoping it wasn't Ross, she went to the door.

Chapter Four

"How's my favourite girl? Thought you might like some help with clearing the cottage."

Surprisingly, Christy wasn't as delighted as usual to see Cameron. His light heartedness should have cheered her up but, instead, it jarred. Maybe she wasn't in the mood to be happy and frivolous today. The thought made her hesitate; when did she start thinking of Cameron's friendly chatter as being frivolous?

"Come in, Cameron. Sorry… I've been thinking about Gran and got a bit emotional."

"Of course you did; it would be strange if you hadn't felt anything."

As she smiled, pleased at his understanding, she thought how easy it would be to rest her head on his shoulder and feel his comforting arms around her, but only in a brotherly manner. That thought surprised her even more.

The moment passed as he stepped inside and closed the door while Christy went to move some of the papers and books from the sofa.

"I see you've made a good start. Anything I can do?"

"Thanks, but no thanks. I'll make us a coffee and you can tell me what you're up to these days."

"I'll come and help and we can chat at the same time. I can't stay long as I'm supposed to meet Fiona later."

Christy noticed that Cameron didn't seem to know his way about the kitchen very well. Perhaps he hadn't come to see Gran as often as his brother. But then, why should he, just because Ross did.

"Are you and Fiona a couple then?" Christy couldn't resist asking.

Cameron looked horrified. "Heavens, no! What on earth made you think that? She's more like a sister to me. You must remember the way she used to follow me and Ross about hoping to be part of our games."

Christy did indeed remember many a summer when the four of them had run about the hills and shores of the loch together, although Ross had never been as pleased to 'look after the girls' as he put it. Fiona often seemed to be a shadow at their play times and was tolerated since she was Mrs MacPherson's niece, until that year they had both kissed the older McKinley brother.

"Anyway, she's always had a bit of a thing about Ross," Cameron continued. "The more he ignores her, the harder she tries to attract his attention. It's not going to happen, but don't tell her that!"

Now Christy was taken aback. So the girl still held a very bright candle for Ross. Perhaps that was why she was so distant when Christy arrived back in the village, since it was Ross who had brought her. Fiona needn't have worried, for he was the last person she was interested in, and he most definitely wasn't interested in her.

They took their coffee into the living room and Cameron had a good look around as he sat opposite her.

"I wondered if you'd thought of getting shot of the cottage and its contents. You'd get quite a price for a lot of the items." Then he seemed to realise what he'd said. "Not that I want you to go away again, of course."

Christy stared at him for a moment, wondering what to say at such unexpected words. Something didn't sound quite right about his nonchalance, but she couldn't think why. She was disappointed he should suggest such a thing when she'd only arrived.

"I've not had time to think of anything much yet." It was all she could manage. It had been an emotional day and, if she were honest, she really wanted Cameron to go away and let her get back to sorting Gran's things since she'd forced herself to begin.

Then he noticed the slim red and gold volume. "Hey, that's quite a stunning book."

As he made to pick it up, Christy quickly placed it beside the other books. "I think Gran must have been reading this before she died as I haven't seen it before." She didn't want him to see the inscription when she'd only discovered it herself.

Cameron finished his drink and stood up, as though sensing her thoughts.

"Look, I'd best let you get back to what you were doing. Of course you won't have thought about the future yet. Forgive me, Christy, love. I'll take myself away before you throw me out."

Christy laughed but was happy to see him go all the same.

When she sat back down amongst her gran's things, she had an uneasy feeling that Cameron had come solely to ask about what she planned to do, not to see how she was coping. He hadn't even told her anything about himself and why he seemed to have time on his hands.

Maybe she was becoming paranoid. Cameron was her childhood chum and hardly likely to have an ulterior motive in asking about the cottage.

It was mid-afternoon when Christy finally stacked the last pile of books into a corner of the room, leaving the *Rubaiyat* aside to read through later. She was suddenly hungry and decided to have a walk into the village before the shop shut, to find something for dinner.

Wrapping up in a warm jacket and scarf, she revelled in the cool autumn air, the most alive and thankful she'd felt since her accident. The leaves were beginning to turn to rich shades of ochre, russet and gold and already the path to the road was carpeted by their kaleidoscope of colours. She had missed the area more than she imagined. The surrounding hills beckoned her to tramp through the heather-clad grass, while the open countryside around the village promised the kind of peace and quietness she had longed for in busy London.

The main village street had several small shops; still no supermarkets here, she was pleased to see. A new inn offered all day snacks and bar meals and the newsagent-cum-general store was just as she remembered. The stone church sat four-square at the end of the street as always.

She pushed open the door of the store, relieved to find an even bigger refrigerated cabinet and deep freezer than in the past. At least she could buy enough goods until able to drive into town. She didn't recognise the man behind the counter and the shop was empty of customers.

"Hello, you'll be Christy Morrison who's staying at the cottage, I expect."

It wasn't a question and Christy smiled; she must be the only stranger to this man.

"Yes, you probably knew my grandmother."

"Aye, everyone knew Mrs Morrison. You have a look of her."

Christy was grateful for his words, delivered without hint of accusation.

"Thank you, Mr…?"

"Ewan MacPherson. My mother works up at the big house. She told me you were back."

So that explained how he knew her. She seemed to remember Mrs MacPherson's son had been away whenever she was at Gran's, but she had no idea where. He was a lot older, so it was likely he'd been in the city. She wondered why he was now working in the local shop. Perhaps he, too, was glad to be back to village life. He seemed pleasant enough though she was uncomfortably aware of his gaze following her as she took a look around before finally choosing several items.

Once she had made her purchases, she said goodbye and carried the bags with her right hand. It would be tiring but she didn't have that far to walk. She hadn't gone any distance when a car drew up beside her.

"Can I give you a lift? They look a bit heavy."

Christy turned at Ross's voice, realising she was happy to see him. She hated to admit she'd be glad of the help, as the bags were filled with potatoes and fruit.

Then she noticed Fiona in the passenger seat and wondered for a moment where they had been. *As if it was any of her business*, she chided herself.

"Thank you. They're heavier than I'd imagined they would be!"

Christy was impressed when Ross got out of the car and after opening the back door for her, he put the shopping in the boot.

"Hello, Fiona, sorry for the detour," she apologised as she sat down.

The girl shrugged as though she didn't care. Once Ross was driving again, however, she suddenly spoke.

"You must miss your life in London, Christy, and your friends. Was there anyone special down there?"

Christy was a bit taken aback at such an intrusive question and noticed Ross glance at her briefly in his mirror, although he didn't say anything.

"No one I can't live without if I decide to stay here. I can work anywhere since I'm freelance and I don't think I'd miss the big city very much." She forced herself to sound matter-of-fact.

There were no more questions after that and Christy was relieved when after a short drive round by the main road, they drew up beside the cottage. Ross insisted on carrying her bags the short distance to the door. As Christy thanked him, he seemed a bit distracted and barely said goodbye before getting back in the car.

She watched them drive away then locked the door behind her, putting them out of her mind for now.

Later that evening, Christy settled on the sofa and began to read the *Rubaiyat*. It wasn't only the words which were beautiful. As an illustrator herself, she appreciated the beauty of the delicate drawings on several pages.

About three quarters of the way through, she found one verse lightly underlined in pencil. Intrigued, she read the words a few times, wondering at their significance.

'For all the Sin wherewith the Face of man
Is blackened, Man's Forgiveness give and take.'

Why would Gran have highlighted such words, if they had not meant a great deal to her? She sleepily wondered if she had done something she regretted, or if something had been done *to* her. Something that needed forgiveness.

Christy yawned and decided to leave the remainder of it until the following day. She was still tired after her arrival and unsettled by the varying reactions to her presence here. She sensed something wasn't quite right, but had no idea why.

But one thing she increasingly did know. At this moment, she had no intention of going back to London.

As Ross drove away from the cottage, he scarcely glanced at the girl beside him, annoyed that Fiona had started quizzing Christy like that. But he was even more annoyed that he, too, wanted to know if she'd left anyone behind, and his curiosity surprised him. Why should it matter if she stayed or returned to someone special in London? As he thought of the slight figure struggling valiantly with two heavy bags held in one hand, he suspected the injury, whatever it was, had been more severe than she let on.

Careful, McKinley, he silently told himself. That girl is occupying far too many of your thoughts since her return, and he was glad when Fiona interrupted them.

"So, do you think she'll stay this time?"

He glanced at her briefly, not wanting to discuss Christy behind her back. "I have no idea, but I'm sure she'll make her decision when she's had time to get used to being here."

"Maybe she'll confide in Cameron. They seem to be great friends." This time, Ross detected a sly note in Fiona's voice. He hoped she wasn't going to start causing any mischief.

"I've no doubt we'll all know soon enough." He changed the subject before she asked more questions. "Have you and Cameron made any decision about the antique shop in town yet?"

"We're still negotiating the price. Since Mr Robson is retiring, he'd like to see it continue after all these years. But it might not happen since Cameron already has a stake in that other place."

They had no more time for conversation as they arrived at the house, but Ross hoped his brother would finally settle down to some definite path in life. At least Fiona had a good business head on her and Cameron seemed to listen to her opinions. But his thoughts soon returned to Christy Morrison and he wondered what decision she would make about her future. He was surprised to find it mattered very much.

Chapter Five

The telephone woke her from a pleasant dream. Christy switched on the lamp beside her bed as she tried to figure out what had disturbed her. She glanced at the time. Eight o'clock. She never slept that late. Sitting up at once, she lifted the phone.

"Hello, is that Christy Morrison…"

"Speaking."

"Don't wait too long before you go back to where you came from. This is a friendly warning, for now."

"What? Who is this?" Christy was wide awake now and her hand trembled as it held the receiver. "Who's speaking?"

The line went dead.

She sat on the edge of the bed wondering what had just happened. Who on earth wanted her to leave this place so urgently, and why? It seemed she'd been right about the push being on purpose, though that didn't do much for her confidence.

She couldn't even decide if the caller had been male or female as the voice was hoarse and indistinct. But the person obviously knew the phone number here, and that she was staying in the cottage, although in such a small village nearly everyone would know she had arrived.

Why did anyone want to be rid of her? There was nothing special about the cottage and no one else who could possibly want it as much as she did. Or could it be another reason entirely?

She couldn't help remembering Fiona's less than friendly manner. Surely the girl didn't seriously think she was a threat to her in any way. Even if Ross was interested in Fiona, which Christy doubted, he certainly wasn't interested in *her*. Then she remembered his kind concern at the dinner table when she dropped the potatoes, and the courteous way he'd helped with her bags. No doubt it was only his old-fashioned good manners.

Christy stood up. She had no intention of allowing her thoughts to be absorbed with Ross McKinley. But what to do about the telephone call? She wasn't sure who to tell. Cameron seemed the obvious choice, if he took her seriously enough. Feeling marginally brighter and resolving to put the episode to one side for now, Christy quickly showered.

She was fixing some eggs when the phone rang again.

"Hello, who is this, please?" She was determined to get in first this time.

"Hello. Christy? It's Nick Anderson, you know, from the dinner at the McKinley's."

"Yes, I remember you, Mr Anderson. How can I help you?" She tried to keep the surprise from her voice.

"Oh, please. It's Nick. I know this will sound a bit presumptuous, but I wondered if you might have dinner with me on Saturday evening. There's a very good country house restaurant a few miles away that I think you'll enjoy."

Christy was silent for a moment, trying to work out why on earth Nick Anderson should be asking her out when he'd only just met her.

"Well, I'm not sure…"

"Please, Christy. I know we've only met the once,

but I'd like to get to know you better. I'm afraid I don't hang around when I see someone I like. But if you'd rather not, then I quite understand."

She took a deep breath. She was curious. That was the only reason she agreed.

"Thank you, Nick. I'd like to accept your kind invitation. I don't know the restaurant and I'd be happy to have an evening out."

"Excellent. I'll pick you up at seven thirty. If you could just confirm the number of your cottage - six, isn't it? Look forward to seeing you then. Bye, Christy."

She ate her eggs with less appetite than she expected. Two strange phone calls in one morning. Coincidence? Of course it was. But she was equally puzzled by Nick Anderson's call as she had been by the other.

Surely he wasn't romantically interested in her after one evening? She'd hardly given him a second look and hadn't particularly taken to him. She wasn't falsely modest and accepted she was reasonably attractive, but under no illusion that she was Anderson's usual type. She had no evidence to suggest this was true, but she had good instincts most of the time and she didn't even know if he was married, or perhaps divorced.

Then she remembered the seeming strain between Ross and Nick and was even more curious. Perhaps she could find out more about the man and why he was so keen to further their acquaintance. Besides, a night out might take her mind off the McKinley brothers. Nick appeared to be a friend of the family, or most of them. It should be an interesting evening.

It was another perfect autumn morning and Christy felt restless after clearing away her half-eaten breakfast. She might not be able to drive, but she could explore her old haunts on foot. She had a longing for the hills which were within easy enough reach. Wrapping up against the slight chill in her windproof anorak over jeans, t-shirt and jumper, she was glad she had brought her flat boots with her. They'd be good for walking and gripping any snow or icy patches when it became colder.

Realising she was already looking forward to winter here, Christy knew her mind had been made up from the beginning. She couldn't bear to leave this place again now she'd returned. With that thought in mind, she set out quite light-hearted, all puzzlement about strange telephone calls and threats pushed conveniently aside for now. She wanted only to enjoy the moment.

She skirted the big house and walked up past the few straggling cottages at the outer edge of the village to negotiate the overgrown path that led to the open hillside. Some of the brambles were already turning from red to black and it reminded her of Gran's homemade jam. No matter where she went, it seemed everything would be filled with memories of her beloved grandmother.

Reaching the plateau, Christy was glad to rest a while and she sat on a flat rock to look back over the hillside she had climbed. It felt so good to be outdoors in this healing place after everything she'd been through in London. She had blocked most of the worst days from her mind, but they often surfaced at odd times catching her unawares and unprepared, and she would relive it again. Or as much as she could remember. Now, in this solitude with only a few grazing sheep for company, she let her mind try to recapture that awful event and her boyfriend's face.

Michael... She now accepted they had been too young for a serious relationship when they met at Art College, but for a few years she'd convinced herself he was the love of her life. Ignoring the little voice inside that cautioned against permanent commitment, she had been carried away by the romance of it all.

London was exciting and she knew he was going to propose, although marriage could wait for a few years. But they hadn't got that far. Christy sighed for the romantic young girl she had been, who never got to have a future with her first love after all. Whenever she tried to think back to the final hours with Michael just before the crash, her mind refused to dwell on it and she knew it was partly because she was going to finish with him. Guilt prevented her from remembering the details.

Pulling up the collar of her jacket, she gazed at the rolling hillside below, the bracken darkening the various shades of green, and inhaled the sweet autumn air. She could see the McKinley house in the distance, lording over the whole village. Even the cottage was almost visible from here if she looked hard enough.

Poor Gran. She had been looking forward to meeting this young man who had seemingly captured her granddaughter's heart. Only she never got the chance. Christy recalled those words of their national poet, Robert Burns, that cleverly summed up many a lost opportunity, or fruitless plan: '*The best laid schemes o' mice and men, gang aft a-gley*'. Plans frequently did go askew.

Christy stood up, brushing her hands down her jeans. Enough of the immediate past for the time being. She obviously still wasn't ready to face the crash and couldn't bear to think again of the lost chance to see Gran one last time. But she had tried to come to terms with losing Michael in such a terrible way and dealing with the guilty knowledge that their relationship would not have worked in the end.

She shivered as the chill reminded her she had probably sat too long for comfort. The meagre warmth from a weak sun had almost gone. Heading back along the trail, Christy saw a tall figure coming towards her, a dog at his side. She frowned at the intrusion, then shrugged. It wasn't her private hillside. Of course other people walked here, but she hadn't expected to see anyone.

As they neared each other, Christy paused. Ross McKinley. Her first inconsequential thought was that she hadn't known he owned a dog. Then she wondered what work he actually did, that he could wander so freely over the hills.

She slowed her pace as he drew near.

"Hello, Christy. Great day for a walk, isn't it?"

She smiled. He sounded friendly enough. "Hello, Ross. Thought I'd get the London smog well and truly erased. I've always loved these hills."

She bent down to pat the black Labrador that patiently waited beside its master. Standing up in time to see a softer expression than usual in its owner's dark grey eyes, she was annoyed for mentioning London, not wanting to remind him of her absence again. Not today, when she was so close to accepting everything.

"I didn't know you had a dog. He's a beauty. At least I think it's a 'he'!"

"He certainly is. This is Darwin, an original specimen if ever there was one." He grinned as he rubbed the dog's glossy head.

Christy was suddenly struck by how much

younger and more carefree Ross looked when he laughed. She recognised a shadow of the young boy she had followed around all those years ago.

"That's a very good name. It suits him." She too laughed when Darwin sniffed at her hand as though thanking her for the compliment.

They stood quietly for a moment, united by the dog. Then Christy made a move to go. "Well, I'd better get back to my chores."

"Is everything okay at the cottage? If you need anything, I hope you know you can ask me for help."

As far as she could tell, there was nothing but genuine concern in his voice.

"Thank you, but I hope it won't be necessary."

As his eyes narrowed, she realised that once again she had sounded less grateful than she meant.

"Sorry, I only meant that I don't need anything and hope to be able to cope when I do. If that makes sense."

He grinned. "It's okay. I know you're fairly independent. But the offer stands, if you should ever need me."

Now he was slightly discomfited, as though aware how the words sounded. She nodded and the moment passed.

"There is one thing you can tell me, perhaps," she said.

Now he looked wary and she wondered what he expected her to say.

"Do you know Nick Anderson well? I wondered if you had worked together recently."

His eyes darkened and he frowned. "Why do you ask?" There was no doubt he was surprised by her question.

"Oh, just curiosity. He's invited me out for dinner

on Saturday and I thought you had been colleagues."

He was silent so long that Christy wondered what on earth was going through his mind. He seemed to be choosing his words carefully.

"I see. We used to be partners in an architect business, but we're not exactly colleagues now." He hesitated. "Christy, it's not my place to say, but be careful. Nick Anderson has a ruthless streak that he manages to hide from most people. I wouldn't like you to be taken in by his smooth talk."

Christy glared in disbelief. She had noticed some strain between the men at the dinner, but hadn't realised it was this bad. Almost as though he was warning her off the other man. And that made her contrary.

"Thanks for the advice. But it may surprise you to know that I'm not that gullible, especially where men are concerned. I'll make up my own mind about him."

The air chilled even more and Christy decided it was time to move on. She was unexpectedly disappointed their pleasant chat had deteriorated with mention of the other man. It wasn't as if Ross McKinley would care who she went out with, yet he seemed displeased at her choice of dinner companion.

"Fine. But don't get in too deep, Christy, or you might drown. Anyway, Darwin has been patient long enough. I'll see you around." He strode off without a backward glance, man and beast in perfect harmony.

Christy was fuming that he'd made the first move. She had wanted to flounce away with her head in the air. Then she grimaced. How childish. That was the last image she wanted to leave with him, though she had no idea why it should matter. She hurried down the path towards the cottage, trying to defuse her anger.

As she skirted the big house again, she suddenly remembered the phone call and realised that Ross's was the second warning of some kind she'd had that day. She was still annoyed enough to shrug it all off, apart from the enjoyment of the hills. She would find out for herself exactly what kind of man Nick Anderson proved to be and perhaps it would be a good opportunity to find out why he and Ross seemed to dislike each other so much. But most of all, it was a chance to dress up and be a carefree young woman for an evening.

Striding along the now empty path, Ross couldn't believe he had fallen out with Christy again. He'd never known anyone so stubborn and suspected he had now made her even more determined to enjoy an evening out with Anderson.

When he had come upon her by herself, she looked so alone that he'd had the strangest urge to put his arm around her. And the way she had patted Darwin caused unexpected tenderness within him that he didn't want to explore too closely. Then he had to go and spoil the moment. Now they would have to start all over again. Ever since his stupid boyish reaction to that long-ago New Year kiss, he suspected it would take a lot to make Christy let down her defences with him, even if she were ever to like him enough again. Besides which, his own armour was pretty intact after an unforeseen betrayal in his love life.

"Heel boy," he called, as he stopped at a spot where he could see the village spreading below. With Darwin beside him at once, he wished, not for the first time, that humans were as obedient. Not that he would ever want to quell Christy's independence or the way her eyes lit up with anger at his words.

Ignoring the direction in which his thoughts strayed, he thought instead about Nick Anderson and why he should so quickly ask Christy out. She was certainly attractive and that vulnerable quality might appeal to many men, but she was not Anderson's usual type. Surveying the land below, he had an uneasy feeling she was going to become part of Anderson's plans for the village. And no doubt he would turn on his full battery of charm from the first date.

His anger rising again, he turned back to the path. "Come boy, that's enough for today," he said to Darwin.

His beloved companion padded beside him at once, as though aware of his master's mood. Ross resolved to keep a closer eye on Christy, for her own protection. Even if she didn't welcome his interference, he hoped she would learn to trust him as a friend. He could make sure Anderson's motives were clear, for he didn't trust *him* one iota.

Chapter Six

Christy surveyed her meagre wardrobe in despair. What on earth should she wear to dinner at a country house hotel? Even if she had her full wardrobe of clothes she'd still be every bit as puzzled. There wasn't much call for dressing up since the accident, especially when she worked freelance from home, and she had only pushed in the dress she wore the other evening at the last minute. But she couldn't wear it again so soon.

Nothing else for it, she'd have to go into the nearby town. She remembered a few dress shops, although they might be a bit pricy. But needs must and a few hours shopping might be good for her. Hopefully, the local bus service still operated or she'd be really stuck here. The nearest railway station was miles away.

She flexed her left arm. Maybe another couple of weeks and she could try driving again. The physiotherapist had told her to begin cautiously, a little at a time. She hadn't exactly named a date to start, but it wasn't just because of the arm that Christy was putting it off. Her stomach clenched every time she thought of getting behind the wheel, yet she didn't want to give up the convenience of a car forever.

As she strolled along to the bus stop in the hope one would arrive, she heard a car gradually slow and guessed the driver's identity before she glanced down.

"Need a lift, Christy?" Ross McKinley had rolled down his window.

What was it about this man? Everywhere she went, he turned up too, although her more reasonable self knew it must be coincidence.

"I'm fine, thanks, just waiting for a bus to town. I expect it'll be here soon."

He glanced at his watch before replying. "You're going to have a long wait. Only one an hour and you've missed the last one by about ten minutes. I can take you into town."

Christy hesitated, then shrugged. Why not? She wouldn't get into town any other way for a while. Against her better judgement, this enigmatic man intrigued her. After the way they had parted on the hillside, she was pleased he had stopped at all.

Aware he still waited patiently for an answer, she smiled in apology. "Sorry, I was trying to decide if I really need to go. If the offer is still on, I'll accept gratefully, thank you."

This time, he leaned across and opened the passenger door from the inside. Amused, Christy realised she had now been in Ross McKinley's car three times in as many days. This was becoming an unexpected habit.

"You're not going out of your way, I hope?" she asked to break the silence. He certainly had none of the easy, outgoing charm of his brother. Yet Christy didn't mind his more reserved nature, as long as he wasn't being disagreeable.

"Not at all. It's sheer coincidence that I'm headed into town myself."

He smiled warmly as he echoed her earlier thoughts. And again, Christy appreciated how attractive he looked when not so stern.

During the twenty-minute drive, neither of them mentioned her forthcoming dinner with Nick Anderson. At first, Christy wondered if she should keep quiet so he could concentrate, but one question kept surfacing and she finally broke the comfortable silence.

"I hope you don't mind me asking, but do you live up at the big house? Or are you on holiday just now? Sorry, you can tell me if I'm being nosy." She smiled, hoping he'd enlighten her. And hoping it didn't suggest she thought of him all the time.

Keeping his eyes on the road, he shrugged. "That's okay; you must be wondering why I always seem to be around. I do have rooms at the house. You know how big it is, so Mother and I don't get in each other's way too much." He glanced at her as though acknowledging that was a good thing. "I've actually taken over the running of the estate now, so it makes sense to live here most of the time. But I still escape to the city now and then for occasional architect consultations when required."

"The estate must be a big responsibility," Christy said, unaccountably pleased that he made his home in the village.

"It is indeed, especially in this economic climate, but we're managing to hold everything together at the moment. Although there's talk of some major changes being made and I expect they'll affect all of us if they go ahead."

Before she could question further, he asked one of his own. "And what about you, Christy? Do you have a job in London?"

Disappointed he'd mentioned her other life, she was determined to remain in the present.

"Fortunately, I'm freelance now. I illustrate children's books, or whatever else comes my way, so I can work anywhere. I'm working on a commission just now, or at least I will be when I get settled in and organised."

Silence greeted her words and she longed to know his thoughts. Did he hope she stayed in the cottage, or would he be glad to see her go back to city life?

"I remember you were always arty, making your own cards and drawing whenever you sat down. As you say, at least you're able to work wherever you choose."

Surprised at his response, she glanced over to catch an odd smile around his lips as he threw her a quick glance at the same time.

"Wow! You have a better memory than me." Christy laughed, appreciating his non-committal remark and amazed he remembered so much about her from their childhood summers.

She was almost disappointed to find they had reached the town where Ross was already drawing the car alongside the kerb. The street itself still looked traditional with individual shops, one good sized supermarket the only nod to modern life. Spying at least two boutique type clothes shops, she remembered buying from one of them before when staying at the cottage in the past.

When he turned off the engine, Ross hesitated a moment, as though wondering whether to say something. "Will you be okay getting home again?" he finally asked.

"Yes, of course. I'll get the bus back. Thanks very much for the lift."

He hesitated again and Christy didn't know what to make of him.

"I have a meeting, so I can't be sure when I'll be

going back."

"Honestly, I'm happy to get a bus. I intend browsing until exhausted, so I've no idea when I'll be ready either." She smiled this time to reassure him. She couldn't imagine why he was taking so long to say goodbye.

"Well, if you're sure. I'll let you out then I'll go and park properly before the traffic warden pounces." Next minute, he was round the car, opening her door before she could say any more.

"Thanks again. I really appreciate the lift." She paused beside him after climbing out as elegantly as possible.

"No worries. Hope you find what you're looking for, Christy." And he returned to the driving seat.

Watching the car drive away, Christy wondered why his parting words sounded more meaningful than they appeared. She shrugged away any more thought of him. He was too much of a puzzle to waste any time over when she had serious shopping awaiting. She headed towards the first clothes shop.

Keeping his eyes on the road, after a quick glance at the retreating figure, Ross couldn't remember when he had last enjoyed a conversation so much. No matter how hard he tried not to let Christy affect him, he couldn't deny his pleasure in her company.

Perhaps she was more like her grandmother than he remembered. That wise old lady had been the only person in whom he could confide for too many years and Christy had the same blue-green eyes. The sprinkling of freckles on her face reminded him of the tomboyish girl who used to follow him and Cameron around on warm summer days. Now he was drawn to this grown-up version, no matter how much he was determined to keep some distance between them.

This would not do, he decided, as he found a space in the car park and locked the doors. He had no intention of getting emotionally entangled with Christy Morrison, or anyone else, and he banished thoughts of her from his mind to concentrate on his meeting with the surveyor.

Christy hadn't had so much fun for ages. By the time she had looked at every possible dress, skirt and top the small town had to offer, she was tired but happy. As often happened, it was the final dress she tried on that she fell in love with.

The boutique was exclusive but friendly and the girl who owned it seemed determined to help her find the perfect outfit; helpful but not at all the kind of nuisance some assistants could be. The larger stores usually irritated her, either because the assistant wouldn't allow her to browse by herself, or because two or three of them were so engrossed in their fascinating conversation they ignored potential customers.

The boutique owner, Sally, introduced herself right away, and after ascertaining what Christy sought and showing the relevant rails, she left her to it. Even if she was a little curious about her new customer, she asked no questions.

Since the shop was quiet, Christy took her time, enjoying the pleasure of browsing through clothes again. Fashion had never been a high priority in her life, but she tried to look reasonably up-to-date and smart, and her artistic eye loved the texture and colours of various fabrics. She had made do since the accident, imagining she'd never be interested in something so basic ever again. Yet it was therapeutic, giving herself over to the luxury of browsing without pressure.

A few skirts and tops caught her eye, but she really wanted a new dress. Something completely impractical and feminine, she decided, but not for Nick Anderson's benefit. Merely for the simple reason of wanting to look her best when out with an obviously self-assured man.

When she finally picked out the multi-coloured dress from the rail, she had a moment of doubt. She loved the silky material and the combination of lilacs, pinks and purples but wondered if it was overkill.

"Why don't you try it on? Those colours really suit you and it should hang beautifully on your shape."

Sally had obviously noticed her hesitation. Christy smiled, quite sure the girl knew exactly what suited her customers.

"Okay, I will. It's difficult to get the right impression when it's on the hanger, isn't it?"

Sally was right. As Christy came out of the changing room and stood in front of the full-length mirror, she recognised at once that it was made for her. It fitted over her body and flared gently from below the hips. She couldn't believe how feminine it made her feel and it would look even better once she added heels.

"I'll take it, thanks." There, no changing her mind. She didn't even care it was the most she had spent on herself all at once for a long time. All the more reason for a treat, to welcome her back to normal life.

She was leaving the shop, when she happened to look across the street. Two men stood deep in conversation: Ross McKinley and Nick Anderson. Christy pretended to rummage in her bag so she could watch for a moment. They appeared amicable enough from this distance. Then she saw Nick offer his hand in a shake and was astonished when Ross ignored it and walked away. So not very amicable after all.

Not wanting either man to see her, Christy noticed a pretty café two doors along, and she nipped inside. She could do with a coffee after the long browse through the shops. It was well after mid-morning so fairly busy. She was searching for a spare seat when she noticed Fiona at a table for two in the corner. The girl looked up at that moment and saw her. After the slightest hesitation, Fiona waved.

"May I take this seat, or am I interrupting you?" Christy asked.

"Help yourself. I'm just finishing anyway."

It wasn't the most gracious invitation or welcome she'd received, but Christy smiled and sat down, determined to be pleasant.

"I've been shopping – as you can see! It's definitely time for a coffee."

"Buy anything nice?" Fiona asked.

"A couple of essentials and a new dress. I haven't bought any clothes for far too long." She held back from saying any more. She didn't quite trust Fiona yet. It was as though the girl had some hidden agenda and resentment towards her.

"Lucky you. Hope you get the chance to wear it."

This time, she heard a note of bitterness. What on earth was wrong with the girl? Christy didn't say anything else and was relieved when the waitress arrived to take her order of a cappuccino and piece of shortbread. That would keep her going until she got a bus back to the cottage.

As the waitress cleared the used dishes from the table, Christy noticed two cups. Fiona must have met someone else before she arrived.

"So, are you enjoying being in your gran's house again?" Fiona asked, as if trying to find some conversation.

"It's a mixed pleasure. I love being back here but I miss Gran so much it hurts sometimes."

Christy noticed a flicker of sympathy in Fiona's eyes. So she wasn't completely hardened. She vaguely remembered the girl having an unsettled childhood which was no doubt why she had hung around with them so much in Kilcraig during the long summers. She could imagine the aunt, Mrs MacPherson, being a good mother-substitute.

"I can imagine." Fiona stood up abruptly. "Well, got to go. See you later." And she was gone before Christy could say goodbye.

Fiona was definitely a strange one, Christy decided, going off like that as though she suddenly didn't want to talk anymore. Once restored with coffee, she gathered her shopping and went to look for a bus. She was in luck, finding one due in ten minutes. As she waited, Christy watched all the people going about their business across on the main street. Then she glanced again at one particular couple. Was that Fiona talking to Nick Anderson? She hadn't realised they were so friendly, but there was no mistaking their closeness as they chatted.

She turned away and hoped they wouldn't glance over at the bus stop. She'd had enough of Fiona for one day and had no wish to meet Nick here. Yet she wondered just how close the couple were, and why he wanted to take *her* out. Hopefully, she might soon find out.

Chapter Seven

Christy was surprised at taking so much care with her make-up and hair. It had been too long since she had dressed up to go on a date – or at least the semblance of one. She certainly didn't fancy Nick Anderson in the least, although she appreciated his male attention.

She had completed her light make-up and slipped into the new dress, when a knock sounded on the door. Hoping he wasn't this early, yet not wanting any other visitor, she opened the door.

Christy stared at Ross for a moment, wondering why on earth he had to appear just at this time. Had he forgotten she was going out with Nick Anderson, or was he trying to spoil the evening for her before it began?

She noticed his hesitation and the appreciative look he couldn't hide quickly enough.

"You're going out. Sorry, Christy, I completely forgot about your… date."

She heard the distaste in his voice, although she believed he really had forgotten. Pulling her shoulders back, she returned his stare. Her dates or otherwise were nothing to do with him.

"No problem, Ross, I'm almost ready. How can I help you?" She sounded formal, as though talking to a business client, but he discomposed her in some way and she was determined to be brisk.

"It'll keep. I don't want to make you late. Is he picking you up?"

"Yes, in half an hour. You can come in if you like.

It really won't take me long to finish."

"You look perfect to me."

She couldn't mistake the admiration in his quiet words. It made her suddenly shy, not quite knowing how to deal with his compliment.

"Thank you." She decided against the flippant remark on the tip of her tongue.

"There's a tiny smudge of lipstick."

Before she could ask where, he stepped close and gently touched the corner of her mouth.

Christy stopped breathing and felt her lips part of their own free will. As he stood back, they stared at each other. Why did her heart suddenly sound so loud? This was Ross McKinley. Disapproving, formal, reserved Ross. Only he looked far from disapproving and his formality added to his intensity.

"Sorry again to get in the way. I'd better go. I'll speak to you another time. It can wait. Have a good evening. But be careful – don't trust too easily."

And he was gone after those unusually disjointed sentences, leaving her decidedly shaken. Christy frowned at the closed door, unsure what had just happened. The only thing she did know was that Ross had indeed most likely ruined her evening, but not quite in the way he had imagined.

Aware that Nick would soon be here, and hoping the two men didn't meet each other, Christy ran upstairs to repair her equilibrium. She wanted to get this evening over now, and hoped Nick Anderson would talk enough for them both.

Striding briskly back home before there was any chance of running into Anderson, Ross swore under his breath. What had possessed him to touch Christy's mouth like that? And where had those sudden feelings appeared from?

Picturing the silky dress hugging her curves and the way her chestnut hair shone and curled around her ears, he tried to convince himself that any warm-blooded male would feel the same. Yet he was honest enough to know his reaction had little to do with the packaging, after his few conversations with her. For some inexplicable reason, Christy Morrison was penetrating his carefully built defences against any hope of love. He had fallen foul of that untrustworthy emotion once before and had no intention of allowing another woman close enough to matter.

As he recalled her startled gaze at his touch, he knew she was every bit as bemused by the unexpected moment between them. And no wonder, since he'd not exactly been the most charming welcoming committee. He left that kind of thing to Cameron, who'd been overjoyed to see Christy again. He frowned at the thought. Surely his brother didn't have romantic feelings for their childhood friend?

Sighing at being completely preoccupied with the girl he'd once awkwardly kissed and then ignored in embarrassment, he reached the house. Going straight to the lounge, he poured himself a dram of whisky to dull the image of Christy being out to dinner with Nick Anderson.

Christy was immediately impressed with the country club as they drove along the curving drive to the entrance. Not just an ordinary restaurant, then, which was little surprise given the man by her side.

He had whistled appreciatively when she answered the door to him and she couldn't help smiling since he too had made the effort to smarten up in dark trousers, shirt and an obviously expensive jacket. She pushed all thoughts of that strange interlude with Ross to the back of her mind.

"Your carriage awaits, ma'am," he said, bowing slightly.

"Why thank you, kind sir." She couldn't resist his good-humoured teasing, and decided to enjoy this evening for what it was worth: dinner with a reasonably attractive new acquaintance. And if he wasn't the man she might choose to be with that was all the better, for she was not nearly ready to let her heart be stirred again.

The dining room was low-key but tasteful, and already buzzed with conversation from other diners. She wasn't surprised when the waiter welcomed Nick by name and took them at once to a table by the window. She suspected he enjoyed, or expected, this treatment wherever he went.

"Thank you for coming out with me, Christy," Nick said, as soon as the waiter left.

"Thanks for asking me, although I must admit it was a surprise." She decided to go for honesty. She certainly didn't want to give him any false notion of being interested in him romantically.

He smiled but didn't answer as he studied the wine list. For a moment, Christy wondered what on earth she was doing here, in this fancy place with a man she didn't know. In fact, it was the first time she had gone anywhere socially since the accident, apart from the dinner that first evening back in Kilcraig.

Yet, as the evening went on, she was relieved to find him an easy enough companion.

"So, tell me about Christy Morrison." He wasted no time in giving her his full attention.

She was tempted to give the stock reply, 'there's nothing to tell', but she wanted to be straightforward, up to a point. "Aged thirty-three, freelance illustrator of mainly children's books, lately of London."

"Well, you don't believe in spinning it out, do you?" He laughed in appreciation. "Are you working on anything at the moment? Or maybe you're too busy with the cottage."

"I do have a commission, actually, for a new children's Bible story book, but it's not urgent. And yes, I do have to clear the cottage."

She saw his eyebrows rise at the commission but he didn't refer to it.

"You must miss your grandmother," he said softly. "I believe you spent most of your summers up here."

Christy almost felt weepy and suspected it must be the kind way in which he acknowledged her bereavement. "Very much, but I'd rather not dwell on memories this evening. So what about you? " She had told him as much as she intended.

"Late thirties, successful business man most of the time, and currently single. Mainly based between Glasgow and Edinburgh."

She smiled at his equally sparse reply which included his marital status. She wondered how she could ask about Ross and was surprised when he suddenly mentioned him.

"So, you'll have known Ross McKinley a long time?"

"Off and on over the years. And Cameron, of course. Why do you ask?"

"Oh, no special reason. We used to work together but our paths have diverged a little. I wondered if he'd asked you about the cottage at all."

Christy stared in confusion. This was the last question she expected and she couldn't imagine why

Nick Anderson would be so interested in Ross. But it was enough to awaken a slight suspicion. She hoped her voice conveyed her reluctance to talk about the cottage with this stranger.

"No, not at all. I haven't spoken to Ross that much and I can't think why he'd discuss the cottage with me. He was a close friend of Gran," she added.

"So I gather. He seemed to look in on her more than anyone else."

Christy really didn't like the way he said it, as though implying that Ross had some ulterior motive for being so friendly with the older woman.

"Anyway, let's forget about it. I can see you don't want to talk about your private affairs." He smiled and changed the subject with the practised charm of a man used to getting his own way.

The short exchange altered the tone of their evening and Christy couldn't wait to get it over and return to the cottage. She smiled and answered when necessary, and tried not to dwell on the uneasy feeling he had caused within her. But she suddenly remembered it wasn't Ross who had asked what her plans were regarding the cottage, it was Cameron. Although why her decision should matter to any of them, she couldn't imagine.

When they finally stood up to go, Christy allowed Nick to help her on with her coat but moved away as soon as possible. Although he was perfectly pleasant and appeared to be enjoying her company, she had no intention of encouraging any further friendship.

By the time they arrived back at the cottage, it was almost completely dark as it only ever is in the countryside. The street lamp further along the path gave the only light. Nick immediately jumped out of the car and was opening her door before she had time to react.

"Thank you. That was a delicious meal and it was kind of you to ask me." She knew she sounded excessively polite.

"You're very welcome, Christy. We should do it again sometime. You're an interesting woman and I'd like to get to know you better."

Surprised at his seemingly genuine expression, she was unsure whether or not to shake his hand. But he made the decision for her by placing his hands on her shoulders and giving her a quick peck on the cheek.

"Goodnight, Christy." He went straight back to the car as she walked down the path to the cottage. She turned and waved as he drove away, before getting her keys out. She couldn't fault his behaviour and was relieved he hadn't expected to be invited in.

As soon as she stepped inside the front door, Christy sensed something was wrong, as though the cottage whispered to her, alerting her to a change in the atmosphere. She shivered, imagining all sorts of noises that didn't reassure her.

Switching on the sitting room light, she held her breath. Everything seemed as it should be it. She breathed out. Maybe it *was* her imagination. Then she heard it: a definite sound from the kitchen at the back of the house. Her first reaction was to run as fast as she could out the front door. Instead, she lifted the poker from the old-fashioned hearth.

Creeping towards the kitchen door, she threw it open as she flicked on the light switch. At first, she thought it was empty. Then she heard the soft meow. A small grey kitten with white socks glared at her from the side of the washing machine.

As Christy gasped in surprise, the kitten shrank

against the wall, still staring at her. What on earth? Fortunately, she wasn't allergic to cats and liked most animals, but this was decidedly weird, finding one in her kitchen.

"Well, hello. How did you get here? At least you're not hissing at me."

At the gentle, if shaky, sound of her voice, the animal inched a little closer.

Christy glanced around the room in puzzlement. The windows were closed with no sign of entry. She tried not to imagine it, but what if someone was still upstairs? Only one way to find out.

Wielding the poker again like some ancient warrior woman, Christy inched up the carpeted stairs, every step feeling like a mountain side. She sensed the movement behind her and turned. The kitten was following her, even more silently.

Strangely, it reassured her. Animals, and especially cats, were supposed to sense when something wasn't right. And this one seemed quite happy to go with her.

When she reached the top landing, Christy threw open every door and flicked on the lights. Definitely no one there. Once she had completely checked everything, she went back downstairs, the cat following behind.

"Well, I've no idea how you got here, but it's rather nice to have someone to talk to." Especially since her breathing had returned to normal after such a fright.

It looked at her as if in understanding and Christy smiled. "Okay, you can stay for now. I expect you'd like a drink."

As she poured milk into a saucer then sat at the table to watch the kitten slowly lap it up, she was still uneasy. Someone must have been inside the cottage. But whether it was to scare her, or to leave her a comforting gift, she had no idea. And if the windows remained locked and the door wasn't forced, it left only one answer. Someone had used a key to enter.

The most obvious person was Ross since he had visited Gran so much. But she couldn't imagine him scaring her like this. Then who else had access to keys? Cameron came to mind, but would he even think of such an idea? She could always phone Ross and ask him outright, but thought better of it. Apart from the fact it was late, she didn't want him to know she was home from her date.

The kitten was quiet enough and seemed very young. She'd wait until tomorrow to investigate how it arrived and wouldn't even bother naming it for now. Ensuring everything was well and truly locked, Christy wondered about the front door. She wouldn't relax, knowing someone could gain entrance. For the moment, she left her own key in the inside key hole; that would prevent anyone opening the door until she could arrange a change of locks.

The little cat followed her upstairs and she was absurdly glad of its presence. When it curled up near the bottom of the bed, she knew she had acquired a new friend. If no one claimed her.

Chapter Eight

The weak sun shone into the bedroom the next morning and played across the bedspread. Hearing a strange mewling sound, Christy stirred. Then aware of unaccustomed warmth on her legs, she remembered the kitten.

"You cry like a baby, little cat."

Sitting up, she had already made up her mind what to do. She would confront Ross first. He knew she was out last night. After sleeping on it, she could only believe he had left the animal as a gift, no matter how unlikely it seemed. Anything else was too disturbing to imagine. Then she'd do something about the locks, or any spare keys.

The kitten followed her down to the kitchen and seemed happy enough to be there.

"I'll need to get you a litter tray and some more food, kitty cat, if you're determined to stay. And a name. How about Misty, and we can be a rhyming couple."

The soft grey fur also reminded her of the mist that rolled off the hills up here and the higher mountains beyond. Odd how comforting it felt to talk to an animal. She'd never have thought of it herself since London life hadn't encouraged pets of any kind.

In the event, she didn't get the chance to ask Ross about the gift before the mystery was solved. She was about to leave the cottage when someone knocked on the door.

She opened it to find Cameron, his wide grin brightening up the morning.

"Mornin', Christy, love. Wanted to catch you. Did you get my wee present last night?"

Christy stared at her friend, astonished he had left the kitten. "*You* put it in the kitchen? I didn't know you had a key! Did you not think I'd be a bit freaked out to find a strange animal here when I got home?"

She didn't care if she sounded angry. It was such an irresponsible thing to do.

"But I thought you'd be delighted to find such a surprise. We have keys up at the house, so Ross could look in on your Gran. We thought you'd not mind."

Christy didn't miss the 'we' and couldn't believe Ross had agreed to such a mad notion. Maybe he'd been the one to tell Cameron the cottage would be empty.

"It was a kind thought, Cameron, but I'd rather you had brought the kitten to me – not left me to worry about who'd been in here."

His smile disappeared at once. "Och, I never thought of that, sorry. Oh, Christy, love, I hope you weren't too frightened."

Once again, she wondered at Cameron's insensitivity. Who wouldn't be upset at the thought of intruders? "Of course, I was, at first."

"So you'll forgive me for being so idiotic?"

He looked suitably contrite and his boyish charm soon asserted itself. She couldn't remain angry but he seemed such a child sometimes. However, she knew she wouldn't forgive Ross so easily for being involved.

"I suppose so. But please don't use the keys again without my knowledge. In fact, perhaps I should take them." It would certainly save the bother of getting the locks changed.

"I promise I won't do it again. Now, how about a trip to Loch Lomond if you're not too busy? I'll pick you up straight after lunch and we can stop for some cat food and litter on the way back."

"But what about Misty? Will she be okay by herself?"

"I see you've named her already – Christy and Misty, sounds perfect! Don't worry, she's old enough to be left in the kitchen for a while."

Christy shrugged. Why not? "That would be great thanks. I'll be ready." When he'd gone, she began to look forward to some time away from the cottage, especially on such a lovely day. And Cameron was an easy enough companion. It wasn't until much later that she remembered he hadn't given her the keys.

Since she had a few hours to kill, she sorted out some final books and papers and knew she had to make a start on clearing out Gran's bedroom. She dreaded this bit, putting off going through all the intimate little items that made up a person's private space. Not that Gran would have minded whatever Christy decided to do, as she was such a practical lady in life and was never precious about material possessions. Still, it was even more heart-breaking breathing in the faint lingering scent of her favourite lavender.

With a couple of black bin bags ready to accept the clothes and knickknacks, either for the charity shop or recycling centre, Christy set to work and paused only now and then when tears threatened at the sight of so many familiar things.

She opened the old fashioned, carved jewellery box that stood on the dressing table. What to do with the contents? Perhaps she should leave that exactly as it was until the lawyer had sorted out the final distribution of the estate according to the will. She already knew the cottage was hers, as Gran had never made secret of that fact when alive. But she may well have left other personal items to various people.

The final service she could perform for her dear grandmother was to strip the bed and wash the sheets and covers, as nothing had been touched since Gran's last journey to the hospital where she died. Now the tears she had kept at bay flowed freely as Christy struggled to fold everything. She had no hope of turning the mattress by herself so that would have to wait until she had help.

As she pulled the edges of the bottom sheet covering the mattress, something drifted to the floor. Thinking it was a white tissue, Christy bent down to retrieve it for the bin, then noticed it was a sheet of paper. Reluctantly opening it, Christy read the spidery writing and frowned. It was in Gran's handwriting and she scrutinised the words, trying to make sense of their meaning.

'*My darling granddaughter,*

I fear my time here on this delightful earth will soon be over and I have much to thank God for in a long and happy life. And one of the most joyful moments happened when you came into my world and brought such blessing. You will never know how much pleasure I experienced in your company.

These past few weeks have been a little more difficult and I know with all my heart that something has prevented you from being here. Whatever it is, I understand that you want to keep me from worrying. You are never far from my thoughts and I only wish I might be able to comfort you in your own need after you have been my solace for so long.

I want you to continue to love this cottage as much as ever, if you feel you could settle here. But the decision is yours and I know you will take time to consider and will follow your heart. Ross McKinley has been a rock and a friend and is exactly the type of partner I would wish for my beloved granddaughter. He is a man of such deep feeling and few words that he needs a special kind of woman, like his grandfather before him.

And now my dear, I must rest for it is too long since my hand has wielded a pen and grows tired. Trust only your own heart and mind, Christy. Too many people hide ulterior motives and false promises. But I digress, child, and will keep any further thoughts until I see you again.

With much love,

Gran

Christy folded the paper as tears streamed down her face. She sat on the edge of the bed. Did Gran mean to post the letter but never had the chance? Or had she hidden it for Christy to find one day? It didn't really matter, as the most important thing was that the elderly woman had known how much Christy loved her and wanted to be with her. And she understood her absence was not her own will.

As for the sentiments about Ross, Christy knew she would read that section many times. But two things puzzled her. She had never heard much about Ross's grandfather before now and wondered why Gran should mention him. And why had she been so concerned about who she might trust?

"Oh, darling Gran," Christy said aloud. "If only you had been able to hold on a little longer, and I had not been in hospital. But thank you for letting me know how much I was loved."

Wiping her tears away, Christy took the letter downstairs and placed it inside the back page of the *Rubaiyat*. She would read both again that evening. Now, more than ever, this cottage was her lifeline to her beloved Gran and too filled with love and memories to ever belong to anyone else.

Chapter Nine

At the knock on the door, Christy felt a lightening of spirits. A few hours away from the village was maybe exactly what she needed and Cameron was a fun companion, even if he irked her at times.

But when she opened the door, Ross stood on the other side. Before she could tell him she was about to go out, he spoke first.

"I know you didn't expect to see me, but Cameron sends his apologies. He and Fiona have urgent business in town and he couldn't put it off. But if you would accept a poor substitute, I'd be delighted to take his place."

From her first disappointment and annoyance at Cameron, to a sudden strange feeling in the pit of her stomach at the thought of a day out with his taciturn brother, Christy took a moment to answer.

"Come in... please. If you're sure you can spare the time. I must admit I was looking forward to seeing Loch Lomond again."

His presence filled the small hall as he entered the cottage and Christy was more aware of his masculinity than ever before.

"Nothing would give me more pleasure, Christy, honestly. It's a while since I've been there myself."

As she led him into the sitting room, a small meow reminded her about his part in the previous evening's drama and she opened the kitchen door to retrieve Misty.

"As you can see, we're beginning to get used to each other, so thank you for your part in the surprise present, even though the idea of someone being here when I was out scared me."

His astonishment seemed real, as Ross stared at the kitten. "My part? Surprise present? I'm sorry, but I have no idea what you're talking about although that's a pretty little kitten."

Now Christy stared in puzzlement, wondering why she always assumed the worst of him. "So you didn't encourage Cameron to leave me the cat when I was out with Nick Anderson? Or give him the key?"

He reached her side in seconds. "I promise you I'd never have thought of such a hare-brained idea. If I'd wanted to give you a gift like this, it would be in person." He frowned as he looked at Misty. "But I think I know who supplied the animal – Fiona. It's exactly the mixed-up kind of thing she would suggest to my susceptible brother."

"Well, I'm sorry I ever thought you capable of scaring me like that, and I've already told Cameron what I thought of him sneaking into the cottage without my knowledge. But it's no matter now and I do love my new little companion. Now, if you don't mind giving me a few minutes, I'll get my bag and jacket."

Depositing Misty back in the kitchen with the remainder of the cat food and some milk, she left Ross in the sitting room and dashed upstairs to finish getting ready. She was absurdly pleased he hadn't been involved in the cat escapade and suspected he'd have a word with his brother about scaring her. Poor Cameron, his motives had been thoughtful and with the best of intentions. But what about Fiona's?

In no time at all, Christy returned to the sitting

room, jacket over her arm, ready to leave. She noticed Ross having a look at her books and smiled. She did the same in other people's homes.

He looked up with an appreciative smile when she entered. "That was quick! And you look great, in case you thought it was a slight."

She had the grace to laugh. "Thank you. And I promise not to misinterpret every word you utter."

It was a rare moment of complete harmony and Christy looked forward even more to some time in his company. She was about to suggest they leave, when he happened to glance at the ornate book lying on her coffee table.

"What a beautiful edition," he said. "Is it yours?"

Christy glanced at him in confusion. "No, well yes, I suppose it is now. It belonged to Gran. But didn't you give it to her? There's an inscription inside."

Picking up the slim volume, he turned to the title page and she saw his deep frown. "I can see why you thought so, but no, I've never seen this before. I can guess who must have given it to her. My grandfather was also Ross McKinley and I believe they knew each other."

Taking the book from him, Christy read the inscription again, remembering that Gran had briefly mentioned Ross's grandfather in the letter she had tucked into the back of the book. She didn't want to share that with him as he had been mentioned too, but she puzzled even more as to what the old lady was trying to tell her.

"Well, I must say I've never heard Gran talk about your grandfather. I found this in amongst her other books and I got the impression it was a treasured possession. Were they close?"

Ross seemed hesitant and Christy wondered how much he knew. "I think they were very friendly at one time but Mother never talks about it and my grandparents died when I was in my teens. Your gran was widowed quite young, of course, and my grandfather was a handsome man as far as I remember."

This was too much to reconcile with the grandmother she had known. Yet for a long time, Christy had only visited in the holidays so didn't know everything about her life in Kilcraig.

Glancing at the man beside her, Christy shrugged. "I have to admit I'm intrigued, but I don't want to spoil our day out. I'll think about it later."

"Good idea. Let's enjoy the rest of the good weather while it lasts."

Replacing the book on the coffee table, Christy made sure that Misty was secure in the kitchen and locked the front door behind them. Although her thoughts were still on the possibility of some clandestine relationship between Gran and Ross's grandfather, she was determined to put them aside and enjoy this time with her own Ross. Though he was far from being that, and did she even want him to be hers? More importantly, could she trust him?

As Ross put the car in gear, he tried to forget the conversation about his grandfather and concentrate on the girl by his side. When Cameron told him he would have to cancel his outing with Christy, Ross had immediately offered to tell her. Only by the time he arrived at the cottage, he'd decided a day out was exactly what he needed and would be made all the better with Christy by his side.

He couldn't doubt she was getting beneath his

skin and he was furious with Cameron and Fiona for pulling that stunt with the cat. *And* taking the key without his permission. No wonder Christy had been freaked. But that inscription put everything else in the shade. Why should his grandfather have given her gran such an obviously expensive and personal gift? His words suggested a close relationship. Ross fleetingly tried to remember anything from his childhood that might be a clue but nothing immediately came to mind.

But Christy was right, this was not the time to dwell on it; today was for getting to know each other as adults a little better. As they drove towards the Erskine Bridge, he broke the silence. "Have you ever been to Conic Hill, at the Balmaha side of Loch Lomond? It's a pretty wee village and the hill attracts a lot of walkers."

"No, I haven't been there, but I'd love to see it. As long as I don't have to climb too high, or I'd have worn sturdier boots," Christy replied.

"Don't worry, it's a good place for a wander and we can take the first section of the path past the forest. It's a bit more than a stroll once we reach the steeper inclines but we don't need to go right up. If you like it, we can come back another day when more equipped and explore a little further."

As Christy smiled in agreement, Ross released the tension in his shoulders and wished he could do this more often. It was too long since he had taken a day off to enjoy the beautiful scenery at the loch and he couldn't imagine anyone he'd rather be with right now. At that realisation, he kept his eyes on the road and hoped he didn't do or say anything to spoil the day.

Chapter Ten

Christy already knew that the scenery in the west coast was even more beautiful all around the shores of Loch Lomond, but had never ventured round to this part of the loch in the village of Balmaha.

Although the car park sat at the foot of Conic Hill, she nodded in pleasure when Ross suggested a walk around the village first. It consisted of little more than several houses, a couple of shops and a combined restaurant and guest house situated on the shores of the harbour area.

They wandered down to the shore where Christy admired the loch stretching into the distance, the mountains a backdrop on all sides. Several small boats bobbed on the narrow inlet and a few families wandered along the loch side looking out for ducks or swans.

"Wait until you see the view from higher up," Ross promised. "We won't need to climb all the way, you'll be pleased to hear."

Once they reached the small shipyard and slipway, Christy turned to look back the way they had come. From behind the car park, the almost conical shaped Conic Hill stretched upwards from a forest of pine trees, a mixture of greens and browns against the light blue sky.

"It's not exactly a Munro, they're over 3,000 feet high, but this is about 1,200 feet and would still make us out of breath if we managed to get to the main summit," Ross explained. "Part of it's on the famous West Highland Way."

"Well I'm afraid it won't be today, at least not to the top," Christy said. "But I'd love to come back when a bit fitter." She turned back to the slipway. "I see boats leave for various parts of the loch from here. Must be great on a warm summer's day."

"Yes, a number of boats ply the loch from a few different areas. It's a good way to get the full impact of its breadth and length. But there's an interesting little island just across that stretch of water."

Ross stood very close to her as he gestured towards a tree-covered island and she was aware of his height and warmth. Resisting the urge to snuggle in even closer, she peered at the inconspicuous blob of land.

"It doesn't look any different from the others to me," she said, partly to break the direction her thoughts were taking.

Ross laughed. "You're right. Nothing interesting to look at from here, but it's often called the Island of Old Women or something like that, although it has an official name that escapes me, most probably in Gaelic."

Now she really was interested. "What a strange name. I'm guessing there's some history attached to it?" Few areas of Scotland escaped historical or romantic tales of one kind or another.

"I don't know the whole story, but there's an information centre back at the car park where we might be able to find out more. Or the Internet will come up with some good stories. All I remember is that a group of nuns used to inhabit the island."

Christy shivered slightly, as a cold breeze drifted in from the east and she pulled her jacket closer to her neck. It would be a cold place for anyone to live all year round, but she'd like to find out more about the Island of Old Women.

"You're getting chilled," Ross said, putting his arm around her and hugging her to him briefly. Just as she was beginning to enjoy the sensation, he let her go and his voice remained light. "Come on, let's go and walk a little before your feet get numb. If we climb up part of the hill first, then we'll be glad of a warm drink."

Happy to get moving, but unexpectedly disappointed at the slight distance now between them, Christy resolved not to get too close to this changeable man, for her own emotional protection.

As promised, the path leading up from the car park was a gentle enough incline to begin with, and other walkers were already coming down from whatever height they had reached. Christy hadn't expected so many tall trees on either side, and at times it was like walking through the centre of a forest.

As they gradually climbed higher to a section of wooden steps, her legs were beginning to protest at the unaccustomed effort. But the sheer exhilaration of being active in such natural surroundings was worth a bit of exertion. The gentle sound of running water accompanied them for part of the way and she guessed there must be a stream somewhere down the mountain side.

"Are you okay, Christy?" Ross asked eventually as they reached a more level area. "Tell me when you've had enough and we'll start back down. There's even more of a climb ahead before we reach the hill itself."

"I think I can manage a little further, maybe until I

can see the loch?"

"There's another level section up ahead after we get past the trees. We can stop and have a look from there."

The short stretch he mentioned had a few more steps, although Christy found it easier clambering over the stone covered path beside them. A narrow brook trickled down on the right side and she noticed a level patch of hillside beyond it with a rough arrangement of large stones, almost like some kind of old burial site or cairn.

"If we carefully step across the wee burn, we'll get a part view of the loch from over near the stones," Ross suggested. "But that's Conic Hill up ahead. You can see it properly now."

Glad to be offered a rest, Christy glanced up at the looming hill before her. If that was only a 'hill', she wondered what it would be like to stand at the base of a Munro. She began to negotiate the many rocks and stones to reach the other side of the narrow burn. At one point, she thought her foot was about to slip into the water but she managed to catch her balance just as Ross put out his hand.

"Oops, nearly," she laughed, jumping over on to the dry patch of grass.

"So was it worth coming this far?" Ross asked, as they stood looking down over part of Loch Lomond.

"Definitely. Even though it's a limited view from here, I can still see the majesty of the loch and the soaring hills in the distance. Anyway, it's worth it for the exercise!" Christy said.

"I know what you mean. It's also good for the soul to be out in such beautiful, natural surroundings."

Christy heard the slightly wistful note in his voice

and was struck by the sudden notion that this man might be lonely as well as reserved. Why had he never married? Or even seem to have a girlfriend? Not that it was any of her business, and she had never mentioned her past love life to him either. They didn't have that kind of friendship. *Not yet*, a little voice whispered in her head.

He suddenly broke into her wayward thoughts. "Would you believe that the Highland Boundary Fault actually runs through this spot at Conic Hill?"

"What's that exactly?" Christy asked, aware of her lack of knowledge about her country.

He smiled down at her. "Evidently the Fault was formed millions of years ago and that's what separates Scotland into the lowlands and highlands."

"Goodness. I've never even heard of it! I suppose that's why the West Highland Way runs through here then."

"Don't worry. My knowledge of geology and geography is sadly lacking though I'd like to explore more of Scotland. Anyway, the rest of the climb is on the hill itself but I suggest we leave that until another day. It's a long way down and the descent can be trickier sometimes," Ross said.

"That's fine by me. I think I've pushed my poor legs far enough today."

As they returned to the path, Ross issued a warning. "Watch out for the slippery stones and scree on the way down, Christy, and the tree roots as we get nearer the forest. I'll stay in front in case you slide."

Hardly had the words left his lips, when Christy stumbled on a giant tree root. "Oops, I didn't see that," she said, as she tilted forwards.

Next minute, Ross had caught her to him and broken her fall.

"Good catch," Christy said, then looked up at his darkened eyes and her amusement faltered.

"Are you okay?" he asked.

Nodding, she continued to return his gaze, wondering what it would be like to feel those firm lips on hers. At such an unexpected thought, she looked down, pretending to rub her leg, although it was her arm that had jarred.

"I'm fine, honestly. Thanks for catching me."

He edged back from her but took her hand. "Any time. I think we can probably walk side by side now so if you don't mind, I'll keep hold of your hand."

It was difficult to tell from his tone or expression whether or not he was just being thoughtful in looking after her, as he would with anyone else. But she was happy to leave her hand in his as they returned to the lower path and the car park.

"Think it's time for a drink," he suggested. "We can leave the car here and wander over to the inn at the loch side. Shall we have a look in the information centre first?"

"Yes please. I'd love to know more about that island."

The building was well laid out with information boards around the walls, leaflets and a hands-on area for children. Her attention was immediately caught by a large board showing the picture of the rare Capercaillie bird and she enjoyed reading about its habitat. That was something she might like to use as an illustration. Then she noticed a poster with a pictorial geology lesson on the Highland Boundary Fault that stretched from the Isle of Arran to Stonehaven near Aberdeen, crossing right through Conic hill as Ross had mentioned.

She picked up a few interesting looking leaflets

while Ross chatted to the girl at the counter. Glancing over, Christy viewed him across the short distance and knew he would be instantly attractive to females, yet he had none of the false charm of some handsome men, nor the flirtatious manner of his brother.

He glanced over at that moment and her face warmed at being caught watching him. "This young lady can tell you more about the island, Christy."

She had already noticed a large information board about a couple of the islands on the loch and was glad to hear more. The girl smiled as Christy wandered over and she imagined from her age that she was probably a student working during the holidays from university.

"You're interested in *Inchcailloch*, I believe?" the girl said. She had a pleasant lilt to her voice as she pronounced the name. "That's the largest of the thirty odd islands on the Loch. It's a great place to walk when you have time. Stunning views from the highest point. The boatman can take you across the short journey from the slipway and you tell him when to come back."

"Why is it called the island of women?" Christy asked.

"Old women, or cowled women." The girl smiled, confirming Ross's earlier words. "That's actually what the Gaelic name means. Evidently, it's because the Irish princess Saint Kentigerna settled there and set up a nunnery. They finally built a church in her memory in the middle ages. It's mostly a ruin now, although the cemetery is interesting."

"It's all so fascinating," Christy said, as they thanked the girl. "I'll definitely come back another day and take that boat across. Thank you."

"Don't forget to pick up the leaflet on the island

from the rack over there. It shows you what wildlife to look out for," the girl added.

Christy's head was full of nuns and Irish princess-saints and she hoped she might use the information one day in her illustration work. She smiled up at Ross, unable to remember the last time she had felt so happy and free.

This was a place to leave troubles and decisions far behind, to soak up the beauty of the loch and mountains and be part of the natural world. And, if she were strictly honest, it was all enhanced by the man at her side. Even Ross seemed to have shed some worries and appeared younger and more carefree, reminding her of the long-ago summers.

"Right, let's get that drink now," he said, taking her hand again as they walked through the car park.

A short wander across the village road took them to the stone-built inn overlooking the water. Whether rustic looking by intentional design or not, Christy admired its charm as it perfectly fitted the surroundings. Wooden tables and chairs held a few hardy walkers enjoying a drink in the cool afternoon. She was glad when Ross suggested they go inside, as she longed to see if the interior lived up to her expectations. It did.

The bar and restaurant immediately welcomed them into its warmth with a large coal fire in one corner, ready for the colder days and evenings. The low beams were hung with hundreds of little china cups, while old items like a big black telephone and ancient typewriter sat at various places around the wide wooden window sills.

Finding a cosy seat at one of the windows, Christy soaked up the atmosphere and decided at once to come back here again. Since it was neither lunch nor dinner time, they ordered mugs of coffee and the special fruit cake, *skeachan*, with its rich mixed fruit and spices, topped with crystallised ginger.

Just as she wondered if the day could get any better, Ross reached over and touched her hand. "Are you enjoying the outing, Christy?" He sounded as though it mattered.

"Very much. I wish I'd known about this beautiful part of Loch Lomond before now." Although she was glad Ross had shown it to her.

"It's amazing how little we know of our own area sometimes. It's years since I've been here," he said.

Hearing that slightly wistful note again, Christy wondered if he had ever brought another female here, then pushed the thought away. But it suddenly brought Michael to mind, and the reminder of how much she had wanted to share her country with him at one time.

"Sad thoughts, Christy?" Ross asked, surprising her with his perception. She was about to shrug them off but decided to start trusting this man a little.

"A few. I was remembering someone who might have loved this wildness. But he's in the past." She stopped there, still unable to share the recent trauma.

"I'm sorry the memories pain you. Sometimes it's best to leave the past where it belongs, perhaps."

She glanced up, but he was staring out of the window as though remembering his own ghosts, and she wondered again why he was still single. Could she ask, in these intimate surroundings?

Before she got the words out, he turned back to her and shrugged off his introspection, surprising her with a question of his own "So, did you enjoy your date with Anderson the other night? I hope he behaved."

Unfortunately, he had spoiled the atmosphere by the tone of his question and it made Christy contrary again. "He was a perfect gentleman, and yes, I did enjoy the evening, thank you."

Her voice must have sounded more irked than she realised, as he took her hand again and looked into her eyes. "I'm sorry, Christy, that was crass of me to question you like that. You've a right to see whoever you choose. I'm afraid Anderson brings out the worst in me. But let's not spoil the rest of our time together thinking about him, or anyone else."

Sensing their former intimacy would be hard to recapture, Christy nodded then picked up her shoulder bag and excused herself to go and freshen up. Her own feelings confused her, caught between the undeniable attraction to Ross and the sudden memories of Michael. Bringing Nick Anderson into the conversation only served to remind her of the animosity between the two men and wonder again at the reason. A quick glance at her watch showed her it was probably a good time to get back to the cottage. She was genuinely tired after the unaccustomed climb, but most of all she needed to sort out her mixed emotions.

Chapter Eleven

When she returned to the table, Ross had already paid the bill and was looking through some leaflets at the desk. He turned at her approach and nodded to the rack. "I see they have some accommodation here too. Great place to waken up to the sound of birds, and gently lapping water beside the loch."

Thanking the woman at the bar, Christy followed him outside, trying not to imagine waking up beside this man in this little haven. "Sounds almost poetic," she replied, avoiding his gaze.

Their journey back to Kilcraig seemed quicker, even though the traffic was heavier. The only thing that kept Christy from dozing to the movement of the car was her tumble of thoughts, not least about the enjoyable time spent in Ross McKinley's company. But he, too, was quiet and she wondered what preoccupied his thoughts.

Breaking the silence at last once they were nearer the village, Christy glanced at her companion. "Thank you so much for the lovely afternoon, Ross. I enjoyed it more than I could ever imagine."

He flashed a quick smile at her before watching the road again. "It was a great pleasure, Christy, and I really hope we can do it again one day."

It was a strangely formal and polite little exchange, but they were both sincere and she very much hoped they would have another outing together. Stifling a yawn, she looked forward to a warm bath then curling up to read with Misty on her lap.

"Oh, I completely forgot! I need to get some more items for Misty. Could you please drop me at the shop?"

"Of course. But I'll wait for you and drive you home. I always see a lady safely to her door."

He spoke lightly and Christy supposed it was almost like a first date, in a way, even if he'd been partly forced into it because of Cameron. But she hoped it wouldn't be their last.

She hurried into the little village shop, pleased to find it still open. Ewan MacPherson was behind the counter again and welcomed her with the same mix of curiosity and courtesy as before.

"You've acquired a cat already, have you? That'll be a good wee companion for you in that lonely cottage. You're in luck, I always keep cat and dog supplies for the villagers."

Although pleased to find him so genial, something in his choice of words about the 'lonely cottage' disturbed her, and again she felt his gaze following her every move. Just then, the door opened and Ross stepped inside, his tall physique filling the shop.

"Thought I'd come and see if you needed a hand to carry the things to the car, Christy."

"Thanks, I'm just about done here." She was absurdly pleased he had come to help and it wasn't only because of the shopkeeper's unnerving stares.

"Good day, McKinley." Ewan MacPherson nodded at Ross. "You're helping our wee visitor settle in then."

Christy caught Ross's guarded glance at the man and noticed he didn't answer the question. "Good day, MacPherson."

"Have you thought any more about Anderson's

suggestion? Even your mother is in agreement with him."

Christy sensed the increasingly uncomfortable atmosphere between the two men and she hurried to pay for her shopping.

"This is neither the time nor place to discuss our business, MacPherson. You know fine my position," Ross said. Turning away from the man's glowering stare, he addressed Christy. "I'll drop you off with these, if you're ready."

"Bye, lass. I look forward to seeing you another day," Ewan called as they left the shop.

Resolving to do most of her shopping in the nearby small town when she could drive, Christy waited to see if Ross would mention the reason for the tension between the two men. But it had only served to make him more distant again, as though worry weighed him down, and she sighed in the realisation that their lovely day was truly over.

As he started up the car, Ross glanced at her briefly. "Sorry about that. We have unfinished business and it's causing a bit of conflict between some of the villagers. But I'll tell you about it another day."

Understanding the subject was closed, Christy thought again of a deep, warm bath that would soothe away any threat of sore muscles after her climb. And much as she enjoyed this man's company, she suddenly needed some time to herself.

When they drew up at the cottage, Ross immediately got out and lifted the shopping from the car, depositing it on the doorstep. "Do you want me to take it into the kitchen for you?" he asked.

"No, that's fine, I'll manage." If he came inside, she might not want him to leave right away and that would be a mistake. As he stood beside her, she looked up and caught a tender expression in his eyes.

"Thanks again for a wonderful day, Ross, and for introducing me to such a beautiful place. I really enjoyed it all."

"It was my pleasure. I'd almost forgotten how to have an uncomplicated day out with a pretty woman." He reached over and pushed a little strand of hair from her cheek.

For a fleeting moment, she thought he was going to kiss her and she tensed. Then he nodded at the door. "I'd better let you get back to your little cat. But I hope we can do this again soon. See you later, Christy."

She watched him stride back to the car, before she turned to unlock her door.

She hardly had entered the sitting room, when a little ball of grey fur launched itself at her feet.

"Hello Misty. Have you missed me?" She bent down to stroke the kitten, then stood up in puzzlement. Why was Misty in this room? She was quite sure she had shut her in the kitchen, and surely it was the kind of door that wouldn't edge off the catch by itself.

She checked the kitchen and took a quick look around the cottage, but nothing seemed disturbed. Then she noticed the *Rubaiyat* book was lying in a different place from where she had left it. She quickly picked it up and flicked through its pages. Gran's letter was still there. But that, too, seemed not quite right, as though someone had opened and refolded it, to read perhaps.

Or was she being paranoid, thinking someone had been inside the cottage again in her absence? Leaving her own key in the locked front door, Christy fed

Misty then went up to run a bath. She refused to be frightened in her new home, in this welcoming cottage. But tomorrow, she would insist on retrieving any spare keys that might be up at the big house. And at least she knew Ross had nothing to do with this little incident since he'd spent the afternoon with her.

His spirits dropped as soon as Ross turned into the driveway. It was so long since he'd taken a day off to enjoy himself that the return was even more depressing. But a large part of his enjoyment had been due to Christy's company, even more than the beautiful location.

That combination of independence and vulnerability got to him every time he saw her, but a deeper feeling had stirred within him today and he hadn't wanted their outing to end. He hoped Christy felt it too, and had forgiven him his previous arrogance enough to enjoy renewing their friendship. Then he had to go and spoil it by mentioning Nick Anderson, like some jealous lover. He'd need to tread carefully, as he had no wish to turn Christy against him by bad-mouthing another man.

And he hadn't liked the way Ewan MacPherson was eyeing Christy's every move in the village shop. But that, no doubt, was partly because of the trouble he was having with the man himself.

"Is that you, Ross?"

The imperious voice from the lounge summoned him and he sighed. What now? He was hardly in the mood for more recriminations. But he entered the room with a half-smile in place.

"Yes, Mother. How are you?" Although he lived here when in the village, his rooms were far enough from the rest of the house to avoid too many confrontations.

"I'm as well as ever, for which I never cease to give thanks. But I want to talk to you about a few items. We'll get the unpleasant business over with first. Why don't you sit down and at least pretend you're pleased to be here." His mother's twisted smile showed it was her attempt at a joke.

"You know I'm always pleased to see you, Mother, even if I don't agree with your plans."

Sitting across from him, his mother studied him with interest. "You look different, more relaxed. Cameron said you were taking the Morrison girl out for the afternoon. I hope you don't get too friendly with her."

Raising his eyebrows that his brother bothered to mention it, and at his mother's words, Ross spoke with deliberation. "Her name is Christy, and I can't see why it should matter to you whom I choose to spend my time with."

Now his mother raised her eyebrows. "It matters who will bear the heirs to this house and estate one day, and I should like to think she will be someone suitable to take the McKinley name."

"Someone like Moira, you mean? How many times must I tell you that I've long known we'd never have suited each other? And I think you're being a little presumptuous about Christy. We've only spent one afternoon together which hardly constitutes an engagement." He failed to keep the bitterness from his voice. "Why have you never liked her? Is it something to do with her grandmother? Or my grandfather, perhaps?"

He knew he had stumbled on something when his mother visibly paled before him. "I have no idea where you get such nonsensical ideas, Ross

McKinley. But I don't want to talk to you about your love life. We need to make a decision soon about the land."

Glad to leave Christy out of the conversation, Ross was no happier about this topic. "You know how I feel about losing parts of the countryside, never mind the few cottages that stand in the way. I can see that we need to raise money for the long-term upkeep of this place, but there must be another way."

"Nick won't wait forever you know. His client is already looking at other areas. We need the income selling some land would bring. Once we added a golf course and more updated accommodation to the house, it's exactly the kind of venue Americans would love."

He didn't doubt it, but it was wrong on so many levels and it wasn't the kind of heritage he wanted to leave for any children.

"Give me a little more time to find an alternative source of income and if I fail, then I guess we'll have little option." Although he had no intention of giving in so easily.

"Thank you. I'll find out the deadline from Nick. But I can't see what else you can do but accept we need to move on. Now, the other thing I wanted to remind you of is the Winter Ball. We need to fix the date so I can arrange the numbers and catering."

He'd forgotten about the annual ball, a highlight for the whole village and an excuse for his mother to play lady of the manor. An unbidden picture came into his mind, of dancing close to Christy and not caring who saw them together. But his mother waited for a reply.

"Let me check the diary. And we'd better make sure Cameron is around, although he seems to have a lot of spare time on his hands recently."

His mother stood up, indication that the lecture was over. "I'm sure he and Fiona will make a success of their antique business, once they get the additional premises sorted out."

Recognising the same over indulgent tone towards his brother that had followed him since childhood, Ross stood and moved to the door. "I'm sure you're right, Mother. My brother has an uncanny way of landing on his feet. I'll go and check that date."

Tired after his climb with Christy and worried over the future of the estate and village, Ross was glad to escape to his rooms and shut himself off by reading for a while before dinner. Maybe he needed a break in the city again. Yet he couldn't rid his mind of the enjoyable time spent with Christy, or imagine removing himself from the village while she was living in the cottage.

Chapter Twelve

Snug in her warm pyjamas and dressing gown after the bath, Christy made some easy vegetable pasta for herself, pleased to see that Misty had finished every morsel of food.

"Just you and me tonight, Misty. Aren't we lucky?"

The kitten looked up as though in agreement and Christy was surprised how quickly she had got used to the comforting presence, even if it did make her talk aloud as though having a conversation. But apart from Gran's stereo with built-in radio, there was nothing else to break the silence. Maybe she should get a small TV and DVD player for the winter nights. Or maybe she should be getting on with the new illustrations. The scenery and quality of light around the area would inspire her to even more creativity.

That thought reminded her of the unexpectedly enjoyable day spent in the company of Ross McKinley. She couldn't deny how much he interested her; such a mixture of thoughtfulness and reticence, the latter almost to the point of dourness at times. There was no doubt about the animosity between him and Nick Anderson, and even the tension in the shop with Ewan MacPherson. What was going on in the village that caused him such stress? Christy very much wanted to find out, in the hope she could ease that frown from his brow.

"Now you're getting carried away, Morrison," she

told herself, and Misty looked up again as though she'd addressed the cat. "Just your foolish owner getting carried away, Misty."

But Ross was the first man she had given any thought to since Michael. Perhaps she was finally moving on at last, even if remnants of guilt lingered to remind her now and then. Would her arm ever be quite the same again? It was certainly getting stronger each week, and she was relieved to be over that initial excruciating physiotherapy.

Picking up the *Rubaiyat*, Christy read Gran's letter again, still moved by knowing these were her own words. Had someone else read this earlier? As well as disquieting her, she was angry that anyone had invaded her privacy like that – or was she indeed being paranoid, imagining an uninvited guest where none existed?

Resolving again to retrieve any spare keys first thing tomorrow, she opened the book and started to read it from beginning to end. As well as the exquisite illustrations of exotic women and men that captivated her, the language and poetry of the words were enchanting. She liked the way in which the drawings were mostly in black and white with only small touches of the same burgundy red as the cover.

She was nearing the end of the book when Misty suddenly stood up, back arched as though she had heard something. Then a knock sounded on the front door. Christy glanced at the clock, surprised to find it only eight thirty in the evening. Not so late for a visitor, then, although she was too tired to be sociable.

When she reached the door, she called out, "Who's there?" She wasn't going to be foolish.

"Ross. Sorry it's so late."

Hearing the one voice she didn't mind, Christy opened the door. "Hello, what brings you here?" She hoped she didn't sound as unwelcoming as the words implied. Then she realised the dog was beside him.

"I was walking Darwin and thought I'd check you were okay after today. But I'm sorry, were you about to go to bed?"

Frowning in puzzlement at his question, she remembered her pyjamas and dressing gown. "Oh, gosh no, I'd had a bath so this was more sensible than getting dressed again."

The incongruity of their conversation made her blush and she bent down to pat Darwin "Hello, boy." She didn't know what to do. Ask him in? What about Misty?

"I'm sorry. I'll go away and leave you in peace." He half smiled as though aware of the awkwardness.

"No, wait. Would you like a drink? I'm about to have a cup of camomile tea and I'd like to speak to you about something. Do you think our pets will get on?"

"If you're not too tired, I'd like that. Let's introduce Darwin and Misty to each other and if there's a problem, I'll go."

Reflecting that it was the first time animals had decided her actions, Christy opened the door wider and let man and dog inside. As she was closing the door, a movement further up the path caught her eye and she had the distinct impression that someone was watching them. She pushed over the door and locked it. Now she really was imagining things.

As they watched, cat and dog eyed each other warily, then Darwin sniffed at Misty and lay down on the floor. The cat hesitated a moment, then sat beside him, licking her paws.

"Well, that's a good omen," Ross said, leaving Christy to work out his exact meaning.

She smiled, glad of the visitors. "It's good of you to call in. I'm not bad at all and the muscle ache won't last long. I was just reading through the *Rubaiyat*. It's really beautiful and I'm sure it's the kind of book to give someone special."

"I have no doubt my grandfather, or any other man, would have thought so of your gran. But I'd still like to know their exact connection. I think Mother knows more than she's letting on."

"Have a look through it while I get the tea, if you like."

It was only as she laid out a tray with cups and biscuits, that she remembered the letter and Gran's reference to Ross, although he didn't seem the type of man to read someone's private mail.

Nevertheless, she hurried back to the sitting room. "Sorry, I forgot I'd put something inside the book, let me take it out of the way." Retrieving the letter from the back of the book, she pushed it inside her dressing gown pocket. "Thanks. Would you mind carrying the tray through in a few minutes, please? It's a bit heavy for this arm yet."

"Of course I will. Give me a shout when you want me through."

By the time, they were sipping their tea, Christy had grown used to the tall man sitting on her comfy armchair and couldn't help thinking how at home he seemed. Of course, he had been used to visiting Gran.

"You said you wanted to speak to me about something, Christy. Is there a problem?" he asked at last.

She hesitated to bring up her earlier disquiet, now his presence had dispelled any lingering fear. "You'll think me paranoid, but when I returned this afternoon, I had the distinct feeling someone had been in the cottage again."

She glanced over and caught a deep frown on his brow. "Sorry, I know it sounds silly and I promise you it wasn't a ghostly presence I sensed or anything like that. But Misty was in the sitting room and I'm sure I closed her in the kitchen. And I think Gran's book had been moved."

"I don't think you're silly, Christy, but I don't even want to consider that anyone would do such a thing." He moved over to the sofa and sat beside her. "I can imagine the fright such an idea must have given you, and I'm assuming you mean someone used a key again?"

She glanced at his dark grey eyes and nodded. "I was going to seek you out tomorrow to ask for any spare keys to be returned."

"Of course. I should have done that at once after the cat incident. But I hardly think Cameron would have let himself in again after seeing how much it upset you." He must have seen her expression as he took her hand. "I'm not saying you're imagining it, Christy, but I can't think why anyone would do this. Do you want me to go and get the keys now?"

Although tempted to say yes, she was also determined not to be intimidated. "No, tomorrow will do, thanks. I can't be absolutely sure I closed the kitchen door completely and if Misty was in the sitting room by herself, it's quite possible she knocked the book out of place." For a moment she actually believed that had happened and she was making a fuss about nothing.

Ross finished his drink and stood up, as though he didn't want to remain sitting beside her and she, too, stood.

"It's probably the most likely scenario, although my brother is still the person who caused your anxiety in the first place. But if you're sure you'll be able to sleep okay, I'll see you tomorrow. Take care, Christy. And phone me at the house any time if you're at all worried." He called to Darwin who came at once.

When they reached the front door, they stood for a moment facing each other. She appreciated his strength and knew it would be easy to seek his protection. But she had to look after herself now.

"Thanks, Ross. I feel a bit foolish now and would never have told you about it if you hadn't called in. But it was good to talk it over."

He reached out his hand and pushed a strand of hair from her eyes. She tensed, aware of his strong masculinity.

"Any time, Christy. I owe it to your grandmother to make sure her favourite girl is safe and well. Sleep tight."

His words broke the spell and she took a step back as man and dog went into the cool night. It was still about Gran and his regard for her.

Before she closed the door, she remembered thinking someone had been watching earlier and she glanced in each direction but the path was clear. Locking the door behind her, she stood against it for a moment, reliving Ross's visit and wishing she didn't feel such a growing attraction for the man.

"And you didn't help, Misty," she told the little cat who seemed as bereft as she felt. "Did you have to get on quite so well with Darwin?"

The kitten padded across to join her on the sofa and Christy allowed her to curl up beside her, glad of the warmth and company. Cameron might have gone about it the wrong way, but she would always be grateful for the kind thought that resulted in her new companion. As for the older McKinley brother, she was pleased their friendship had cemented a little more, even if his motives might still be a tad suspect.

Chapter Thirteen

Before Ross had the chance to return her keys, Christy opened the door next day to a chastened looking Cameron on her doorstep.

"I bring two humble apologies. Forgot to give you these, Christy love," he said, holding out a set of keys. "And I'm sorry about letting you down yesterday, although I hear my brother was a poor substitute and filled in as best he could."

Smiling in spite of herself, Christy opened the door to let him in. Had Ross asked him to bring the keys? And if he didn't, why had Cameron suddenly remembered them? Knowing she was in danger of seeing conspiracies where none existed, she concentrated instead on Cameron's chat.

"My brother would have handed them in himself but he's away into Glasgow with Fiona. They both had business in town so it made sense to go together."

A slight pang of envy struck her as Christy imagined another girl with Ross. Surely it didn't matter who else he spent time with, especially Fiona. Then she remembered Cameron mentioning that the girl had always fancied Ross, and she felt uneasy. Perhaps Fiona had wangled the trip.

As she made coffee, Christy realised Cameron was telling her something else. "I'm sorry, I missed that. Did you mention a dance?"

"It's officially called the Winter Ball and we're expected to dress up a bit in our finery, which means a pretty dress for the women and kilts for the men.

Not bothering with a tray so she didn't have to ask for help in carrying it, she put a mug of coffee down on the table beside Cameron and one for herself before replying.

"That sounds fun, like a ceilidh only bigger and posher."

Cameron laughed. "That's it exactly. And I hope you'll do me the honour of dancing with me."

"Am I invited?" she asked, since this was the first she'd heard of the evening.

"Well of course you are. My mother's fixing the date and then the invitations will go out. Most of the villagers will be there, and other guests of course."

She had to admit it sounded an event not to be missed and it was a long time since she had been at any kind of dance, even with Michael. A rogue image came into her mind of Ross in a kilt and she pushed it away as quickly.

"You might even get to meet the one that got away from my brother. Although he won't be pleased she's invited."

At first, she wondered if she had misheard Cameron's words and glanced across to find him watching her closely. Was he trying to gauge her friendship with Ross?

"You mean an ex-girlfriend?" she asked, trying not show it mattered.

"She was a bit more than that, I think. My mother was all set to put an engagement announcement in the *Scotsman* and *Herald*, then suddenly it was all off and Ross refused to speak about it again. He's never told me the whole story and you don't ask my brother personal details unless he volunteers any information. Think it might have had something to do with

Anderson as they detest each other."

Christy tried to process such news while hiding the extent of her interest. "I expect he has his reasons for not talking about it," she said. "I suppose many of us have past incidents, or even present ones, we'd rather not remember or discuss too much."

Cameron drained his cup and stood up. "Well I'd better not take up any more of your time. Thanks for the coffee, Christy, and look out for the invitation."

Surprised at his sudden desire to leave, she wondered if Cameron had his own secrets he'd rather not think about. Or he might only have other pressing things to do, she admonished herself.

"Thanks for bringing the keys down. And Misty is a lovely companion, by the way."

He hesitated, then smiled with his usual open friendliness. "To make up for our lost day out, would you like to come and visit the antique shop Fiona and I are involved in? We've been building up an interesting collection."

"Sure, I love antiques. Is it in town?"

"No, we changed our minds about that. It's over at Loch Lomond. In a shopping complex with a view, not the area you visited with my brother. I thought we could take a drive over on Saturday morning, and I promise not to let you down this time."

"It's a date. I'll be ready."

He nodded, gave her a perfunctory hug then was gone.

Christy locked the door and sat down on the sofa going over Cameron's revelations. Why should she be so surprised that Ross had almost got married, when she'd wondered often enough why he had no wife or girlfriend. But it did perhaps explain his reticence, if something had gone wrong. On the other hand, she had no idea which of them had ended the relationship. And how was Nick Anderson involved?

She put the mugs in the sink and decided to leave all speculation aside in the hope that Ross might confide in her himself one day. And perhaps she could encourage him by beginning to talk about her own past. Meantime, she allowed her thoughts to drift to the idea of a winter ball. For that, she would certainly need another new dress.

First of all, she needed to get on with her illustrations. Now that the cottage was mostly cleared and cleaned, she had decided to use the front bedroom as a studio. She was happier sleeping in her old room at the back, and more light flooded into the front room in the mornings. It would give her space for a desk and all the paraphernalia she liked around her as she drew and painted. She had a feeling photography would become even more of an interest, after her visit to Loch Lomond. Autumn and winter should provide some stunning images of light and shadow, especially when snow arrived on the mountains. She could put her laptop on another small table and use that for digital images, as well as emails and research.

That reminded her that she hadn't even fired up her computer since arriving. So much for the Internet age – it seemed to have left her behind. But she still had a couple of friends in London and an agent who might have been trying to get in touch and she decided to get onto that first. She had never got around to replacing her trusty old mobile with a smartphone that had Internet connection.

Once she switched the laptop on, the familiar Windows tune played on the opening screen and the desktop icons came into place.

It was only as she clicked on the Internet icon that

she suddenly remembered. Gran didn't have a computer and there was no Internet connection in the cottage. Sighing in frustration, she shut the laptop down again. Now that she'd got this far, it was annoying not to be able to access her emails. Unless... Perhaps Cameron would let her bring the laptop up to the house. They were bound to have Wi-Fi and she could maybe access her mail that way.

As she picked up the telephone, she realised she didn't know the number, and the thought made her nervous as she wouldn't be able to phone anyone if there was a real disturbance at the cottage. Cameron had only kept in touch by email when arranging to pick her up at Glasgow Central the day she returned. Nothing else for it, she would take the laptop and walk up in the hope Cameron was still at home.

Making double sure Misty was comfortably shut in the kitchen, she put her jacket on and packed the laptop in its black case. It was mostly used for her illustrations, and she'd packed it in between her clothes on the journey north, but she really must get a smartphone.

Glad the rain had stayed away, she set off up the path towards the big house. She hadn't been back since that first evening and hoped she would be welcome arriving unannounced like this. She grinned, realising she sounded like someone from a previous century who needed an invitation to call. Ross should still be in Glasgow with Fiona so he at least wouldn't be around.

Chapter Fourteen

There was no reply at first and Christy was about to give up when the door opened and Mrs McKinley stood in front of her, eyebrows raised at sight of her visitor.

"Christina, this is an unexpected pleasure. Come in. Were you looking for one of my sons?"

Swallowing her reservation at taking up this woman's time, she hesitated. "Yes, sorry. I saw Cameron earlier and thought he might be here. I don't want to bother you, but I'm trying to check my emails and realised I don't have Internet access yet. I wondered if you perhaps have Wi-Fi here."

"Don't stand on the doorstep, dear. Come through to the kitchen and we'll have a cup of coffee. I've not had the chance to chat to you properly since you returned. Neither of the boys is here at the moment and I tend to leave computers to them."

Feeling more like a servant not allowed to enter the drawing room, Christy followed her hostess through the hall. She could hardly refuse hospitality when it was offered, although she still suspected this woman didn't care for her that much.

At sight of the large wooden table in the centre of the kitchen, Christy remembered childhood days when she and the boys had called in for a drink in the middle of their outdoor games. And Fiona always hanging around with them, yet seeming more of an outsider than Christy.

"Have a seat, dear, and I'll pour the coffee. There's some in the pot not long made."

Placing her laptop at the other end of the table, Christy sat down and glanced around the spotless room as Mrs McKinley brought over two pretty mugs and a plate of shortbread.

"Homemade by Effie - Mrs MacPherson. They're delicious."

The mugs of coffee and plate of biscuits made the woman opposite her more approachable and Christy relaxed. Perhaps this was a good chance to get to know each other a little better.

"So, how are you settling in, dear? I hope the cottage isn't too much for you. Or are you thinking of going back to London?"

Christy put down her mug and wished the woman would stop calling her 'dear' in that patronising way. And so many intrusive questions. Then she felt guilty when the woman was trying to be friendly enough.

"I love the cottage, thanks, and it's looking great, although I sorely miss my grandmother's presence." She lowered her eyes, as sadness unexpectedly engulfed her again.

"I expect it will take a long time to get used to her absence. Death always affects us more than we realise. What about London? Or perhaps it's too soon to make that decision yet, if you have no one special waiting for you?"

Glancing at Mrs McKinley, Christy had the distinct impression her decision mattered to the woman for some reason and she resented the veiled question about her personal life.

"I'm pretty sure I'll be staying here. I can work anywhere and can't imagine being back in the city. I might have to go down to see my agent occasionally, but I can keep in touch with her by email. Once I get Internet access in the cottage," she said, reminding the woman why she'd come up here. She certainly wasn't going to tell this woman anything about Michael.

"Oh, you have an agent? I didn't realise you were that far on in your career."

The raised eyebrows and condescending tone annoyed Christy and she wondered if she could ever really like this woman. She nodded, but didn't bother answering the statement.

"My sons seem pleased you're up here again. I expect they're glad of some pretty female company besides Fiona, while they're making up their minds about settling down. I'm hoping Ross will soon be patching things up with his girlfriend when she comes over for the ball."

Christy couldn't mistake the way Mrs McKinley watched her while delivering these words and she wondered why the woman was at pains to emphasise Ross's ex-girlfriend. Did she think he might be interested in her? Unlikely as that seemed, why should it matter? Either the older woman was deluded, or Cameron had misunderstood his brother's feelings and intentions.

Determined to show no reaction whatsoever, Christy smiled. "It's great to see Cameron and Ross again and they're both being very kind."

As she was beginning to work out how to escape gracefully, she heard the front door open and she inwardly sighed with relief. Maybe Cameron had come back after all.

But the footsteps that brought their owner to the kitchen belonged to Ross. He stopped at the sight of his mother and Christy sitting drinking coffee together.

"Hello, Christy, this is a lovely surprise. Hello, Mother."

"Christina was looking for some help with her computer and I invited her in for a chat," Mrs McKinley said. "I thought you were in Glasgow with Fiona, Ross."

"I didn't stay long and Fiona wanted to get the train back as she was meeting someone. So hopefully I can help you. What's the problem?"

She looked up and smiled ruefully. "I'd forgotten I have no Internet access and was hoping you might have Wi-Fi so I could check my emails, if it's not too much trouble. Though my laptop's so old it might be a bit slow."

He sat down beside her as he answered and his mother faded into the background. "You should be able to get a connection for the cottage okay. We can check that out later. But for now, why don't you come and use my computer."

Glad of the excuse to escape his mother's gimlet eye, Christy nodded. "That would be brilliant, if you don't mind. I don't expect I'll have many but my agent might have got in touch to chase up the illustrations. And a couple of friends might be wondering why I haven't replied to emails."

"Then let's go and try it now, if you've finished your coffee." He turned to the older woman. "You won't mind me taking Christy away, Mother?"

Christy stood up at once as his mother replied. "Not at all, Ross. We've had a nice chat but I must get on now. And I'm sure you'll have work to do yourself."

It was a clever dismissal, combined with a warning not to monopolise too much of her son's time and Christy was relieved the interrogation was over. "Thanks for the coffee and letting me take up your time, Mrs McKinley."

The woman nodded as she watched Christy and Ross leave the kitchen and Christy would love to have known his mother's thoughts.

"My rooms are up here," Ross said, as he led the way up the grand staircase and along to the left.

"Are you sure you're not too busy?" Christy asked.

"Not at all, especially when helping a damsel in distress." He smiled as he opened the door and Christy noticed again how much more relaxed it made him.

The large room overlooked the countryside beyond the back of the house and was obviously a kind of sitting room and study, with book shelves floor to ceiling along one wall. A very tidy medium sized desk sat at the bay window but no computer was in evidence. A comfortable looking sofa and chairs were tastefully arranged in front of a modern electric fire and surround.

"The computer is over here. Have a seat while I fire it up," Ross said, walking over to a corner of the room where a more work-like desk and computer with various other office paraphernalia sat ready for use. "I like to keep the other desk free for paper work."

Christy hadn't noticed the computer desk and approved of the arrangement. "May I look at your books?" she asked.

"Of course, although I must warn you that many of these have been handed down from my parents and grandparents and don't necessarily reflect my own taste!"

While Ross readied the computer, Christy enjoyed reading the spines of almost every type of book imaginable and it showed an eclectic taste in literature. She found several volumes of poetry and idly lifted one down. As she opened the title page, she had a feeling it would belong to his grandfather, the one who had given Gran the *Rubaiyat*. And so it proved. Glancing over at Ross, she hesitated about asking questions since she had arrived uninvited into his home. It seemed the wrong time for serious conversation. She should check her mail and leave Ross and his mother to their business.

"Here we go," he said, and Christy put the volume back on the shelf. "I've connected to the Internet, so it's all ready for you to go online. I'll be over at the desk so you can have some privacy."

"Thanks. I really appreciate this," Christy said, as she sat at the computer and logged into her emails.

As she suspected, only two friends and her agent had been trying to contact her, apart from all the junk mail. Deleting adverts and offers, she opened her agent's message first. A friendly reminder about the deadline for the Bible story illustrations and a 'hope you are well' type of message.

Christy certainly couldn't fault Brenda's sensitivity and willingness to adapt to her move so far away. But she'd worked with her for a couple of years now and they had a trusting relationship.

Her friend Annie's chatty email sparkled off the screen with her 'hope you've found a hunky Scot in a kilt for me!' and Christy hoped the fun-loving children's writer would pay her a visit at some point. Typing a quick reply to both ladies, she assured them everything was great and that she enjoyed being back in Scotland.

That left Fran. At least she had emailed. Opening her message, Christy read it quickly.

'Hi Christy. Hope you're well and surviving the wilds. I miss you down here, but understand your need to get away. Keep in touch. Fran x'

No 'love, Fran' she noticed, but at least it was friendly enough. Her friend had been looking forward to welcoming her as a sister-in-law and their strained relationship since the accident had added to Christy's guilt. Did Fran blame her for Michael's death?

Christy closed the emails deep in thought and sat staring for a while until she heard Ross move.

"Everything okay, Christy? Not bad news, I hope."

She shook her head, but couldn't answer at the sudden sadness that threatened to overwhelm her.

He was beside her in a minute, realising something had upset her.

"What is it, Christy? You've gone pale."

His kind voice only made her worse and she stood up, trying to smile. "Sorry, it's a silly reaction to something. Please ignore me."

"Of course I can't ignore your obvious distress. Come and sit over here for a moment and you can tell me about it if you like. I promise I'm discreet and won't interrupt."

How much should she share? Although she felt a growing closeness between them, that conversation with his mother had put doubts in her mind. Was he over his ex or not? Yet she had a sudden need to talk about the email from Fran.

Taking a risk, she sat down beside him on the sofa. But where to begin?

A large hand gently covered hers. "Take your time, Christy, and only tell me as much as you can."

Taking a deep breath, she kept her eyes on those clasped hands. "It's all to do with the accident." She released her breath. At least she had got that far. "You know I hurt my arm, but I still can't remember some of the details. And I wasn't alone." She hesitated again but he only squeezed her hand in encouragement.

"My boyfriend, Michael, and I were late for a party and all I remember was the car skidding. It was pretty bad..." Her voice trailed away and she looked up at his kind eyes.

"And he died?" Ross asked softly.

Christy looked away again. "Yes. But our relationship was already in a bad place. I can't remember all the details before the crash. Sometimes, I can hardly get over the guilt that it was my fault. The email was from his sister and my once best friend, Fran. She doesn't know I was already having doubts about remaining engaged, before the accident."

Shaking slightly, and feeling nauseous, she couldn't say any more. "Sorry, I can't go on."

For answer, Ross took her in his arms and held her against his chest. It was completely platonic, one person comforting another, but Christy rested in his arms as though it was the most natural place to be.

He finally pulled away and wiped the few tears spilling from the corner of her eyes.

"Thanks, Ross. I appreciate you not asking questions. To be honest, that's all I know. I was in hospital for quite a while and the doctors are sure I've only blocked it out because of the trauma."

He gently took her hand. "Thank you for trusting me with your confidence. Now I know what kept you from your grandmother's side, it's my turn to feel even more ashamed of my attitude at times." He let her go and sat slightly away from her as though to let her recover.

"I didn't altogether blame you," Christy assured him. "It's taken me a long time to get over not being here in time."

"Then let's agree to leave the past behind for now. I want to mention a happier event." He smiled in the hope of cheering her up. "I hope you'll come to the ball. At the very least, it will let you meet many of the villagers again. It's always well attended, probably a throwback to the old Lord of the Manor days."

Christy had no trouble imagining him as such, but after her own honesty she had to ask a question and risk annoying him. "And I hear your girlfriend will be there?"

Had she meant to add the word 'ex' or did some devilment make her stir him? But she was unprepared for his reaction.

His eyes became flints of ice and all trace of his earlier understanding disappeared. "I see my mother has been filling your ears with her version of my past. I don't have a girlfriend, Christy, and the person of whom she speaks will not be at the ball through my invitation. But I'd rather not discuss it at the moment, if you don't mind."

Disappointed he refused to share his own confidences, Christy was about to stand up and apologise for taking up so much of his time, when a knock sounded on the door.

"Sorry to disturb you, Ross, but Nick is here and asked to speak to you. If Christina is finished with the computer," Mrs McKinley called.

At least she had the courtesy not to open the door uninvited, but Christy was gratified to see Ross's annoyance at the interruption. Whether or not it was because of his mother or Nick Anderson, she couldn't be sure, or maybe it was both.

"We'll be down in a few minutes, Mother," he replied and Christy presumed she had gone back downstairs.

They stood and looked at each other unsmiling.

"I'm just going anyway, Ross. Thanks for everything. I'm sorry to offload my troubles onto you and to stir up your own unhappy memories."

"Come here, Christy," he said, and held out his arms, his smile taking away any hint of command. "You can confide in me any time you are troubled. Promise me you won't hesitate to contact me, day or night. Please forgive my dark mood just now. I'm afraid my mother has a knack of interfering when it is least appreciated. I'll tell you more about my boring past another time."

His eyes conveyed his intensity and she nodded. "I promise, and there's nothing to forgive."

Hugging her tightly as he would a sister or friend, he placed a quick kiss on her cheek and let her go.

She was strangely comforted by his manner, and grateful no hint of romance had got in the way. But she also knew her feelings had shifted for this enigmatic man and she would relive that moment being held against his heart.

As they reached the bottom of the stairs, common sense returned and Christy sensed that the shadows of her boyfriend and his girlfriend, ex or not, lay between them and would have to be resolved before she could allow herself the luxury of romantic feelings for someone else.

Nick Anderson sat chatting to Mrs McKinley as they entered the kitchen and he stood at once.

"Hello Christy, it's lovely to see you again. We must have another evening out."

Did he mention the meal on purpose, Christy wondered later, as she noticed Ross's mouth tighten as he glared at the man? Mrs McKinley, on the other hand, seemed surprised.

Christy remained non-committal. "Hello Nick. Thanks, but I have a commission to finish so I'll need to get on with that first." She turned to Ross's mother. "It was good to see you and thank you for the coffee. Bye for now, Ross, thanks for the use of the computer."

She made her escape, as three pairs of eyes watched her with various emotions. But she wanted only to be back in the safety of the cottage to shut out the world and the sad memories that were beginning to surface.

Chapter Fifteen

Biting back his annoyance at being disturbed at such a moment with Christy, and curious at his mother's motives towards the girl, he reluctantly took Anderson up to the study away from listening ears.

"She's a fine-looking girl, that Christy Morrison, and a stubborn one I suspect," Anderson said as they sat on either side of the desk.

"I trust you haven't come to discuss Miss Morrison," Ross replied, making it clear the subject was off bounds.

The other man shrugged. "Not unless she gets in the way of progress."

Ross stared at the smug looking man he once worked beside. Why had it taken him so long to see his true nature? "You'd better tell me exactly what you mean by that," he said quietly.

"Ah, so you're not entirely immune to her charms, McKinley. But I'm talking about the cottage, as you well know. We had a similar conversation when the grandmother was alive."

"And I warned you then about the futility of anyone trying to buy that piece of land. It's not for sale."

"But what if your mother thinks differently? She still has some control over the future of the house and its land."

Ross sat back in his chair and wondered, not for the first time, why his mother favoured this man.

Quite apart from the big age difference, there was nothing romantic in their friendship but he was dashed if he knew what his mother was up to sometimes.

"Leave my mother to me. I can't imagine she wants to see people turned out of their homes in this economic climate. And the development, if it goes ahead, need not affect that piece of land."

The twisted smile on the other man's face annoyed him even more. But losing his cool would hardly help.

"I've brought a copy of the plans for you to study, in case you've misplaced the others. My client is willing to give you until the end of the year for a final decision. Your mother is already aware of this. Don't throw away the best chance you have to keep this place going for your heirs, if you ever have any."

Ross stood up, indicating the impromptu meeting was at an end. "I'll have a look at the plans, but I make no promises. Now you'll have to excuse me, as I've work to do for the estate."

Anderson smiled as he stood. "You know this is a stunning position. A golf course and exclusive accommodation would undoubtedly attract the well-paying American market. Think about it before someone else cashes in on such a great opportunity."

As he saw the man out, Ross watched him drive away in his sporty Saab. Much as he disliked him, with good cause, he considered his words. Was it the right direction for the estate, much as he hated the idea of turning his ancestral home into a commercial enterprise? Like so many other old houses, it ate up whatever money was available in repairs. But he couldn't contemplate revoking the leases on the few cottages, especially now that Christy had taken over her grandmother's. And he was quite sure that she had never understood the exact terms of the will, probably imagining the cottage now fully belonged to her. It was a conversation he would have to broach before she heard it from someone like Nick Anderson.

Turning at the sound of his mother's footsteps, he presumed she was about to offer her opinion.

"I don't want to discuss Anderson's visit right now, Mother. But I do want to know why you felt the need to mention Moira to Christy, since she is no longer in my life."

His mother had the grace to look guilty and he waited for her reply with interest.

"I meant to tell you, dear, that she's back home and will probably be coming to the ball with her mother. Elizabeth mentioned her when we were playing golf and I forgot to tell you. It just slipped out when I was telling Christina about our traditional event."

Ross knew his mother wasn't guileless enough to forget something like that, unless on purpose, and for some reason she had made sure to tell Christy about his *ex* - or perhaps she'd neglected to include those two important letters.

"Whatever you and Elizabeth Rutherford have plotted between you, it's not going to happen, Mother. Please understand that. If Moira accepts your invitation then I shall be pleasant as I would to any other guest, but no more. Now I have to go and check the next item on the repair list."

Returning to his study, Ross stood at the window and wished he could rewind the last hour or two to that moment when he had held Christy in his arms. Although careful to make it nothing but a friendly gesture, he had felt the first stirring of something akin to desire deep inside and it scared him.

The day at Conic Hill had moved their friendship on a little and now Christy was beginning to breach the emotional defences he had carefully built around his heart. The fact that she, too, was emotionally vulnerable gave them something in common but made his behaviour even more important. Yet too many shadows seemed to stand between them at the moment and he should tread carefully. One of the first things he must tell her was the true legacy of the cottage her grandmother had left her and assure her that he would never willingly take it away from her.

Chapter Sixteen

Saturday dawned cold and bright and Christy realised that September had crept up on her already. She was beginning to feel as though she had always lived in this cottage in the village and increasingly couldn't imagine ever living in London again.

This week, she needed to arrange the Internet connection and send her illustrations away by the end of next month. She was fairly happy with the figures and scenes now completed, although a bit surprised to find that one of the shepherds had a distinct look of Ross McKinley. To compensate, she had made another loosely resemble Cameron. Shepherd brothers seemed appropriate.

Hearing the knock on the door at the promised time, Christy smiled. Cameron wouldn't let her down a second time. When she opened the door, his smile lit up the morning even more.

"Your chauffeur reporting for duty, m'lady." He bowed, then kissed her cheek. "Hope you have a warm jacket for a walk around the shores. Don't worry, the antique shop is inside."

"Morning, Cameron. Do you want to come in first?"

"No, it's fine, thanks. Let's get going and not waste what little sun there is. Besides, I've told Martin we'll be along soon."

As she settled into the passenger seat, she glanced in question. "Martin?"

He was already pulling away from the cottage as he answered. "My partner. We're running the business together."

Christy frowned, wondering if she had misheard something a few days ago. "But I thought Fiona was your partner."

He laughed. "Unofficially, she thinks she is. Fiona and I take care of all the buying of goods and clearing of houses for the shop, but Martin is the money behind it and he and I lease the premises. But Fiona is a great asset. We'd been looking at a possible shop in town a while back but it makes more financial sense to keep to the one at the Loch side for now."

Christy remained silent while she absorbed this news, wondering why Cameron had never mentioned Martin before. But, then, why should she know everything about his present life in so short a time.

The first part of the journey was the same as the one she had taken with Ross, over the impressive Erskine Bridge as it spanned the River Clyde below. But Cameron turned off in a different direction towards Loch Lomond, eventually negotiating a large spread-out car park to find a space. It was already getting busy by mid-morning.

"I see it's the weekend for one of the Farmer's Markets down by the shore. It's your lucky day," Cameron said, taking her arm as they wandered along the pathway.

Sure enough, Christy was delighted to find a whole row of colourful stalls laid out with a variety of fresh goods. She caught sight of glorious red Scottish beef and another with delicious looking salmon.

"If you don't mind, I'm going to have to do some shopping here before we leave. This is brilliant! In fact, why don't I arrange a small dinner party for you,

Ross and Fiona and we can reminisce. Do you think that would work?"

"Anything involving food is okay by me. But let's have a short walk round the shore and then I'll take you up to the shop."

Christy didn't know where the idea for a dinner party had come from but was glad she had been impulsive. She still hadn't had a chance to chat to Fiona since that awkward day in the cafe.

"So this is also part of Loch Lomond? I can't believe I've never been here before," Christy said, as they walked along a path by the side of the water, ducks quacking in unison while young children fed them.

"Aye, that's right, although these buildings are a more modern addition. It's the longest loch in the UK, so you'll find lots of different areas where you can get close to the water." He laughed. "I'm beginning to sound like a tourist guide. But one of the best ways you can see the whole length and breadth of the loch is to take a boat trip on a good day."

Christy was quite determined to do just that, maybe in the spring, and she could start to explore a bit more of this magnificent beauty spot almost on her doorstep. The light this morning was less intense than on the day with Ross, and in the distance a lingering mist covered the highest mountains. Again, she had the urge to capture some of it for her illustrations and mentally added a good camera to her list of things to buy in the city.

"Well, if you've seen enough water, let's go and meet Martin. Our premises are just back here."

Christy had noticed the row of glass fronted shops along the loch side, opposite where the stalls had set up business. Cameron steered her through one of the doors and the warmth hit her cold face.

"You can have a look through the clothes shops if you want when we come down," Cameron said, "and we'll not forget the market. The antique shop is just up these stairs."

When he opened the door, Christy's first reaction was that 'shop' had been misleading. Virtually the whole floor was taken up with a veritable cornucopia of wonderful items, from large furniture to glass covered display shelves of tiny figures and antique jewellery, plus hundreds of open shelves and surfaces with too many items to identify at first glance.

"Wow, what an Aladdin's cave! Just leave me here for the rest of the day," Christy said.

"I think you'll need a few visits to find everything. But, look, I told you Martin would be waiting for us."

The man who greeted them was around Cameron's age, but shorter with a boyish face and a devastating smile. "Cameron, my love, and Christy, I presume. Welcome. Come and have a cup of coffee with me."

As he ushered them into his small office, it took Christy no time to decide the gorgeous looking Martin might be gay. His friendliness was infectious and he soon had Christy laughing about one story or another about the shop. The biggest surprise, however, was Cameron. He positively grinned the whole time and Christy began to wonder if Martin was only a business partner.

How could she have missed it? Then again, she had only seen Cameron on his own and he'd always been the more outgoing of the two brothers. It did explain, perhaps, why she had never been romantically interested in him, or he in her. *Don't jump to conclusions*, she told herself. But she did observe Cameron a little more closely.

"Have a wander round, pet, while I bring this lovely man up to date with our latest acquisitions," Martin eventually suggested. "We might even throw in a discount if you see something you like."

Not exactly feeling dismissed, but aware the two men had business to discuss, Christy took pleasure in wandering around the store, stopping at almost every surface to examine its wares. She ignored the larger items since the cottage already had its fair share of old furniture, but the various Dinky toys, old fashioned telephone and gramophone made her nostalgic. Every old, well-loved book called out to her and she had to harden her heart against bringing more books into the cottage after removing so many. Although those she had disposed of were not worth anything and some of these might be fairly valuable. One particular volume almost tempted her: an edition of Keats' poems. Hesitating, she replaced the book. Now she knew this place existed, she could easily return by herself to browse and buy once she was used to driving again.

One corner kept her amused for a while as she looked through a rail of vintage fashion and she couldn't resist trying on a handsome grey top hat. What a haven for drama groups. She wondered if there might be one in or near the village. It was something she might enjoy, if only to help with painting any background scenery.

Her final browse was through the boxes of old postcards. Being visually minded, nothing appealed to her more than finding pictures of the past in old postcards and magazines. The written messages from long ago were a bonus, bringing some of the people alive. Another reason to return by herself and take time to enjoy the many on offer.

She spotted Cameron beckoning to her and made her way back to the office area.

"Perfect timing," she said. "That was wonderful, but I need to come back by myself and have another good browse. I've already got my eye on one or two items."

"Come over any time, my lovey. Fiona comes in a few days a week and I'm sure she would bring you," Martin said. "But I hear you're off to spend at the market now. It's good quality fair so don't hesitate to buy the products."

Christy had almost forgotten about the market and her idea for a dinner party. She hesitated. Should she ask Martin, or was that presuming too much? Maybe she should consult Cameron first. She'd wait until they were at the market.

She was about to shake Martin's hand when he gave her a big hug. "I'm sure we'll be friends, Christy. Glad you enjoyed the visit." He turned to Cameron. "Bye for now, love, see you later."

As they wandered outside towards the market, Christy stopped. "Could we have a walk along by the shore first, Cameron? I want to ask you something."

"Aye sure, I don't think they've run out of food yet."

As they wandered past the quacking ducks again, Christy took his arm. She'd read that men found it easier to talk about personal matters if they were side by side rather than facing. And this was about as personal as she could get!

"Tell me if I'm out of turn, Cameron. But would you like me to ask Martin along to my little dinner?"

She smiled at Cameron's astonishment, as he

stopped walking. "Well it didn't take you long to suss me out! Or did Fiona tell you?"

"Absolutely not. I've hardly spoken to her since coming back. Something about the two of you together suggested a close friendship, but I was afraid I might be jumping to conclusions."

They walked on a little and Cameron smiled brightly. "I knew it was a good day when you returned to Kilcraig, Christy Morrison. My mother would have apoplexy if she knew and that's why I don't stay at the house very often. Martin has a wee bungalow over on this side of the river and I'm never happier than when I'm there. Even Ross doesn't know for sure, although I think he's suspicious about my love life. But he's such a man's man that I don't know how he'll react to the truth."

Christy had a feeling his brother would say exactly the right thing. "Well, it's just a suggestion, but perhaps a small intimate dinner would be the best place to break it to him, before you confront your mother."

"I can see why my brother is growing so fond of you, Christy. I've never known anyone so understanding and non-judgemental."

His words warmed her heart and she almost asked about Ross's ex-girlfriend, but stopped herself in time. She wouldn't dream of discussing Cameron's love life with Ross so why should she expect Cameron to talk about his brother.

"So, do you think it's a good idea? The dinner invitation?"

He stopped in the middle of the path and hugged her. "I think it's a wonderful idea and I'm sure Martin will be glad I'm not hiding him completely away from my family any more. My mother I'll leave till

130

another time!"

They decided to shop for meat and veg first, then go back up and invite Martin. The choice was so great that Christy ended up buying enough for a week plus the dinner party.

Martin was surprised to see them again but Christy spoke right away.

"I would love you to come to the little dinner party I'm giving for Cameron, Fiona and Ross. And if you haven't met Cameron's brother properly yet, then maybe it's time you did."

Martin looked from one to the other, eyebrows raised in question. When Cameron nodded, Martin hugged Christy. "I would be honoured, dear girl. Thank you."

"Great! Cameron can let you know the arrangements as soon as I've fixed a date. Look forward to seeing you then."

As they said goodbye, a few customers arrived and they left Martin to it. On a wall near the door, Christy noticed a poster about the shop. It seemed they also bought items to sell for clients. That was useful to know, in case she decided to change any more of the cottage.

As Cameron drove her home, he was even more garrulous than usual and Christy knew he was relieved to be completely himself. He wasn't the kind of man made for secrets and prevarication. *Unlike his brother perhaps*? A small voice whispered inside.

"Thank you for being such a lovely person, Christy. You don't know what this means to Martin, and to me."

"I can guess. We all need to feel accepted, don't we? But Martin seems a really great guy and I'm sure we'll have fun. Maybe you could get your mother used to him before the ball. That would be a good time to introduce him to the wider society."

Cameron snorted. "I must say you're full of surprises, my gorgeous friend. But you'll have to give me time to think about that one!"

When he dropped her at the cottage, Cameron got out of the car and gave her a long, warm hug. Then he kissed her cheek. "You're the sister I never had, Christy, although we never know what might happen." He winked as he left her staring after him.

As she was about to turn away to the path, she noticed Ross heading towards her and knew he'd seen Cameron's exuberant embrace. Since he possibly didn't know the truth about his brother, she wondered if the hug caused the dark expression on his unsmiling face.

Chapter Seventeen

Christy waited until Ross reached her side. "Not walking the dog today?" She reminded him of the excuse he had made the last time he walked to the cottage unannounced. Besides, a perverse part of her enjoyed the fact he'd seen Cameron being so warm towards her.

"No, I came to see if you might be in as there's something I wanted to discuss with you."

Although tired after her day out, Christy was intrigued and curiosity won out, never mind that she enjoyed this taciturn man's company. "As you can see, I've just returned home but if you're willing to help me put away this food, then you're welcome to come in. Cameron took me to a different part of Loch Lomond and I bought up half the food market!"

Again, she was struck by the way Ross's presence filled the cottage, but in a reassuring manner. She could get used to having him drop in more often. She quite understood how her grandmother must have enjoyed this man's company, in quite a different way from she did.

"I see you're not exaggerating too much," he agreed, as between them they took the shopping through to the kitchen, where Misty immediately purred around Ross's leg.

"Hey, you're supposed to greet your owner first," Christy admonished the kitten. But she smiled to see such a discerning animal quite comfortable with her visitor.

"Maybe she smells Darwin from me and wonders why he's not here this time." Ross grinned, and they were back to that closeness they'd shared in his study before being interrupted.

"I'm glad you had such a good day out," he said. "My brother is charm personified at times, I believe. At least you have enough food here to last a good while."

Christy was sorely tempted to tell him about Cameron but it was not her place. But she could invite Ross to the dinner party.

"I've decided to have a small dinner for Cameron, Fiona, you, if you will come, and Martin, Cameron's partner." She needn't say what kind of partner the man had turned out be.

Eyebrows raised, he looked at her rather more intensely than before. "So you met the vivacious Martin. He's a nice chap. I think that's a lovely idea, thank you."

It was a strange way to describe a man, and as Christy continued to look at Ross, she understood. He knew, or had guessed the truth. She hoped so for Cameron's sake, but she couldn't openly acknowledge the possibility right now.

"The antique shop is wonderful, so I expect to make a few trips there when I'm driving again. But come and sit down for a while. You said you had something to discuss. Thanks for the help just now."

As they returned to the sitting room, Ross continued making small talk first. "How is your arm? Do you think you might get the car out soon?"

"It's definitely much stronger, although I don't think it will ever be perfect. But what is?" she joked. "I'm going to try out the car soon, once the dinner party is over."

Conversation dwindled to a halt and Christy waited to see what was so important. Ross picked up the *Rubaiyat* instead and fingered the embossed cover. She frowned. Was it that difficult, whatever he wanted to say? And her heart flipped a little. Maybe it was something to do with his ex.

Putting an end to her increasingly wild speculation, she couldn't stand the suspense any longer. "You wanted to talk to me about something in particular, I believe."

He raised his eyes to hers and replaced the book on the coffee table. "It's a delicate subject, Christy, and I'm trying to find the right words."

She was right. He still had feelings for his ex and didn't want Christy to get the wrong idea about his availability. "Why don't you just tell me, then we can both relax."

He half smiled in the way she was beginning to adore and she took a deep breath to steady her resolve for whatever he had to say.

"I applaud your directness, Christy, and it's one of the things I love about you."

Now she was confused. Surely he used the term in a general way? She waited for him to continue.

"You know, of course, that your grandmother left this cottage to you, but I'm afraid it isn't quite as straightforward as you might have believed. I don't know if the solicitor gave you all the details and you may not have read the official documents at all." He paused.

Whatever she had expected, this was not even on the radar and Christy waited, dreading to think what was coming. "You're quite correct. I have no idea about the official blurb yet as I was just glad to be here. Is there a problem?"

"Not a problem as such, but it's something you need to know. Your grandmother never actually owned the cottage outright. It was leased for her lifetime and for her heirs, if they choose to live here."

He watched her reaction but gave her time to absorb his words. Christy had never thought much about the ownership before, assuming it was now hers outright. But leased from whom? Ross McKinley?

"I see, or at least I think so. You mean I would be allowed to live here for as long as I choose but could never sell it?" Not that she would want to. She tried to keep her voice steady, although she unaccountably felt like weeping.

Instead of replying straight away, he sat beside her. "I know this is a shock, Christy, and a lot to take in. But it need never have come up at all at one time."

"And now? Something has changed, hasn't it?" She noticed his mouth tighten and knew instinctively it was not his choice.

"It's complicated." He smiled ruefully at those words beloved of TV dramas. "It partly involves the estate and the village. You may have noticed the ill feeling between Ewan MacPherson and me that day at the village shop."

When he saw her nod, he carried on. "Nick Anderson is acting on behalf of a client who wants to buy some of the land belonging to us to build a golf course. But part of the deal involves us being able to offer luxury accommodation to paying guests. Anderson quite rightly thinks it would attract a lot of overseas visitors, especially Americans."

At first Christy thought he meant only the big house, then she realised why it would affect her.

"You mean these few cottages are part of your

land, therefore you can evict the tenants and convert the cottages to luxury accommodation. And that way, you make a huge income to help with the upkeep of the estate."

She couldn't keep the slight trace of bitterness from her voice and noticed him wince, but it was largely due to disappointment that Ross could consider such a move.

"It's neither my idea nor my wish, Christy, but my mother still has the major side of any vote."

"But how does Ewan MacPherson come into this? I know his mother works at your house but surely he owns the village shop?"

"MacPherson has big ideas for the village and hopes that attracting more visitors means he can expand and open a larger supermarket. He's already in talks with one of the major conglomerates and they would look at it more favourably if there was general expansion in and around the village."

"And the character of the village would be lost forever in the process, like so many other places," Christy said.

They were both silent as she tried to take in the enormity of the problem. Not only because of Gran's cottage but everything combined left her with a horrible sense of looming loss again.

As she glanced at the man beside her, she saw the concern etched on his face, though she didn't know how to respond to the revelations.

Ross reached out a hand and gently took one of hers. "I'm deeply sorry to be the bringer of such worrying news, Christy. Believe me, I'm still fighting every step of the way. I'm also trying to think of ways to raise money without ruining the whole ambience of the village, and the estate. But I needed to tell you before someone else did."

Part of her appreciated his sensitivity and she guessed Nick Anderson would eventually have found a way of telling her why he was so interested in the cottage, after softening her up a little more.

"Does Cameron know all this?" she asked, finding it hard to believe he could be so secretive. Then again, he'd managed to keep his private life pretty quiet.

He shrugged. "Not that I'm aware. He's never been that interested in the house or village and his life is pretty much taken up with the antiques shop. Strangely enough, Fiona is more interested in everything that's happening here."

His remark hardly registered until later, as she was so pleased Cameron hadn't hidden all this from her, since he probably neither knew the details nor cared. A sudden tiny meow interrupted the tense atmosphere between them as Misty rubbed her small head around Ross's legs.

"Well I'm glad at least one female is still talking to me," he quipped, bending down to stroke the kitten.

Christy stood up, suddenly unable to sit so close beside Ross when her thoughts and emotions were in turmoil. "I'm sorry, I think I need some time alone to process all this, if you don't mind."

He stood at once but remained close beside her. "I can't tell you how much it pains me to upset you like this. I'll find a way through it, Christy." He gently touched her cheek then raised her chin a little until he looked into her eyes. "I promise."

Caught in the charged little moment between them, Christy nodded, not able to deny his sincerity at least. "Thanks for being honest." She had to give him that.

"I'll see myself out. Please try not to worry, but if you can think of another way we could raise funds and benefit the village and its traditions, I'd be very grateful!"

After he'd gone, Christy sat with the comforting warmth of Misty on her lap. "Even you feel his power and attraction, don't you little cat," she whispered. Between the day out with Cameron and now this traumatic discovery, Christy was worn out.

She made a quick snack for herself and Misty then curled into the sofa with the *Rubaiyat* and her sketch book. No more thinking for tonight, she promised herself. Instead, she let the old cottage and memories of her grandmother's presence lull her into a semblance of serenity.

Ross put one foot in front of the other, hardly aware of walking home. He hated causing Christy so much worry but her shock would have been worse had someone like Anderson told her about the proposed plans.

All he had wanted to do was put his arms around her and tell her he would protect her, but it wasn't the right time for serious promises that he might not keep. And he suspected she didn't need, or want, a man to look after her. Of one thing he was becoming increasingly sure: his life had changed for the better since Christy Morrison returned to Kilcraig and he couldn't bear the thought of her moving away again.

Although she seemed to enjoy his company, each time they met some bigger problem lurked in the background waiting to tear them apart. The only light-hearted day they had spent together was at Conic Hill and he longed to recapture those first tentative steps to a deeper friendship, or something stronger. Instead, he had difficult decisions to make that would affect her future, and most definitely *their* future, if they ever had any hope of forming a lasting relationship. Increasingly, nothing would please him more.

Hopefully Christy would still hold her little dinner party as it was time he met Martin socially and if what he suspected were true, Martin would be glad of the welcome from at least one McKinley. Then the Winter Ball would be upon them and thanks to his interfering mother and her friend, Moira might well be a spectre at the feast as far as his friendship with Christy was concerned.

Entering the house, he retreated to his study to try and work out what he was going to do about the future of the estate.

Chapter Eighteen

The sharp telephone ring woke Christy from a disturbed sleep. Misty stretched and yawned from the bottom of the bed as Christy turned over to glance at the clock before lifting the receiver. Seven thirty on a Sunday morning. Not very thoughtful.

She was unprepared for the nasty whispering voice at the other end of the phone.

"I told you to go back to where you came from. You're not wanted here and there's no place for you in the McKinley's life. You have until the end of the year to pack your bags and give up the cottage."

Shaking uncontrollably, Christy was unable to put down the phone until the venomous words abruptly finished and the dialling tone was all that remained. Who would do such a thing? Again, she couldn't discern if it was a male or female voice, so shocked was she at the threatening words.

Completely awake now, she was gladder than ever for Misty's company and allowed the kitten to snuggle up on the cover beside her. Coming on top of Ross's revelations about the cottage, it unnerved her and spoiled the new life she was trying to make up here. Maybe she *should* go back to London, and find a permanent art position somewhere.

Then she remembered her awakening feelings for Ross McKinley and the easy friendship with Cameron, and hopefully Martin in time. She could never give up that easily. She felt close to her grandmother here and the area had so much beauty and light that her art could be inspired forever.

With sudden resolve, Christy got up and showered and dressed. After a leisurely breakfast, she was going to check out the local church service. She had need for a little calming contemplation and the hymns would soothe her bruised spirit.

She vaguely remembered the small church had stood in the village for a couple of centuries and recalled the Christmas Eve service when she stayed with Gran over Christmas.

Waiting until a few minutes before the service began, Christy was welcomed at the door by a pleasant lady she didn't know and once inside, she slipped into a seat towards the back. About half full wasn't too bad in today's secular society, she decided, and the ages appeared to range from half a dozen children at the front to various generations evenly distributed.

Since only one couple shared her half row and sat a few spaces away from her, Christy sat back against the wooden pew and closed her eyes for a minute. Already, the organist's voluntaries were starting to calm her spirit, reminding her that she was but a tiny part of the vast world. Throughout the service, she stood at the hymns, prayed when appropriate and listened to the wise Biblical words the middle-aged minister spoke from the low pulpit.

It was an hour well spent and Christy rose at the end more resolved than ever to remain in this village that was becoming her home. As she was about to slip from the pew, she looked up to smile at anyone passing by and was surprised to see Fiona and Mrs McKinley observing her. They returned her smile but moved on towards the door. Why wouldn't they attend church, she chided herself? Next minute, she noticed Mrs MacPherson and her large son from the shop, but they were up ahead and didn't turn round.

At the door, the minister clasped her hand in a warm welcome. "How lovely to see you here this morning. Christy, isn't it? Your grandmother would be pleased to know you are settling in the cottage. Do please come again. This is my wife, Eileen, who teaches at the primary school."

Christy was cheered by their friendliness and liked Eileen immediately as soon as she spoke in her soft Irish lilt.

"Hello, Christy. It's great to see a new young face here, so it is."

"Thanks, I'll certainly visit again," she said to them both. "I very much enjoyed the service."

She had turned to walk back to the cottage when she sensed someone coming up behind her. She spun round and almost knocked into Ross.

"Whoa, I was only coming to say hello!" He joked as he caught her arm.

Her relief was out of proportion and she knew the phone call had spooked her more than she cared to admit. "Sorry, I didn't know it was you. Were you at the service too? I didn't notice you."

"I sometimes attend for my sins, and I must say you brightened the place up this morning." His grin was genuinely admiring and Christy was glad she'd worn her red winter jacket. "Occasionally, I stand in for the regular organist," he added nonchalantly.

Christy's smile was replaced by amazement. "You play the organ? Wow, I'm seriously impressed. You were good."

He grinned again. "And the guitar and the fiddle sometimes, but not necessarily at church. You see, you don't know everything about me yet."

By the time they reached the cottage, Christy wondered what other surprises this man hid from her. "Would you like to come in for a coffee and say hello to Misty?" she asked. *Who was she kidding?* It was completely for her benefit. But it would be good to dispel the sombre mood of their last meeting.

"I'd love to but I daren't be any later. Mother likes us to sit down to a family lunch on Sundays if everyone is around and I have to give more notice if I'm absconding." He hesitated. "But I'm sure you'd be welcome if you wanted to join us."

Christy was equally sure she would not be particularly welcome and declined gracefully.

"Maybe another time, thanks. I'm going to get on with some work this afternoon and maybe take a walk later." She almost told him about the phone call, but this wasn't the right time.

As she reluctantly said goodbye, Christy remembered the dinner. "Oh, is Friday evening okay with you for the dinner party? Then I'll check with Fiona and Cameron."

"As far as I know, that's fine. I'll look forward to it. Do you want me to mention the date to them?"

"Might as well, thanks. Perhaps you could ask them to let me know if it suits." She waved him off before turning into the cottage.

Her own lunch seemed lonely and dull, apart from the comical antics of Misty, but she wouldn't have been able to face a meal under the watchful eye of Mrs McKinley.

Her afternoon passed in the creative pleasure of putting the finishing touches to her main illustrations. Although digital work was becoming more popular, she still preferred to do the first drafts the old-fashioned way then post them to her publisher. She'd take them to the post office tomorrow. That completed, she pulled her jacket on and opted for a walk to clear her head before darkness set in.

She headed for the country road which was just far enough at this time of year. A few families had the same idea and she returned the friendly smiles, resolving again to stay in this place, if she were allowed. As she eventually turned back, she was surprised to find Ross walking his dog towards her.

"We meet again," she said, and bent to pat Darwin.

"I'm glad we have. May I walk back with you? Fiona and Cameron said Friday is perfect by the way."

"Great. But has Darwin had enough of a walk yet?" Much as she enjoyed Ross's company, she didn't want to deprive his dog of the exercise.

"I think we've both been out long enough. Won't be long till it's dark and all good children should be tucked up asleep."

"And are you good," she couldn't resist asking.

"When I want to be." He grinned.

As she returned his gaze, Christy had a moment of inner certainty that she never wanted this man to be out of her life. To hide her sudden confusion, she kept her eyes on the ground as they chatted.

"Is that coffee still on offer?" he asked when they reached the cottage.

Glancing at him, she nodded. Maybe this was the right time to tell him of the phone calls. "I'd like a chat anyway, if you have time. And I'm sure Misty will be happy to see her new pal again."

She saw his raised eyebrow at her request and he followed her inside. As she suspected, Misty was soon purring around Ross and allowing Darwin to reacquaint himself with her scent.

"Coffee first, then chat," she said, heading for the kitchen. "Make yourself at home," she added, and had never meant those words more literally.

When the coffee was ready, she found him looking at her illustrations.

"These are excellent, Christy. I had no idea you were this talented." He looked up in genuine admiration.

"Thanks. I can lose myself for ages in drawing and painting and fortunately my left arm was damaged and not the one I most need. Talking of which, would you mind bringing the tray through please."

Once settled on the comfortable sofa, they sipped their coffee in companionable silence for a few moments, Christy intensely aware of his masculine presence sitting so near her.

"You sounded a little worried about something, other than the news I gave you earlier, I mean," Ross said at last.

Placing her mug carefully on the mat, Christy hesitated, not wanting to sound foolish. "I think someone is playing a prank on me, at least I hope it's a silly prank - or else it's a threat."

He, too, placed his mug down and gave her his full attention. "I think you'd better start at the beginning. What's going on, Christy?"

As she told him about the push on the back when returning from the dinner the first night and then the phone call, his lips tightened but he allowed her to continue. "That's partly why I was so freaked out about someone putting a cat in the cottage while I was out. Then I was pretty sure it was entered again and someone had picked up the *Rubaiyat* book."

She paused to gauge his reaction, but he certainly looked as though he believed her. "I had another phone call early this morning but this one sounded even nastier. He or she told me to leave the cottage and go back to London by the end of the year."

This time he took her hands. "Why didn't you tell me about this before instead of worrying about it by yourself?" Then he shook his head. "You didn't know who to trust."

She nodded and returned his gaze. "It sounded so foolish, as though someone was just playing games, or didn't want me back here for good."

"Let me set your mind at rest on one account, Christy. None of this is my doing. I adored your grandmother and I see much of her in you. I could never do anything to hurt you."

Much as she believed his words, she still didn't know what place, if any, his ex-girlfriend might still have in his life and it increasingly mattered.

"Thanks, Ross. I never really thought this was your style." She deliberately kept the words light-hearted in case she allowed herself to draw on his intensity too much. "But I don't know what to do about the phone calls."

"The first thing to do is go ex-directory, then it's your choice who gets your number. Don't worry, I'm pretty sure someone is only out to scare you away for whatever warped reason."

At least he took her seriously. She could get used to having him around like this. But he stood up regretfully.

"Well, it's time we headed back. Seriously, Christy, please phone me any time you're concerned and I'll jump on my steed and be here in no time."

She laughed, pleased he had lightened the mood and at least she now had his number stored in her mobile. "What maiden could resist such a sight?" she said.

As she was about to open the door, he stood beside her and she had to look up at him. Then he dipped his head and kissed her gently on the cheek. "Goodnight, Christy, sleep well. And make sure everything is secure."

She felt bereft as soon as man and dog had gone then she checked the windows and two doors, closing all the curtains against the darkness. Although slightly reassured she'd be able to do something practical about her phone number, it still didn't tell her who was responsible for the calls.

As Ross walked Darwin up the long path home, he was aware it had taken all his resolve to tear himself away from Christy. Never had he felt so protective of a young woman, and he hated to think of her being alone at the cottage feeling insecure or frightened. Although he had to admit she'd seemed more worried than scared and he admired her courage. She obviously had the same stubborn grit as her grandmother.

But he could scarcely believe someone was being so malicious and he tried to consider each person he knew, before discarding the possibility as being absurd.

Why on earth would anyone want the girl to leave badly enough to scare her? This wasn't Anderson's style, although he certainly wanted the cottage as part of the golf club deal.

Since it was beyond him for now, he resolved to make sure Christy's phone number was changed as soon as possible. And he'd also ensure he was always available if needed.

Chapter Nineteen

In the week leading up to the dinner party, Christy was amazed at how much she had achieved. The phone number was changed, she had Wi-Fi Internet connection for her laptop and she was fitter and stronger than before she arrived. After the diligent exercises for her arm, she was determined to get the car out in the next week or two.

Her friend Annie had emailed again, hinting she would like to visit the cottage and Christy put her off until spring. With winter approaching, it was the worst time to be travelling up to a country village in Scotland and, besides, she wanted to make sure she wasn't going to be evicted. But she'd look forward to seeing her again.

She had some sympathy for Ross, as his responsibility and sense of duty to the estate was eclipsed by his mother's advantage as majority owner. But she also hated the thought of the village being changed beyond recognition, its values being eroded by monetary gain. At least the minister and his wife sided with Ross in wanting to maintain the sense of community.

She had enjoyed an invitation to the manse and again felt that instant friendship with Eileen in particular. They were exactly what the villagers needed and she was sorry she hadn't met them until now.

"Sure we both knew and liked your grandmother,"

Eileen confided over coffee. "A wise and gentle lady. I believe you've been living in London for some years."

Christy didn't mind answering the unobtrusive questions as they were asked out of genuine interest. Besides, they might wonder at never having seen her before.

"Yes, and I'm afraid a terrible accident prevented me from coming up in the months before Gran died, which almost broke my heart. We were very close." The words were out before she had time to consider telling them.

Eileen gently touched her hand. "If you were close, then your grandmother knew exactly how much you loved her. Don't you agree, Hamish, darlin'?" She turned to her husband.

Hamish returned his wife's smile and nodded. "She spoke of you on more than one occasion and it was obvious how much she loved you and how proud she was of your art."

Glancing at his friendly expression, Christy knew he didn't say the words only to comfort her and she was glad Gran had spoken of her.

His next words surprised her. "We wondered if you might do something for us, Christy, but I'll let Eileen explain."

Intrigued, she waited to hear what she could possibly do for them.

"Well, it's actually two favours, so it is," Eileen said with a smile. "I don't know what you think of Sunday school, or children for that matter, but we could do with an artistic pair of hands for some of our projects, especially as we near Christmas."

A warm feeling of belonging crept over Christy at thought of being part of the local community in this way. But it was overshadowed by concern about the cottage and where she might live if things didn't work out. She hesitated before replying. "I think I'd love working with the children," she said at last.

Eileen smile broadly at her husband before turning back to Christy. "Now didn't I say you were the very person we needed as soon as we were introduced!"

"Believe me, my wife is very perceptive and usually correct in her judgement, which is quite terrifying at times," Hamish said.

"Sure, can you ever imagine my husband quaking in his shoes, Christy?" Eileen laughed. "But I did mention two favours, so I'll come right out and say it. We'd also greatly value your help with the village pantomime. Behind the scenes, I mean. The lad who used to do it has moved away and we've been struggling to find a replacement with enough time and talent to advise on the background scenery and such like."

The idea immediately appealed to Christy. She'd always loved the theatre but had no ambition to act, even in amateur productions. Behind the scenes would suit her very well.

"You know, I love the sound of everything you've suggested and I'd be very happy to help wherever possible. But...I may not be here permanently."

They both looked at her in understanding. "Oh, will you listen to me, Christy. I've jumped in impulsively as usual. I hadn't even thought you might be going back to London," Eileen said.

Glancing at the kind faces beside her, Christy wondered if she might confide in them and suddenly made up her mind. Not about the problem with the big house and the implications for the cottage, but she could mention the phone calls.

"I don't want to leave the village. Apart from the fact I feel closer to my grandmother in the cottage, there's nothing really attracting me back south. But something has been disturbing me and I'm not sure if I should take it seriously."

At their prompting, Christy told them about the nasty phone calls. Their reaction was not disappointing.

"Well, I'm that glad you've changed your phone number at least. But who would behave in such a shameful way?" Eileen asked.

Christy shrugged. That was the big question. But they didn't know the whole story and she wondered how much they had heard, if anything, about plans for the village. When she asked, it was obvious both had heard rumours but knew no details.

"You know, Ross McKinley seems a very honourable man, to use a slightly old-fashioned word, and I'm sure he'll have everyone's best interests at heart," Hamish offered.

"I'm sure you're right," Christy agreed, "but it seems his mother has the major voting power and I'm not so sure about her plans. Anyway, I'd love to help out while I'm here."

By mutual unspoken consent, they talked of general things in a 'getting to know you' fashion and Christy left their company secure in the knowledge she had made two more friends in the village.

However, it hadn't resolved the problem of the threats. She could try and ignore anonymous phone calls and change the number, but she had an uneasy feeling that this was only the beginning, that the threats would strengthen and change unless they discovered who was behind them and why.

Chapter Twenty

Christy enjoyed preparing her dinner party meal. A long time had passed since she'd entertained her own guests and the cottage already felt like home.

She kept the starter a simple carrot and sweet potato soup, made the day before and requiring only a heat through and garnish. The main course of Scottish beef and ale casserole was equally simple to prepare and serve and she made a refreshing pineapple mousse to leave in the fridge for dessert. She couldn't claim to be a Master Chef or Cordon Bleu cook, but she stuck to what would work with minimum fuss so she wouldn't miss too much of the conversation.

Trying to calm her nerves by breathing deeply, she avoided sipping any of the wine ready to serve. For some silly reason the only guest who made her apprehensive was Fiona, perhaps because she hadn't really spoken to the girl much, and always sensed a strain between them. She had looked forward to renewing their childhood friendship, although that word made her question her memories. Had they ever been true friends in the past either?

Checking all was well in the kitchen, and that Misty was happily curled up in her favourite spot near the fire, Christy ran upstairs to put the finishing touches to her hair and face. As with the meal, she had kept it simple: a smart but casual skirt and top with toning low heeled shoes, minimum make-up. Hair brushed and soft lipstick applied, she reached the bottom step as the doorbell rang.

Hoping that Ross might be first, she was delighted when his tall frame filled the doorway.

"I believe you're expecting guests this evening, Miss Morrison?"

Christy smiled and returned his banter. "Indeed I am, Mr McKinley. Won't you please come in?"

It was the perfect note to set the tone for the rest of the evening.

As each guest arrived, Christy relaxed a little more. Soon the cosy room was buzzing with laughter and conversation and she thought how much it suited the old cottage. Ross helped her pour the drinks and she placed a little bowl of savoury nibbles on the coffee table until the starter was ready to serve.

"It's good to finally meet you socially, Martin," Ross said as he proffered a glass to the man.

"Likewise, Cameron's brother," Martin replied with a grin and he turned and winked at his partner.

Christy could see the evening certainly wasn't going to be dull, as Martin and Cameron proceeded to entertain them with tales from the antique shop and life in general. Although Fiona was a little quiet, she too smiled and added a few of her own experiences. When Christy moved through to check the soup and heat the *focaccia* to go with it, she caught Fiona's eye.

"Do you need any help?" the girl asked.

About to decline, Christy paused. What better way to get a chance to chat to her? "Maybe you could put the bread on the table, thanks."

As Christy took the warm tray of *focaccia* from the oven, Fiona suddenly asked a question. "You do know they're an item, don't you? Cameron and Martin."

Christy was glad her concentration was still on the bread so it would hide her discomfort at Fiona's obvious wish to gossip. "Yes, Cameron told me. I expect he wants to tell Ross now too."

"And hope he paves the way to his mother." Fiona laughed.

Unwilling to speculate about the family, Christy turned the conversation to Fiona, genuinely interested in the girl she once knew fairly well.

"And what about you, Fiona. Do you live with your aunt all the time now?"

Shrugging, she answered briefly. "Not much choice at the moment."

Guessing she wouldn't get any further, Christy cut the bread, placed it inside a basket and held it out. "Thanks for your help this evening. Could you put this on the table, please? The soup's ready so perhaps you would ask the others to sit at the table."

Face flushed as though pleased to be appreciated, Fiona nodded and left the kitchen. At least it was an attempt at friendliness, and Christy was grateful for the short conversation.

She seated them informally, placing herself at the head of the small oblong table to give the illusion of equal numbers. It also meant she could slip in and out of the kitchen easily. Surprisingly, Fiona immediately offered to be helper, carrying dishes to and fro and Christy had to admit she made a big difference. As the evening progressed, the girl became friendlier and Christy wondered if perhaps the copious glasses of wine had played a part.

"Mm, this is a delicious casserole," Ross remarked at one point. "You know what they say about the way to a man's heart." And he grinned straight at Christy.

Feeling the warmth creep up her neck and face, Christy wasn't sure how to respond in front of everyone. She smiled and said nothing, but noticed the sharp glance Fiona threw her.

"Aye, and she's lovely to look at as well as being a good cook. Lucky man who nabs you, Christy, love," Cameron said in appreciation. "Just as well I'm already spoken for." He winked at Martin and everyone laughed.

Christy was pleased that Ross treated Martin with the utmost friendliness and respect. No doubt he'd known his brother better than anyone. Once dessert had been consumed with as much pleasure as the other courses, Christy suggested they take their coffee back to the more comfortable chairs around the fireplace. This time, she gratefully accepted when Ross offered to clear everything into the kitchen.

"Just push the plates into the sink and I'll clear the rest up later," she said. "Perhaps you could take the coffee tray through and I'll bring the pot." She didn't intend missing any more of the conversation than necessary.

As she glanced around her unusually crowded sitting room, Christy was overwhelmed by a sense of belonging. Even in this short time, she had settled into the village and still felt comforted by so many wonderful memories of Gran. If only things could remain this way. She pushed the little frisson of fear aside, determined to enjoy the moment and leave the future to itself for now.

She was bringing the refilled coffee pot through when she heard Martin mention the *Rubaiyat*.

"Wow! I've never seen such a gorgeous copy of this – look at those illustrations." He held the book reverently as though afraid to hurt it. "Sorry, you don't mind if I have a look do you, Christy?"

"No, of course not," she said, understanding that Martin took great care of all old items.

"You know, I think this might well be worth a bob or two, if I'm not mistaken. What do you think, Cameron love?" Martin handed it to Cameron.

They waited to hear his verdict and were not disappointed. "Think you might be right, although we'd need to check up on its provenance of course."

Mixed emotions coursed through Christy: surprise, uncertainty, disbelief. "Well, I love the book but I had no idea it might be valuable. Not that I'd ever dream of selling it since it's such a precious memento."

"You'll probably find it's no more than one of many mass-produced copies," Fiona said. "It's not that old, is it?"

Christy wasn't the only one who glanced at the girl as she delivered the words in a slightly dismissive manner. Exactly how did Fiona know the age of the book? At that thought, Christy remembered the distinct feeling that someone had moved it when she wasn't in the cottage. Surely it couldn't have been Fiona? Fortunately, she had already taken Gran's letter out of it and didn't mind them all having a look through the *Rubaiyat's* pages. Then she saw Cameron's eyes widen at the inscription and the quick questioning glance he threw his brother. Christy saw the brief shake of the head from Ross before Cameron's next words.

"That was Granddad's name. Gosh, he must've given this to your Gran. Wonder why?"

Since Christy didn't know the real reason, she kept quiet and noticed Ross didn't offer an explanation either.

"Maybe the old codger wasn't as saintly as everyone supposed," Fiona said with a laugh.

"May I have some more coffee, please, Christy?" Ross said, "I think we'd better put the book over on the sideboard out of harm's way."

Christy threw him a grateful glance and while Ross poured the coffee she did as he suggested. Everyone ignored Fiona's barbed comment, and soon conversation became more general. By the time Martin and Cameron got up to leave, Christy knew she had another friend for life in vivacious Martin and hoped Mrs McKinley would accept this genuinely nice guy in her younger son's life.

"Thank you, darling Christy, for making me so very welcome. Hope to see you over at the shop soon." Martin hugged her warmly, as did Cameron who whispered "thank you" in her ear.

Any thought Christy might harbour about being alone with Ross for a short time was soon laid to rest by Fiona.

"So, you'll walk me up the lane, won't you, Ross? I'd feel safer with a strong man on my arm."

"I can't think why you should need protection, but of course we can walk some of the way together," Ross gallantly replied.

Christy watched with interest, noticing Fiona's satisfied smile and Ross's hesitation. She mentally shrugged, deciding to clear what she could of the evening's meal then collapse into bed.

Ross took her hand when he was ready to leave, not to shake but to hold in his. "Thank you for a truly delightful evening and dinner, Christy. It was kind of you to include Martin. Let me know if you need any help putting things away and I'll come down in the morning."

Before she could reply, Fiona threw her thanks from the door. "Great evening, Christy, thanks for the invite."

"You're welcome." Christy replied to both. "Thanks, Ross, but I'm sure I'll manage fine," she added in response to his offer and he released her hand.

After they'd gone, she sat on the sofa for a while. On the whole, she couldn't have wished for a more enjoyable evening. She would never be bosom pals with Fiona but at least they were talking in a reasonably friendly manner.

Picking up the *Rubaiyat*, Christy stared at the inscription that was seemingly indicative of some measure of love between Gran and Ross's grandfather. *What happened between you*? Christy silently asked. As she turned the pages, admiring again the delicate illustrations, she paused at the fine pencil underlining of verse seventy-three.

'Ah, Love! Could thou and I with Fate conspire,
To grasp this sorry Scheme of Things entire.'

Another meaningful sentiment that only added more confusion. Perhaps Mrs McKinley knew more about the truth behind the words and the gift. And that might explain her slight unfriendliness. Christy closed the book, resolving to find out the answer to what sorry scheme of things might have taken place between their grandparents.

Chapter Twenty-One

Choosing a clear, crisp October morning to liberate Gran's little car from its long rest in the garage, Christy checked it had enough petrol for its first outing. Since Ross had reassured her it was well maintained, she had no doubt it would take little more than a short run to get it going again.

And so it proved. To avoid parking problems, she drove it as far as the village main street and once round the perimeter of the park. Nothing too taxing while her left arm became used to each gear change.

Pleased to feel only an occasional twinge, she smiled at the sense of freedom a set of wheels gave her. "Thank you, Gran," she whispered in the silence. Since she needed a few groceries, she parked just along from the village store in the one space that didn't require much manoeuvring.

Ewan MacPherson stood in his usual place behind the counter, nodding in welcome at sight of her. A younger woman was helping to serve and she smiled at Christy. A few other villagers were browsing for items in the shelves running down the length of the shop and she relaxed. Why should the man bother her when they had no quarrel?

"Good day, Miss Morrison. I'm glad to be of assistance again."

Christy smiled in response to his friendly enough greeting. As long as he made no mention of Ross, she could be perfectly civil to the man.

"So, you'll be well settled in the cottage now, lass," Ewan said, as he placed her shopping into a couple of bags.

Detecting no undertones in the question, Christy replied. "Yes, thanks, Mr MacPherson. It's beginning to feel even more like home now."

"Ach, call me Ewan, makes me feel less old." He grinned. "My mother remembers you as a wee girl."

"That was a long time ago. But thank you, Ewan. And you must call me Christy."

"Well, let me know if you ever need anything, Christy lass, and I'll try to oblige."

Although delivered with a grin, his words sounded vaguely suggestive and she only nodded. Why did the big man have this effect on her? Or maybe it was partly his animosity towards Ross that disturbed her.

During the remainder of the day, her natural optimism reasserted itself. The cottage enveloped her like a warm blanket, its homeliness increasing. Misty was the ideal companion and the latest illustrations were developing well. She flexed her arm after its unaccustomed use, relieved to find little discomfort. Even getting behind the wheel had been less traumatic than she feared.

She was beginning to hope that whoever had threatened her was giving up, when the phone rang.

"Hello, can I help you?" She'd got used to getting the first word in now.

"Christy! Oh, I'm glad you're in." Fiona's breathless voice answered.

"What is it? Has something happened?" Christy's stomach flipped. Please let it not be Ross.

"It's Mrs McKinley. She's speaking oddly and her eye looks strange, sort of droopy. I don't know what to do and no one else is here!"

Trying to calm the girl's panic, Christy spoke quietly. "I'm on my way. Call an ambulance, Fiona."

Throwing on her jacket, Christy hurried up to the house. By the sound of it, the woman was in the throes of a stroke and it was imperative they got her to hospital as quickly as possible.

A few minutes after she arrived and ensured that Mrs McKinley was as comfortable as possible, the ambulance's klaxon alerted them to its presence. Time passed in a blur as the paramedics took over. Christy stood back to allow Fiona into the ambulance beside the patient, promising to wait for Ross or Cameron.

"Thanks," Fiona said, as she took up her vigil beside the older woman before the doors closed.

Christy stood anxiously aside, watching as the flashing lights resumed and the ambulance set off towards the hospital. She didn't have long to wait. Ross drew up to the door, alarm in his eyes.

"What's happened, Christy?"

"Oh thank goodness you're here, Ross. I'm afraid your mother seems to have had some kind of seizure. Fiona went with her. She phoned me in a panic as no one was here."

"Thanks for coming up right away. I'll go after the ambulance. Could you phone Cameron for me and tell him what's happened. I don't think he was due over here today. I'll let you know how Mother is later."

Christy was thankful she'd added both their phone numbers to her mobile and she dialled Cameron's as she watched Ross drive away. It was answered at once.

"Hi Cameron? It's Christy. Don't panic, but I'm afraid your Mum's been taken to hospital with a possible stroke. Ross just arrived and has gone after the ambulance. Fiona went with your mum."

Christy listened to Cameron's hurried voice, hearing the underlying concern. She agreed as he told her to wait for news at the cottage and he would phone Mrs MacPherson.

Once she was back in her own little home, Christy couldn't settle, wondering about the situation at the hospital. She hoped Mrs McKinley wouldn't be left paralysed; she had no doubt the woman would be a difficult patient for anyone who had the caring of her. But she also wished her well and fully intended visiting her in hospital if she were in for any length of time, and certainly once she was home again.

"Oh, Misty, it's at times like this I'm glad of your presence," she told the little kitten who'd leaped up beside Christy when she sat down.

Any kind of incident such as this reminded her how fleeting life could be and how instantly it might change. Images of Gran and Michael as she last saw them crowded her mind until she needed a distraction from sad and regretful thoughts.

Once she had made a cup of coffee, she fetched the *Rubaiyat* and read through the immortal words again, finding comfort in knowing Gran had read this same book many times. Turning to her favourite lines, she nodded in agreement.

> *'The Moving Finger writes; and having writ,*
> *Moves on; nor all thy piety nor wit*
> *Shall lure it back to cancel half a line,*
> *Nor all your tears wash out a word of it.*

Surely no truer words were written or spoken? She couldn't cancel out the past, but she could determine how she dealt with the present and approached the future.

A knock at the door interrupted her musings before she mulled too much on the past again and she glanced at the clock to find time had moved on quicker than she realised.

Ross stood before her and she fleetingly knew the evening had become brighter for his presence.

"Come in, Ross. How is your mother?" Presumably that was the reason for his visit.

Misty immediately came to greet him and Christy envied the kitten for a moment when he bent down to fondle her neck and ears. Ignoring such inappropriate thoughts, she sat down beside him on the sofa.

"Mother's going to be fine," he said. "Thanks for being there so quickly and remaining calm. The damage is minimal and she should make a good recovery. She was very lucky to get to hospital right away."

"I'm so pleased it's not as bad as I feared. It must have given you all a shock."

He nodded and took one of her hands. "It's only when something like this happens that we really think about what matters." He stopped as though searching for expression while still holding her hand.

Christy waited, not wanting to spoil the moment, reluctant to read too much into his words.

"I don't know what the implications will be for the estate now. I suppose it will depend on Mother's recovery," Ross said. "But she's still determined on the ball." He smiled at her. "It's a bit of an institution around here and she won't let everyone down if possible."

Christy nodded. She certainly couldn't fault Mrs McKinley's determination, or stubbornness, which should stand her in good stead for her recovery. "Perhaps it's helpful for her to have something to look forward to."

"And you, Christy, do you look forward to anything in particular?"

She glanced away for a moment, unsure of her life choices. "A better year than the one almost over," she said, smiling to avoid any suggestion of self-pity.

"Then I wish you all you wish yourself. Now, I'd better get home and see what needs to be done before Mother returns, although it should be a day or two before they let her out."

He stood up and Christy did the same, reluctant to bring their impromptu chat to a close.

"Thanks again for your help," Ross said softly.

She was about to move towards the door when Misty entwined herself around Christy's legs and knocked her off balance.

"Oops, I think Misty is trying to say goodbye." She laughed, trying to stay upright.

Ross put out a hand to steady her and then she was standing close enough to his chest that she felt the heat radiating between them.

"Christy..." His hand cupped her chin.

She looked into his darkened eyes and his words dwindled away as they stared at each other without speaking. Then, tentatively, his mouth claimed hers in a gentle kiss. All thought fled as she responded, her lips parting as he pulled her ever closer, her arms holding him tight.

Ross drew apart first, leaving her unsteady. "I'm sorry. I didn't mean to do that. Better say goodnight."

Before she had the chance to respond, Ross headed for the door and she could do nothing but follow. After he had left with a brief smile but no more words, Christy closed the door and stood with her back against it, waiting for her pulse to return to normal, every nerve still longing for more of his touch. She eventually sat down, glad to welcome Misty up beside her.

"Well, I don't know what to make of that," she said, as she stroked Misty's silky fur.

She did know, however, that the kiss had reached into her heart and body and given another minute, she would have responded ever more passionately. Feelings she hadn't realised had deepened quite so far now surfaced to leave her bemused and confused.

But why had he reacted so quickly to stop the kiss going any deeper? The man was still as much an enigma as ever. Yet beneath that controlled exterior, lay great passion, she was sure of it. So, did something or someone else cause his hesitation? Someone like his ex? Perhaps he wasn't free to have feelings for her, or maybe worry about his mother and the estate superseded all other considerations for now.

And what of herself? She had no doubt of her growing attraction for Ross over the past weeks, even though she had imagined her own recent past too traumatised to allow space for another man. But that kiss proved her wrong and brought long-suppressed teenage feelings for him to the surface. Yet, once again, he had pulled away.

"What complicated creatures we humans are, Misty." She stroked the kitten, eliciting an answering purr. What now for her and Ross?

Chapter Twenty-Two

Over the next few days, Christy tried not to dwell on the fact that Ross had not contacted her since that meaningful kiss. Did he regret it so much that he couldn't face her?

To make it worse, she had never heard from Cameron either and could only assume both men were completely tied up with their mother's rehabilitation. She'd half hoped Fiona might contact her but she too was silent. Christy hadn't even seen any of them about when out walking, although she didn't go near the house.

So her response when Nick Anderson phoned again was warmer than she meant it to be.

"Hi Christy, Nick Anderson here. I hoped you might agree to meet me for coffee in town. Tomorrow morning, if you're free?"

After her initial hesitation, she agreed. "I could make myself free and I need to go into town anyway." Surely that wasn't too eager. She could perhaps find out what he was up to and he might know more about Mrs McKinley.

Next morning, confident and pain-free enough to drive to town, Christy parked at the furthest end so she could walk past the shops. She was mildly surprised that Nick had chosen the same humble cafe she'd been in before. Perhaps he *had* been the person meeting Fiona that day.

"It's good to see you again, Christy. You're

looking good."

She might not fully trust him, but Nick Anderson was a practised charmer, and having a good-looking man pay her such close attention made her smile.

"Thanks." She didn't add any reciprocal compliment lest she inadvertently gave him the wrong idea. "What can I do for you," she asked, getting straight to the point of the meeting.

"Whoa, what happened to coffee and small talk between friends? At least I hope we can be friends, Christy."

That all depends what you want, went through her mind. "I didn't want to take up too much of your time," she said.

"The next couple of hours are yours," he replied at once, with his usual grin. As though she were lucky to have that length of time with him.

"Have you heard how Mrs McKinley is doing?" he asked once he'd ordered coffee.

"Not recently, although I believe she's recovering well." He obviously hadn't been updated either.

He nodded, then got to the heart of the matter. "So, have you decided to stay up here after all?"

Christy had the impression this was no idle question, as he watched for her reaction.

"I'm pretty sure I could make my home in Kilcraig since it holds such happy memories." She didn't intend giving him a definite answer before the practicalities were finalised.

"I see. And you plan to stay in the old cottage? Only, I noticed there's a great new modern development with houses for sale."

Christy stared at him without replying. What to make of that? Why should he care where she lived? Because he needed the cottage as part of the development at the estate? Well, she wasn't going to tell him that idea might be shelved anyway.

"Thanks for your concern, but I have no plans to give up my grandmother's cottage just yet." If she were going to discuss her future plans with anyone, it would be with Ross. There was something ruthless about Nick Anderson and she wondered again exactly what had caused the animosity between the two men?

"Have you known Ross a long time?" she asked, determined to change the subject.

"Long enough," he said with a grin. "I'm afraid he's never got over his girlfriend preferring me. Not that we lasted, as it turns out."

Trying not to show the extent of her shock, Christy glanced away. So Moira had dumped Ross – for Nick Anderson? No wonder the men didn't get on. Yet, she couldn't help thinking Nick might be exaggerating, or was that her wishful thinking. She didn't want to imagine Ross pining for someone who'd thrown him over.

"What about you, Christy. Surely there's a man somewhere?"

"Not any more." She refused to tell him any of her private business. "Anyway, it was kind of you to invite me out again, but I must get back. I've promised to help with the village pantomime and need to finalise some ideas for scenery."

He took her sudden departure with good grace and a knowing grin. "Maybe we'll get a chance to resume our conversation another day. Take care, Christy."

As she stood up, he did too and before she could move away, he kissed her cheek as though they always parted that way.

"Thanks again," she said, before hurrying from the cafe without a backward glance. That was enough time in his company and she was in no hurry to repeat the experience. She could never trust a man like him and hadn't liked his 'take care', as though she had cause to do so. Or perhaps she was becoming paranoid about everyone.

All the way home, she couldn't rid herself of the thought that Ross might not be completely over his ex, no matter what he said. It must surely rankle that Moira had preferred someone like Nick Anderson.

When Christy finally let herself into the house, she immediately knew something wasn't quite right. Then she saw Misty happily ensconced on the sofa licking her paws. Yet, she had made sure to shut the kitten in the kitchen. Someone had been in the cottage again.

Her skin tingled as she glanced around, alerting her to a change in the air. A lingering scent, perhaps? Not as obvious as perfume or aftershave, but a strong sense of another presence in this room not long ago. The scare tactics were working, even as she went again from room to room to reassure herself she was alone with Misty. But she couldn't go on like this, whether it was her imagination or not. The phone threats were all too real.

She was reluctant to bother Ross when he hadn't been in touch for so long, but maybe Cameron could reassure her. She pressed his mobile number and held her breath. He answered on the third ring.

"Christy, love, sorry I haven't been around lately and apologies for not thanking you for helping Mum."

She waited for a space then jumped in. "Don't worry about that, Cameron, but I wondered if I could talk to you soon."

"Of course. I'm just about to leave the hospital. I

could call on my way over to the house. I need to collect something from there. See you soon."

After a quick check of all the rooms, Christy stroked Misty as she waited for Cameron. Maybe she was getting worked up for nothing.

When he breezed in half an hour later, Christy was ridiculously pleased to see him and gave him a tight hug.

"Hey, it's good to see you too, Christy. Is everything okay?" He held her at arm's length.

"Sorry. I should ask about your Mum first. How is she?"

Cameron sat beside her on the sofa before answering. "She's okay, thanks. They want to keep her a bit longer but she should be home in a couple of days. Anyway, tell me about you. How've you been?"

Normally, the usual 'fine thanks' would be automatic but she hesitated before telling Cameron about her suspicions.

"You sure someone's been here? Anything else to make you think so?"

Christy understood his reasoning – she could hardly believe it herself. "Not really. But I've been very careful to make sure Misty is in the kitchen."

He stood up suddenly. "Let me check the kitchen door. Maybe it's not secure enough. It's an old house."

It was an obvious suggestion and Christy had meant to double check that herself. She watched as Cameron opened and closed the door. Maybe the click wasn't as satisfying as it should be.

"Hmm, it closes okay, but I'm not convinced it stays tight shut."

For some reason, Christy had the impression that Cameron was a bit distracted and she didn't want to push it.

"You're probably right. Don't worry about it. I'll arrange for someone to come and check it out." After a few more minutes general chat about the antique shop, Cameron made his excuses to leave.

"Better get on, but we'll need to get together soon. Martin is looking forward to seeing you again."

"That would be great. Thanks for calling in and reassuring me."

When he'd gone, Christy made a pot of tea, wondering why Cameron was so distracted. Perhaps it was something to do with Martin. The sooner his relationship was out in the open, the better for everyone involved.

The phone rang as she was finishing the dishes and she hoped it was a genuine call. At her 'hello, who's calling', Eileen's voice answered and Christy relaxed.

"I wondered, or rather hoped, you might do me a big favour please, Christy. Could you help out at Sunday school this weekend at all? Sorry it's short notice, but one of our teachers is ill and it might be a good chance for you to meet the kids."

Pushing aside her reservations, Christy tentatively agreed. "I've not had much experience with this kind of thing. Are you sure I'll be of use?"

Eileen laughed kindly. "Believe me, you'll be a breath of fresh air, so you will, and we really do need your help. Sure, you'll be fine. You won't have to teach as such, for Jean Simpson is more than capable of taking charge, but we need another person to assist according to regulations."

Christy relaxed even more. "That's okay then. I'd like to help if I can."

The phone call had cheered her up and she made

sure the doors and windows were secure. A relaxing bath next, then another read through the *Rubaiyat* to see if it held any more clues to Gran's life.

Once cosy, with the open fire crackling beside her, Christy went through to fetch the book from the top of the old-fashioned sideboard where she had left it. She stared in confusion. It wasn't there. Puzzled, she searched every surface and around any part of the floor that might hold a dropped book. No sign of it. Had she taken it upstairs?

Rushing up to the next floor, she explored every conceivable place she could have left it. Definitely not there. Returning downstairs, she had to face the awful thought that someone had indeed been inside the cottage and he or she had taken the book.

But who would be interested in it enough to steal it? For its value perhaps? She remembered Martin mentioning it might be worth something. Or was it another reason entirely? Something to do with the inscription, or yet another way to freak her?

An unexpected longing for Ross's reassuring presence almost propelled her to the phone. But she stopped herself, refusing to be the one to do the running. Whatever had almost begun between them was halted by Ross's silence. But one thing was for sure. Tomorrow, she would arrange a change of locks. Getting all the keys back, as far as she knew, hadn't been enough to stop whoever was determined to scare her back to London.

Chapter Twenty-Three

After a fitful sleep, when arguments about staying up in Scotland or going back to London played over in her mind, Christy got up more tired than when she went to bed. Her first hope was that maybe she had only misplaced the *Rubaiyat* last night.

She was in the middle of a thorough search again when the phone rang. It was Ross.

"Hello, Christy. Sorry I haven't been in touch but I've had a few problems to sort out. Anyway, I'm phoning to ask if you could possibly visit Mother with me this evening. She's asking to see you."

Silence, while Christy absorbed the sound of his voice and the fact that Mrs McKinley wanted to see *her*.

"It's fine, Ross. I know you'll have a lot on your mind. I can't think why your mother wants to see me but of course I'll visit."

"Great. Thanks. I'll pick you up at six thirty to give us time to negotiate the traffic. We can catch up then. Bye."

Christy held the phone receiver as the engaged tone told her Ross had gone. Bemusement was uppermost, both at his business-like conversation and his mother's request. Although conversation was the last way to describe their brief exchange. He hadn't even asked how *she* was. Then she admonished herself, remembering Ross had an estate to take care of as well as worrying about a parent. And she could hardly tell him about her own worries over the phone.

After breakfast, she walked to the village and asked Ewan MacPherson about the possibility of finding a locksmith nearby. He was probably the most likely person to know everyone around here.

"Aye, I do know someone, lass. He's retired now but was one of the best. Is it for the cottage?"

Of course he was going to be curious about her reason for a locksmith, but the fewer people who knew her fears the better. "Yes, the front door. I'm finding the key a little awkward and would prefer something more secure."

"Ach, these old houses start to need a bit more attention eventually. Give me your phone number and I'll tell Bob to let you know when he can come round. Is it safe enough for now?"

"Yes, thanks. It can wait another day or two. I'll take a loaf of that delicious wholemeal bread while I'm here, please, and some milk."

After a few more pleasantries, Christy left the shop, aware Ewan's curiosity was peaked. Thankfully, no one else had been around to hear her concerns. She'd just have to be patient, wait until Bob phoned and trust that he'd be able to do something fairly quickly.

For the remainder of the day, she absorbed herself in her drawings and further ideas for the children's Bible stories. She'd been given a fairly wide remit and a list of the stories to illustrate. So far everything had been approved but she had about a quarter of them to finish. At least it took her mind off the missing *Rubaiyat*, for most of the time at least. But what could she do? She had no wish to get the police involved at this stage. Maybe Ross could help her look once more, move a few of the heavier pieces of furniture, check it definitely hadn't fallen down behind something. It was grasping at air but she still couldn't believe someone had stolen it.

By the time Ross was due to arrive, Christy had eaten a light snack and was ready and waiting for him. Deciding casual was more practical, she dressed up the black slim trousers and light sweater with a pretty red and black scarf.

Although Ross greeted her with a peck on the cheek, Christy sensed the strained atmosphere between them. Surely one full-on kiss hadn't scared him off for good?

"How have you been, Christy?" Ross broke the silence as he negotiated the traffic on the busy main road.

"Fine, thanks. And you?" She couldn't tell him about the missing book while he was driving. Best keep to banalities.

"Not so bad. Hospital visits keep me out of mischief." He threw her a brief grin before concentrating on the road again.

"Is your mother much better? Cameron said she might soon get home."

"I didn't know you'd seen Cameron." He threw her another glance. "Yes, any day now. Fortunately, it hasn't done too much damage and she should be able to live a normal life, albeit a slightly slower one."

"That's good. Do you know why she's asked to see me?"

Christy noticed his frown before he answered. "Not really, but I assume it's because you were one of the first to help her."

They remained quiet in their thoughts after this exchange and Christy wondered what lay ahead. She hadn't forgotten that Mrs McKinley still owned the major share of the house and its cottages.

The hospital car park was already jam packed with visitors' cars when they arrived and they had to park some distance from the door. Fortunately, the rain had stayed away and it was a pleasant enough walk. Christy was pleased to see it wasn't one of those tall, prison-like buildings she'd seen in other places. Only a few stories high, its various buildings sprawled over a wide area linked by paths.

As they entered, she couldn't hide the sudden reaction to the claustrophobic lack of air and overwhelming heat. Such impressions she had retained of the London hospital since the accident came rushing back and sweat broke out on her brow.

Ross was certainly sensitive, as he immediately knew she was uncomfortable.

"You okay, Christy?" He took her hand.

"Sorry. I don't like hospitals much and it takes a few minutes to psych myself up to get through it." She glanced at his concerned expression.

"Then it's doubly kind of you to visit my mother. It's not far to the ward and we needn't stay long." He gave her hand a reassuring squeeze.

By the time they reached Mrs McKinley's bedside, Christy had herself under control, although she still couldn't believe she'd been summoned like this. The lady herself was sitting on a large, supportive chair, an expensive looking lavender dressing gown tied at the waist. She looked a little pale, but Christy detected no real difference since she was sitting down. And she already knew the voice wasn't affected by the stroke. No doubt her walking might be slower.

"Hello, Christina. I am so pleased you could visit me."

Hesitating a moment over whether or not to kiss the patient, Christy was relieved when Mrs McKinley held out her hand.

Clasping it in hers, Christy smiled in response to the friendlier tone. "How are you, Mrs McKinley? You look very well."

"Thank you, dear. Why don't you sit down? Ross, come and greet me, then you can fetch another chair for yourself."

With a raised eyebrow at the command, Ross pecked his mother on the cheek and went to do her bidding while Christy sat next to his mother.

"I've brought you a glossy magazine in case you're bored by now," Christy said.

"That was kind, thank you. Now let me say what I must before I start wilting." Mrs McKinley waited until Ross was settled at her other side then she turned to Christy.

"I want to thank you for your help and quick actions on the day of my little episode. Evidently, Fiona went to pieces and if it hadn't been for you, I might have been worse off."

As Christy squirmed in embarrassment and was about to deny she'd done much at all, Mrs McKinley continued. "It might have seemed second nature to you, my dear, but it is my good fortune you were so close."

Christy briefly glanced at Ross to find him smiling and she finally found her voice. "I'm so glad I was able to help, Mrs McKinley, but I'm sure Fiona would have coped had I not arrived."

"Perhaps, but that is not my recollection, and you were the person the paramedics praised."

Christy glanced at Ross again, hoping he would say something, but he seemed quite happy to leave the conversation to the women.

"Will you soon be home," she asked, floundering for anything more interesting to say.

"The day after tomorrow, if all continues to please the doctors. I confess I'll be very glad to return to my own bed and food."

Christy nodded in sympathy; she well remembered that desire.

"However, this has made me rethink the plans for the estate," Mrs McKinley said.

A quick glance at Ross convinced Christy he'd heard this already.

"The golf course is too big a project since Ross has made his feelings clear. But we may still look into converting the house in some way."

So where did that leave her and the cottage? She couldn't ask outright since Mrs McKinley had never brought up the subject with her.

Ross spoke for the first time. "It's all very vague at the moment, but the less disruption the better for my mother."

"I am quite able to speak for myself, Ross, thank you. But my son is correct for now."

Since Christy had no idea how the new plans might affect her, she hoped Ross could explain later.

"Now, I expect you to come to the Winter Ball, Christina. I would like you to meet a few more people, including Moira, Ross's... friend."

Thrown by the sudden change of subject, it took Christy a few moments to register the words. She wasn't surprised to see Ross's mouth tighten.

She didn't wait to hear his comments. "I'd love to go to the ball, thank you, Mrs McKinley. It's a good excuse for a new dress apart from anything else."

"Good. Now, I am rather tired after all that

talking. You must visit the house once I am back to normal life," the older lady said, effectively dismissing them.

Christy stood up. "It's good to see you recovering so well, Mrs McKinley. Goodbye." She touched the patient's hand in farewell, quite sure a kiss was neither expected nor desired.

She gathered up her coat and scarf while Ross said goodbye to his mother. She was about to walk on but he was soon beside her. They remained silent until the cold evening air breathed through Christy once more and her shoulders relaxed.

"Sorry about the summons and dismissal," Ross said, as they headed towards the car.

Christy laughed, as it exactly described the evening. "No need to apologise. I honestly didn't mind visiting your mother. I expect she doesn't like growing older and relinquishing control."

Ross stopped walking. "Considering my mother has never been over friendly towards you, that's very perceptive and understanding, Christy Morrison."

The approval in his voice warmed her a little more. Then she remembered the problem of the missing *Rubaiyat* and the veiled hints about Ross's *friend*.

Chapter Twenty-Four

"Can I talk to you about something that's bothering me, Ross? You can come in and say hello to Misty," Christy said when they reached the cottage.

Did she imagine his hesitation before he replied? "Yes, I'd like that, thanks. I wanted to ask you something too." He didn't elaborate as he followed her to the door.

As soon as she opened the kitchen door, Misty made straight for Ross. At least she hadn't got out this time.

"Maybe she's looking for Darwin again," he offered, bending down to fondle the animal.

Christy filled the kettle while Ross made himself at home. Too much at home for her peace of mind. It was good to see him in the cottage again and she hadn't realised quite how much she'd missed him the past few days.

"So, what's been happening?" Ross asked, when they were settled on the sofa, each remaining at enough distance to stop it being too cosy.

She kept her eyes on him. "You'll think I'm imagining yet another incident, but the *Rubaiyat* has gone. I mean someone has taken it."

"Are you sure? When did this happen?"

His reaction certainly proved he had no knowledge of it, not that she ever thought he did.

"I'm fairly certain someone got into the cottage again, as Misty was in the sitting room and I had definitely shut her in the kitchen the other day. Then I discovered the book was missing. Don't worry, I've arranged a locksmith through Ewan MacPherson. But I can't imagine why someone would take the book."

Except for its possible monetary value, and sentimental value to her, but she didn't want to cast suspicion on any of the friends who'd been here when it was discussed.

Ross had frowned all the way through this and now he moved nearer and took Christy's hand.

"Why didn't you tell me, Christy? You must have been worried."

She glanced away before answering. "I hadn't spoken to you for a while and didn't want to bother you with your mother ill. Cameron made me agree to a locksmith."

Now he looked almost hurt. "You told Cameron?"

"Only because he called in on his way home from hospital yesterday evening. And he doesn't know the book has gone as I only discovered that later. He thought the kitchen door might just be faulty and that's how Misty gets out."

Ross stood up. "Let me have a look."

Since there was no point in dissuading him, Christy watched as he did exactly the same as Cameron.

"It's not completely secured, but I can't imagine the door opens that easily. When is the locksmith coming round?"

Pleased he hadn't belittled her concern, she explained about waiting for the man's phone call to confirm a time. "Don't worry about it. I just wanted you to know I'm getting the locks changed at last.

Ross still stood, looking undecided. "Do you want me to have a search with you?"

"That might be a good idea as you can move the heavier furniture aside," she agreed.

"Lead on and I'll follow."

After checking behind and under everything that moved, Christy hesitated about going upstairs. Surely she would have remembered if she'd taken it up to her room? But Ross suggested it himself and she almost ran up the stairs, conscious of him behind her, heading for the bedroom.

When she entered, she could hardly look at Ross, every nerve too aware of him. Quickly, she indicated the chest of drawers.

"That's the only place I might have laid it down but I don't think I did."

Nodding, he pulled it away from the wall enough for them to check behind.

"Definitely not there," she said and was about to leave the room.

"What about the bed?" He asked.

Glancing at him, they both seemed to realise the incongruity of the situation at the same time and Ross grinned.

"I've already checked there and I don't remember ever reading it in bed. I'm sure it's not in the cottage now. We might as well go back downstairs," she said.

And before the atmosphere became even more loaded with unspoken desire, she hurried from the room. Now her dreams would be filled with the image of Ross McKinley standing next to her bed.

Downstairs, she poured another drink as Ross came and sat beside her, neither of them referring to her haste.

"Maybe the book will turn up when you're not looking for it," he suggested.

She shrugged. "Maybe." But she knew without

doubt that someone had deliberately removed it. "Anyway, what did you want to ask me?"

"I was wondering if you'd like to go along to a music gig with me at a country inn," Ross said. "I think you'd enjoy it – a friend of mine plays in the band. It's a week on Saturday evening."

Surprised by the unexpected invitation, she took a moment to reply. "I'd love to go, thanks. What does he play? Guitar?"

"Ah well, it's not that kind of band. In fact, I'm pretty sure you won't have seen, or heard, anything like it!"

Christy laughed at his teasing. "So are you going to tell me, or is it a surprise?"

"Both. Even when I tell you, I think they'll still come as a surprise. They're a Scottish tribal drumming band."

He watched her reaction, a broad smile on his face. He was quite correct, she wasn't any the wiser, but mightily intrigued.

"Now I can't wait. Should I dress up, or is it casual?"

"Definitely casual. We can get something to eat at the inn before they play. I'll be able to introduce you to a few friends at the same time."

"Looking forward to it already. Sounds great. Thanks for asking me, Ross."

"My pleasure. Now I'd better get home and take Darwin out for his final evening stroll." He stood up and Christy accompanied him to the door. "Please let me know when the locks are changed, or if you have any problems with them."

He took her hand and Christy nodded, aware of the air of expectancy between them. But he only leaned down to kiss her cheek as he said goodbye.

She watched until he was driving away then locked the door and, for extra security, she pushed a chair under the handle. Then she did the same with the back door before checking all the windows. She'd never been this neurotic before and was glad she'd arranged the locksmith for her peace of mind. At least Ross had left her intrigued about the Scottish tribal band and she couldn't wait to see how they might differ from anything else she had seen.

As for the scene in the bedroom, she would try to banish it from her mind else her imagination would only heighten her longing for a deeper relationship with the annoyingly reticent man.

Ewan was as good as his word and the friendly, elderly locksmith arrived two days later.

"Ach, they were built to last were these old houses, lassie," he said, as she brought him his second mug of coffee. "The locks are a wee bitty different from those in the modern boxes they call houses."

After his assurances that neither the front nor back door would defeat him, Christy continued with her final draft sketches so she could get them away to her agent and be reassured she was on the right lines before adding the fine coloured detail.

When she took the proffered new keys for the cottage, relief was mixed with a strange feeling that she had made a major change to her grandmother's home. Yet, she would have been the first to convince Christy it had to be done.

Once the sketches were finished, she turned her thoughts to the Sunday school class she'd agreed to help with. Eileen had reassured her again that she only needed to be a presence rather than a teacher. The children all met together but did different activities so it might only be a matter of amusing the younger ones for the session and they had plenty of books and table games. Maybe she could take along a copy of the previous book she'd illustrated before the accident. Appropriately enough, it was stories of animals and she could always tie it in with Noah's Ark, if allowed.

At a loose end by Saturday, she decided to go back to the antique shop. Maybe Cameron or Fiona would be there, and she'd be delighted to see Martin again. The evening out with Ross was a week away so she'd have plenty of time to decide what to wear. And if she remembered correctly, the complex beside the loch included a good quality department store. She could have a browse while there and even better if it was the right weekend for the Farmer's Market.

The weather was on her side, the late October sun glinting on the river as she drove across the Erskine Bridge. In less than half an hour, she was parking the car at the loch side. A quick flex of her bad arm gave her no more than a twinge. It was a good day to be out and about beside such a beauty spot.

She walked down to the shoreline first and discovered it was indeed another market day. The food stalls were doing a good trade already. Wandering along the path by the loch, she watched the families feeding the ducks before heading back to the antique shop.

At first, she thought no one was around so she browsed through the vintage jewellery cabinets before seeking out her favourite sections of books, magazines and postcards. She often found good illustration ideas from old magazines.

Some of the obviously rarer and more expensive books were displayed in a glass fronted cabinet. A few of the hard-back books caught her eye, amongst them an edition of John Donne poems. Earmarking it as a possibility for later along with the Keats she had seen last time, Christy stared at the locked case in puzzlement. If she were not mistaken, one of the slim volumes looked very familiar. Surely it must be a coincidence that one cover embossed in red and gold was similar to her missing *Rubaiyat* book.

It was wedged between other books and before she could get a closer look through the glass, a female voice called to her. Fiona was walking towards her.

"Hello, Christy. What a surprise to see *you* here."

Christy noticed she didn't add, 'pleasant' to surprise as most people would have done.

"Hi, Fiona. I liked it so much the last time when I came with Cameron that I wanted to come back by myself."

"Oh, I didn't know you'd been before," Fiona said.

Was it her imagination, or did Fiona seem uncomfortable?

"Is Martin around? I'd love to see him again," Christy said

"Sorry, he won't be here till nearer closing time. He and Cameron had some business arrangement but they don't tell me everything. We have a Saturday lad to help out if it gets very busy, though it's mostly just browsers these days. Don't know how long this place will last."

That was news to Christy. Cameron had never hinted that they might be struggling. But why should he tell her his business affairs?

"I'm sorry to hear that. It has a wonderful variety of items. In fact, I was having a look at some of the books in the glass cabinet over there, or at least what I could see of them.

Fiona followed her glance. "Anything in particular?" she asked.

"Well, I'm pretty sure I'd love the volume of Donne poetry. But another book caught my eye and I couldn't see it properly. Can you let me have a look at it, please?"

Fiona turned her attention back to Christy and shrugged. "I'll see if I can find the key. Haven't looked at that cabinet for ages."

While Fiona went back to the office, Christy had a closer look at the books behind the glass. One of them definitely resembled the *Rubaiyat*, though she couldn't see the title. A few minutes later, Fiona returned to her side.

"Sorry, Christy, I've no idea where the boys have put the keys to specific cabinets. You'll have to wait until one of them is here."

As far as Christy could tell, Fiona seemed to be speaking the truth. "That's a pity. I'll catch them another time."

She didn't want to hang around for the whole day in the hope that Martin returned, when it was most likely a waste of time. But the incident bothered her. Surely Fiona or Cameron hadn't stolen the book from the cottage? Yet it was a bit strange that Fiona had no access to the cabinets when left in charge. Not exactly the way to make a much-needed sale.

Thanking Fiona and leaving her to deal with a customer, Christy browsed through the clothes in the department store, recognising several well-known labels. She settled for a pretty multi-coloured shirt that would go with her jeans. She had no idea what to expect on the forthcoming evening out with Ross and couldn't even remember the band's Gaelic name to

Google them.

Before returning to the car, Christy wandered along by the market stalls and bought some salmon, cheese and a couple of pork chops, adding a small piece of fish for Misty and some freshly baked wholemeal bread. She responded to the friendly greetings automatically, her mind still on the promised evening's entertainment. It was time she went out more and the combination of an undoubtedly handsome escort, and the promise of stirring music made her heart lift. At least she could forget about vague threats, missing books and future decisions, although she was determined to examine that familiar looking book in the locked cabinet as soon as possible.

Chapter Twenty-Five

It felt comfortable being in the local church again and Christy smiled in acknowledgement at the many greetings until her face muscles hurt. It wasn't even so much about the religious side of the service, although she appreciated the well-known hymns and modern songs. In a church this size, it was more about the sense of community, of fellowship some would call it, and she could easily imagine becoming a regular part of this.

The Sunday school class turned out to be uneventful and good fun. After being introduced, she was happy to amuse the three younger children with the animal stories and soon had them drawing which animals they would let into the ark.

"You're a natural, so you are," Eileen said later. "You'll fit in here with no bother."

The praise warmed Christy and convinced her even more that she wanted to remain in this village. She didn't see Ross or his mother this time but she noticed Fiona leaving with Ewan. They were cousins of course so she supposed they were bound to see each other often.

"Remember we're beginning the pantomime rehearsals next week in the village community centre, if you're still interested," Eileen told her as she said goodbye.

"Looking forward to it, as long as I don't have to act in it!" She was perfectly happy to stay behind the scenes and help calm any nerves if necessary.

The rest of the week dragged as Christy contemplated the forthcoming evening out with Ross. He'd called her briefly to tell her his mother was home and he would pick Christy up on Saturday around six.

She busied herself walking around the local countryside, photographing ideas for future illustrations and trying not to dwell on the problem of the missing *Rubaiyat*.

Later in the week, Cameron phoned. "Hi, Christy love, Fiona mentioned you'd been to the shop the other day. Sorry Martin and I were missing. Let me know when you plan to come again and I'll make sure I'm here. We could grab a coffee."

"That would be good." She wondered why he didn't mention the request to see the volume in the locked cabinet. "Did Fiona tell you I was interested in one of the books?" she asked.

Was it her imagination that he paused rather long before answering?

"Oh, yes, she mentioned the Donne poems. I can bring the volume over so you can look at it, if you're not heading over this way soon."

No mention of the red and gold book. "That's okay, thanks, Cameron. I'll make a point of visiting again as there was another volume that caught my eye. I'd like to see it properly."

"Right you are. Let me know when. See you."

As she put down the phone, Christy's imagination went into overdrive. Did Cameron know the book she meant and even worse, had he taken it? No, of course not. He was too open for such subterfuge. But Fiona was another matter altogether.

Ross settled his mother into her room once more, trying to keep his mind from dwelling on the problem of Christy's intruder. At first, he'd been inclined to believe the kitchen door was faulty but too many strange things had bothered her, including the supposed theft of the *Rubaiyat*. At least the locks were now changed and only Christy had the key, although it might be wise if she were to trust one to him eventually in case of emergency.

"That's enough help, Ross, thank you. I'll manage quite well myself now."

His mother's command recalled him to the task in hand. Thank goodness the stroke had been mild enough not to destroy what independence his mother enjoyed, although it might be a while before she returned to the golf course, if at all. No doubt she would find something else to occupy her time and mind.

"Now, about the Winter Ball. I want to go over the guest list with you once I'm settled in again. The invitations will have to go out soon."

Ross suppressed a sigh. It was at times like these he wished for a sister who might have enjoyed being drawn into such events.

"Perhaps we could have a discussion about it one morning near the beginning of next week, if that suits you," Ross suggested. The sooner the better, once he'd had his date with Christy.

Thankful to be dismissed at last, he gave thought to the Saturday evening ahead. He hoped Christy would enjoy the particular brand of music, but he'd be surprised if it didn't stir some deep elemental part of her as it did him. And he wanted to be there when it did. However much he might deny it, his attraction to Christy was irreversible. It only remained to see where it might eventually lead once they had sorted out the niggling demons in their lives. The first item on the list was to ensure his mother had no lingering illusions that his well and truly ex, Moira, would ever figure in his life again.

Christy was glad she hadn't overdressed for this date. As soon as she stepped inside the old-fashioned inn, the atmosphere wrapped itself around her and she could have been in any period of Scotland. The low beams and subdued lighting added to the ambience. Ross seemed like a different person, casually yet smartly dressed in jeans and open-necked dark blue shirt that emphasised his slate grey eyes and dark brown hair.

"Hope you don't mind a more enclosed venue than before," he'd asked when picking her up.

"As long as it's not in a lift and there's a way out, I'll be fine," she'd replied with a grin. Even the drive there was enjoyable, eventually skirting part of Loch Lomond until they reached the small building that was tucked into the foot of the hills.

She understood his warning about it being enclosed but the inn had such a welcoming air that she ceased to notice its size. The tables were already filling up and a few hands waved to Ross in greeting.

"Come and meet a few of the guys, Christy," Ross suggested, leading her to a corner table where three men and a girl sat with half pints and various plates of tapas before them.

"Christy, this is Shona, Graeme, Malc and Spence. Malc's brother is in the band."

"Great to meet you, Christy," several voices said. "Come away and sit down with us. Bring a couple of chairs over, McKinley," Malc said.

Returning the friendly greetings, Christy couldn't believe the transformation in Ross. It was as though he had shed his more responsible side and could be himself for a change. His easy laugh and banter with his friends boded well for the evening. She was grateful he remembered to include her in the conversation. A seemingly endless supply of food appeared every now and then and the inn soon filled to capacity at promise of the forthcoming gig.

Shona soon engaged her in friendly chat, difficult though it was above the level of voices around them.

"How long have you been going out with Ross?" Shona asked. "He's a deep one!"

Stumped for the best way to answer, Christy finally settled for the truth. "We're not exactly going out, but we are old friends."

"Well you're an improvement on the last one – not that I had much to do with her."

Conversation levels had increased even more, so Christy decided she didn't have to reply to that revelation. Besides which, Ross had brought a round of drinks over for them all and a sudden murmur of expectation filled the inn.

"The band is just gearing up to come out," Ross said close to her ear.

His nearness filled her senses with anticipation even before the band came on and she couldn't remember being this happy for far too long. She sat back, intrigued to see this Celtic band at last. The lights dimmed and all conversation ceased as the four-man group appeared and set up their position under a single spotlight. Her eyes widened and she glanced at Ross to find him grinning.

"Wait till you hear them," he whispered.

The sight of them was a good enough start. Each

of the young men was dressed in a dark tartan kilt, while the top half was in various states of undress or with minimum covering, such as a tartan plaid casually thrown over one bare shoulder. Two of the men held huge drums before them and another sat behind smaller drums, while the fourth member of the band held bagpipes at the ready. She couldn't begin to imagine the kind of sound they would produce between them but there was no mistaking their effect so far.

Christy could scarcely take her eyes from the tallest, most brawny drummer in the band. Naked from the waist up, his huge arm muscles rippled in readiness as he wielded the drum before him, hands holding the sticks.

And then the music began.

The sheer power of sound reverberated through the intimate surroundings of the inn and Christy's eyes remained riveted on the band. As one particular number gradually increased in tempo and power, Christy felt the thrum of the music reach into her soul to release all the passion she had scarcely acknowledged before. Her breathing quickened until the final triumphant drumbeat faded.

Silence reigned for about a second, before the tumultuous applause and whistles rang out. Speechless at the depth of her emotions, Christy was aware of Ross's eyes on her and she returned his smile. "Wow!" she whispered.

Instead of speaking, his fingers found hers and she grasped his hand. All around them, conversation lulled again as the band struck up their next piece of stirring music. This time the skirl of the bagpipes played a slower lament until one by one each of the drums entered to increase the tempo. Christy gave herself up to the experience, warmth coursing through her at the wild tribal sound and the touch of Ross's hand in the subdued lighting. It was no time for words as none could express her feelings.

By the time the entertainment was drawing to a close, Christy had become one of the gang at their table and she had a clearer insight into what their future might include if she and Ross were ever a couple. It was good to push unwelcome thoughts of his ex and the troubles with the cottage aside to enjoy the evening with this man by her side.

Before they left the inn, Ross introduced her to his friend, Rory, the large drummer. His hand was as strong and firm as his muscled torso and Christy returned his grin.

"It was absolutely wonderful," she said. Anything else was unnecessary.

"Glad you enjoyed our wee performance. Ross should bring you to the Hogmanay shindig. Then you can really let your hair down and join in the ceilidh."

"You're right, Rory. Good to see you again," Ross said, squeezing Christy's hand.

"Great idea." Shona had come up behind them with her friends. "I'd love to meet up with you again, Christy, and it's good to see a smile on Ross's face again."

After the goodbyes and promises to get together again soon, they wandered out to the car and Christy smiled to see the moon almost full in the clear midnight sky. Could it get any more perfect?

The road back home was deserted and she loathe to spoil the peace inside the car with inane chatter, as well as the fact that one piece of music was still running through her mind. She watched what she could see of the darkened countryside with a glow in her heart. At one point, the shimmering moonlit loch was partially visible and she felt truly at one with her surroundings and with this man.

"Happy?" Ross asked, as they eventually neared the outskirts of the village.

"Very. Thanks for that wonderful experience. I can still hear and feel the thrum of that music."

"It's the kind that gets into the soul, isn't it? But it's even more meaningful in the right company." He glanced briefly at her before watching the country road ahead.

Anticipation suddenly gripped Christy as she wondered where this was leading. What exactly had the evening meant to Ross? Or to her for that matter? Yet it wasn't only the drumbeat that had made her heart respond to the music's ancient message.

They remained silent for the rest of the journey and Christy was still undecided what to do when the car drew to a halt. But she couldn't let the evening end so abruptly.

"Coffee, tea?" she asked, having a sudden absurd notion to add "me?" to the question.

"If you don't mind, I'll see you to the door but I won't come in this time," Ross said.

Christy was glad the darkness hid her confusion. Maybe she had read him wrong and imagined their closeness at the inn. For whatever reason, he obviously didn't want to spend any more time with her this evening and she was fine with that. Or so she convinced herself.

"Of, course. I had a really lovely time, thank you."

"I'm glad, Christy, I did too. Let me get the door for you."

She waited until he came round and opened her door and he stood back to let her clamber out.

"Sleep well," he said, briefly kissing her cheek, before going back round to the driver's side.

She hardly had time to react at his sudden departure; as though he hadn't wanted to risk kissing her lips again. She watched as he drove away and soon he was out of sight, but far from out of mind. Much as she hated to admit it, she had well and truly fallen for Ross McKinley completely against her better judgement. But why had he left her so quickly after such a wonderful evening together?

Ross drove the short distance home with reluctance. How easy it would have been to accept that invitation into the cottage and to see where it might lead them both. He was in great danger of losing his heart to Christy and the idea worried him, even scared him a little. Was he ready for another relationship? Was she? Once they went down that road, there was no turning back. Why spoil their friendship? Yet that music had well and truly stirred his senses and he'd tried to convey his feelings in their clasped hands. But he knew fine well that wasn't enough, for either of them.

His heart sank when he discovered his mother still downstairs. Just what he didn't need.

"Is that you, Ross?" The voice still carried even after her illness.

Resisting the urge to say 'who else would it be?' he entered the lounge.

"I didn't expect you to be waiting up. Do you feel all right, Mother?"

"Very well, thank you. Did you enjoy your evening out?"

No doubt she was hoping to find out how far his friendship with Christy had progressed.

"We had a wonderful time and I was able to introduce Christy to some friends, though the music was a bit loud to hear ourselves talk." He tried to lighten the atmosphere but no one was more tenacious than his mother.

"Do you think she'll decide to stay up here?"

Ross had no intention of discussing Christy and he didn't sit down. "I've no idea. You'll need to ask her when you see her. Now if I can't get you anything, I'm off to my room. The music's given me a headache. Goodnight, Mother." And he headed for the door.

"Ross…"

He turned and waited.

"I hope you'll be pleasant to Moira when you see at her the ball."

"Am I ever unpleasant? Sleep well."

He knew what his mother was up to but getting back with Moira was never going to be an option, even without his increasing attraction to Christy.

Chapter Twenty-Six

By the end of October, the pantomime was providing a distraction and a pleasure as the rehearsals progressed and Christy threw herself into whatever she was asked to do.

"You've been a blessing with all that artistic work," Eileen said more than once. "Aren't we the lucky ones to have you involved."

"Honestly, I'm glad to have such a fun project while I'm in between commissions."

She hadn't seen Ross since their night out and she was beginning to think he'd been avoiding her on purpose. The ball was still ages away and she was having second thoughts about attending, yet it seemed most of her new acquaintances in the village were going, even the minister and his wife.

"Are you going to the fireworks display next weekend?" Eileen asked.

"I hadn't thought about it but I'm glad to know it's still a tradition. Is it by the side of the local loch?" Christy asked.

"That's right. Most of the villagers turn out so hopefully the weather will hold up. Hope to see you there." Eileen waved as someone else claimed her attention.

As Christy neared home, she was aware of footsteps behind and turned. Ross. She waited until he caught up wondering how he'd explain his silence after the evening out.

"How are you, Christy? Sorry I've not been in touch, again."

"Fine, thanks." Like him, she didn't bother elaborating and they strolled on in silence until he spoke again.

"Hope you're intending going to the jamboree at the loch," he said.

"Funnily enough, Eileen just asked me the very same question. Yes, I'll come along for a while. I like that kind of event, especially in the cold."

At his puzzled glance, she laughed. "I mean I love getting all wrapped up and enjoying the cooler air. There's something cosy about this time of year."

"If you say so." He shrugged. "Give me a bright spring evening any time!"

When they reached the cottage, Christy hesitated. But she needn't have worried whether or not to ask him in as he immediately made his excuses.

"Is it okay if I call for you for the fireworks display? We could go together in one car."

"That would be good. See you then."

With a brief wave, he strode on towards his home as though they were nothing more than friends. Maybe that was all he wanted from her. But her emotional defences had been breached the other evening and she didn't want to build them again until she figured this man out and had decided he was worth waiting for.

The Saturday evening in early November turned out to be ideal conditions for a fireworks display: very cold with clear skies but seemingly no threat of rain or wind. When Christy and Ross arrived at the parking area near the loch, most of the villagers were already gathered. As they strolled across the grass, she caught sight of Cameron and Martin. They waved them over and both hugged her.

"Isn't this fabulous, Christy darling?" Martin said, as he linked arms with her.

Throwing an apologetic glance at Ross, Christy agreed. "I'm looking forward to the fireworks," she said.

Cameron was as charming as ever and she kept glancing over at Ross hoping he didn't feel left out. But he excused himself for a moment to speak to a few other people and she shrugged. Just because they'd arrived together didn't mean he had to look after her, she reminded herself.

She caught sight of Fiona and Ewan at one point and was surprised to see Nick Anderson arrive and seek the girl out. They hadn't noticed her yet and she remained beside Cameron and Martin while everyone greeted each other. She loved the sense of community and cheerful atmosphere. Men, women and children were warmly dressed with zipped-up jackets, hats and gloves. She knew her own face must be glowing by now as the sharp evening air nipped at any exposed skin. Exhilarating, that was the only word for it.

As the bonfire flared into the night sky, the dark and brooding hills were just visible beyond the flames, light dancing over the still loch. Up near the car park, someone had set up a table providing mini baked potatoes wrapped in tin foil and hot dogs from insulated bags.

"Fancy a bite to eat?" Cameron asked, "Before the fireworks display starts. It'll keep us warm."

"Okay, thanks. I'm impressed that they've bothered with all this food!"

Ross re-joined them and the four of them wandered over to the food table. Christy was amazed at such organisation and realised the annual event must have been perfected over the years. All the same, they needed willing hands to take charge of it all.

After their warming snack, Ross touched her arm. "I'll go and fetch us a drink."

"Thanks. I'll have a wander around for a while," Christy replied. It was so long since she'd been at a bonfire and fireworks display that she wanted to absorb every minute. The scent of sausages mingled with the peaty smell of the fire while the sound of the younger children's excitement reminded her of the happier days of her own childhood.

Cameron and Martin were chatting to a few people further away and Christy strolled over the grassy verge, enjoying the vista of the gleaming loch and firelight that competed with the stars. It was one of the pleasures of living in the countryside, being able to count the stars on a clear night. She smiled at the sight of all the families enjoying the evening and it warmed her heart to be part of it all. She paused near the bonfire to watch the flames licking the darkness above.

Next minute, she felt a hard push from behind.

Startled, she lost her balance and was clutching at air, the heat from the bonfire already reaching for her. She must have cried out as someone suddenly grabbed her arm and pulled her back.

Christy was aware of all the people gathered around her as it became obvious a nasty accident had been averted.

"Are you okay, Christy?" Fiona's anxious face was the first she saw. "I thought I wasn't going to catch you in time."

Christy looked at the girl in surprise. She'd

imagined a stronger arm than Fiona's had saved her. But Eileen and her husband were fussing over her and next minute, Ross had his arm around her.

"What on earth happened, Christy? You could have been badly burned." He pulled her close to him.

She buried her face against his chest before answering. "I don't know. One minute I was admiring the stars, the next I was falling towards the fire."

She glanced around in embarrassment but everyone was giving Ross the space to attend to her. "I'm pretty sure someone pushed me," she said in a low voice only he could hear.

He held her away from him and stared into her eyes.

"Are you sure? Who on earth could wish you that much harm? Not that I don't believe you," he quickly added as she was about to protest. "I only meant that it might have been some of the younger teenagers messing around and one of them could have accidently knocked into you."

"It's possible, I suppose. But why wouldn't they just apologise since I wasn't harmed?"

"You know kids – probably frightened they'd get into trouble. I don't want to think of it being anything else."

Christy didn't either and was soon hugged tightly by both Cameron and Martin when they realised what had happened. A few minutes later, she caught sight of Fiona talking to Ewan a little further away. The light from the bonfire illuminated them in the darkness and as far as she could see, they seemed to be arguing. Strange that Fiona appeared to be the one to save her, yet she hadn't stayed around to be thanked by Ross.

"Do you want to go straight home, Christy?" Ross

asked.

"No, absolutely not. I'm determined not to miss the fireworks." And she was not giving into her paranoid fears. Besides, she was enjoying the feel of Ross's arm around her and wanted to prolong their closeness. She refused to dwell on what might have happened but kept well away from the bonfire.

The remainder of the evening passed in a kaleidoscope of colourful fireworks lighting up the night sky and Christy was soon caught up in the general excitement. Surrounded by Ross, Cameron, Martin and Eileen, she felt safe and perhaps even loved.

When Ross dropped her at the cottage, he hesitated. "Shall I see you in and make sure all's well?" he asked.

She nodded, glad the decision had been made for her after his quick departure the last time. Thankfully, everything seemed as it should and she had to release Misty from the kitchen. It always felt even more like home with this man here beside her.

As usual, Misty entwined herself around Ross's legs and he laughed, bending down to stroke the soft fur. For a second, Christy wished he was touching *her* hair in such a tender way then she stopped her wayward thoughts.

"Drink?" she asked.

"Why not? I'd love a coffee please after all that cold air. Let me know if you want help."

Once settled side by side on the sofa, Christy was amused to see Misty make herself comfortable on the floor at Ross's feet.

"She's definitely fallen for you." She smiled at him.

"I don't often have that effect on females, of any

species," he said.

"I find that hard to believe." She was reluctant to say any more, but he grinned.

"I used to think Cam would be the one to charm all the ladies," he mused. "But I got that wrong. Thanks for introducing Martin into the community. It must have been tough for Cameron to hide his true feelings. Now I expect most people won't even notice or care, for all the time he spends here."

"They suit each other so I hope your mother welcomes him too. We all hope to find lasting love one day," Christy said.

"I don't think she has any option." He laughed but didn't take the chance to talk about their own love lives so she changed the subject.

"Did you find out anything more about your grandfather?"

Ross put down his mug. "I mentioned him to Mother but she conveniently changed the subject. I'll try again as she must know something about her father's past."

Christy nodded. "I was thinking about Gran of course and all the parts she underlined in the *Rubaiyat*. I reckon they must have loved each other but for whatever reason, they ended up married to someone else."

"Unless they fell in love after they were married," Ross said. "It happens sometimes and maybe they didn't want to upset their families."

When he didn't expand on his words, Christy decided the moment was right to share a little more of her own story.

"I thought I'd found the right person once, but even before Michael died, I knew we wouldn't have lasted." She kept the emotion from her voice but Ross took her hand. She kept her hand in his and let his warmth flow through her.

"That must have been tough, not getting the chance to talk things through with him, but sometimes it's difficult to tell if it's the right person until after marriage." He paused before continuing. "My father soon decided he'd made a mistake and ended up abandoning Cam and me along with Mother. No wonder she is slightly bitter, but it did make her a strong parent."

Christy squeezed his hand. "That must have been terrible for you two boys, not to mention your mother. At least I had loving parents, although they were taken away far too soon. And I always had Gran."

She waited to see if he would say anything about his ex but when he didn't mention her, she changed tack.

"Ross, may I ask you something?"

"Of course," he answered readily enough, though she noticed his eyes were wary.

"Why do you and Nick Anderson dislike each other so much?"

He hesitated at first and sat back against the sofa then he shrugged. "It's old history now but I discovered him doing some shady business when we shared a company – cut price, inferior fittings for large premises we were working on. That kind of thing."

"I can imagine that would anger anyone if your good name was dragged into it," Christy said. "Not to mention the risks attached to shoddy work."

He nodded. "It's not the only reason I don't have time for him." He kept his eyes on her. "You know about my ex, Moira. Well our break-up was as much to do with Anderson as anything else. He managed to turn her against me with his insidious lies then proceeded to wine and dine her himself."

There was no self-pity in his emotionless words but Christy understood the humiliation it must have caused this proud, reserved man. She suspected he didn't give his love lightly, much like herself.

"She couldn't have known you very well if she believed him."

Ross lifted their clasped hands and dropped a light kiss on hers. "Thanks for that vote of confidence. It wasn't all her fault – Anderson is far too persuasive and I didn't defend myself enough in her eyes."

Christy remained silent for a moment, wondering if Ross still carried lingering feelings for the girl.

"Anyway, I think that's enough about me, but perhaps it explains a little of my warning against Anderson, unwelcome though it was. No wonder you got mad at me." He grinned, dispelling the serious moment.

"Okay, I admit I didn't take kindly to being told what to do. It was bad enough when we were younger. Do you remember that time you warned me not to jump over the stile after Cameron and I wouldn't listen?"

He laughed. "How could I forget, especially when you fell flat on your face and just missed a cow pat. But I admired your determination even then, though you'd never have guessed."

Their shared memories of long-ago summers in Kilcraig warmed Christy even more and she didn't want the evening to end. But even as the thought entered her head, Ross stood up.

"I think it's time to go before I outstay my welcome, and Darwin will be waiting for his last short walk of the day. I'm glad you've no lasting effects from the incident at the bonfire. Hopefully, some of the young people have confessed to larking about too much by now."

Christy stood too but neither moved towards the door.

"Honestly, I'd forgotten all about that while we were chatting so thanks for keeping me company for a while."

"It's always a pleasure." As though he'd just realised how much he meant it, he stopped speaking. Then he dipped his head and kissed her very lightly on the lips. But instead of moving away, his arm tightened around her and she pressed closer to him. As his mouth explored hers, her passion rose to meet his and she wanted nothing more than to take it even further.

With a groan, he broke away. "Definitely time to go," he said as he tucked that stray strand of hair behind her ear again, except this time it didn't feel like such a brotherly gesture. "Much as I want to stay a bit longer, I don't want to risk our friendship."

Please don't go! She wanted to tell him, but his excuse had thrown her. She still wasn't sure exactly what was happening between them, although she could no longer deny that their *friendship* had deepened too much to go backwards.

When he turned towards the door she had to follow.

"Goodnight, Christy. Let me know if you have any more trouble of any kind and I'll be straight here."

"On your white charger, I hope," she answered with a smile.

"Well, probably with Darwin at least." He grinned and next minute he was gone taking all the warmth with him.

Closing the door, she snuggled up with Misty. "Just you and me again, little kitten, but I suspect we're both a little bit in love with Ross McKinley."

As Ross left the cottage, he couldn't get the image of Christy's smile out of his head, or the taste of her sweet mouth under his. How he had wanted to make that kiss even more lingering yet he daren't take that final step while they both had issues to resolve. Even though they could probably move on better together. Was she completely over Michael? Maybe she needed to recover those lost memories in order to stop feeling guilty about his death. He hoped he had reassured her about Moira, but had he actually said he was well over her?

There was no doubt he had fallen hard for Christy Morrison, if he could let himself trust again. He hoped that disturbing incident at the bonfire hadn't made her rethink her decision to stay in the village, although she was becoming a part of the community already. Surely no one had physically threatened her in such a way? He would be keeping a closer watch on those around them, although he still couldn't imagine anyone with a strong enough motive to actually want to hurt the girl.

Chapter Twenty-Seven

The rehearsals for the pantomime were in full swing over the following weeks and Christy threw herself into it with heartfelt pleasure at being so accepted by everyone. It also allowed her to stop dwelling on the phone calls and the worrying escalation of the threats with that push near the bonfire. At least Ross was aware of it and didn't think she was imagining it all, although he hadn't discovered who was behind the threats.

The children of all ages were a delight to work with and half the time was spent in laughter as each tried to learn their words and get used to performing on the make-shift stage in the village hall. Acting in Cinderella gave them plenty of scope for hilarity as a couple of the older boys took the parts of the ugly sisters.

But the real revelation was the morning she arrived to find Ross in conversation with Eileen.

"Ah, here she is," Eileen said, turning in Christy's direction. "I was just telling Ross how thankful we've been for your artistic help."

"Hi, this is a surprise. Eileen is exaggerating but I've been happy to get involved."

"I'm glad to hear it," he said. "The village pantomime is a highlight of the year."

They stood smiling at each other until Eileen coughed discreetly before taking up the conversation again.

"We're just going over the musical sections with Ross who's a whizz with different instruments, for which we're very grateful. One of the other lads has had to call off so Ross is filling in."

"Oh, that's good," Christy said. So that meant they would be spending time together at rehearsals now and then.

"I don't need to be here all the time," Ross said, as though reading her mind, "until nearer the performance, at least."

A noise from the stage area alerted Eileen to the possibility of too much high jinks from the young people and she excused herself.

"So you're enjoying helping here, Christy?" Ross smiled down at her.

"Very much. They're a great bunch of youngsters and I love painting any extra backdrops required. Just as well you're seeing me at the start of today as my overalls will be splashed with even more paint once I get started."

"And very cute you must look in them. I'll be around for a short while so I can get to know the sequence of it all. But no actual playing yet."

"That's a shame. I look forward to hearing your repertoire." She ignored the 'cute' reference and only hoped she didn't look a total fright once covered up with a scarf around her hair.

"I try my best but I'm not a professional musician, much as I love music. Do you play an instrument at all?" he asked.

"I had piano lessons many moons ago and probably wouldn't remember much but I do love listening to music and have quite an eclectic taste."

"Then we need to continue this topic another time so I can discover your favourites. But I'd better not keep you back or Eileen will be after us. I'll maybe see you later."

Ross touched her shoulder briefly before they headed off towards the others, Christy immediately disappearing behind the scenes to don her overalls. She could still feel the warmth from his hand and smiled like a teenage girl with a crush. But it was much more than that.

She was so engrossed in painting a forest scene that Christy was unaware of how much time had passed until Eileen called a halt to rehearsals.

"Thanks for your great work this morning everyone, it's going well. Don't forget to keep learning your lines!"

Christy smiled in sympathy – it was one of the reasons she was happy to be stay behind the scenes. She took the paint brushes to the sink and stretched to release the tension.

"Maybe you need those shoulders massaged." She whirled round to find Ross watching her. "Sorry, I didn't mean to startle you," he said.

"I was surprised you were still here." Had he waited for her?

"Thought I'd take the afternoon off and wondered if you'd like to come with me. I think you'll like the venue."

"Intriguing. Let me think if I can take time off… yes, of course I'd love to go with you." She laughed, enjoying the light-hearted moment.

"Excellent. I have a few things to catch up on first but I'll pick you up about one thirty if that's okay with you."

"Perfect. Looking forward to it."

He was about to leave when she remembered he hadn't told her where. "Ross – where are we going?"

He turned back. "Have you been to Kelvingrove Art Gallery and Museum in Glasgow?"

She smiled in pleasure. "Far too long ago. I'd love to visit it again!"

"I guessed you might. See you after lunch."

Her spirits rose even more at the thought of visiting the famous art gallery, especially with Ross. When Eileen and the others waved goodbye after rehearsals, Christy felt again the warmth of belonging and she hoped that whoever threatened her peace had realised she wouldn't be leaving the cottage or village anytime soon.

Chapter Twenty-Eight

Christy's memories of the huge art gallery were so vague that it was like visiting an Aladdin's cave of creativity and inspiration. From the moment they entered the impressive Gothic looking red sandstone building she felt at home.

Although a massive size, the space and height of the ceiling created an airy ambience that made it a pleasure to explore.

"Wow, that's some organ," she said, as she took in the immediate main area inside the entrance and noticed the huge instrument on one wall.

"It's massive, isn't it? I believe they sometimes have free lunch time concerts," Ross said.

"I'd love to hear one." Christy smiled at Ross, hoping they both might return together to hear the organ one day.

The ground floor was largely taken up with museum items, including a good variety of stuffed animals and birds and a life-like dinosaur. She smiled at the antics of one very small girl who hid behind her dad and peeked out every now and then to make sure the dinosaur hadn't moved. She then caught sight of the spitfire hanging from the ceiling in perpetual flight and suspected there would be more delights as they wandered around. She stopped at an enormous elephant.

"That's Sir Roger. Magnificent, isn't he," Ross said

"Wonderful. I imagine he'll be popular with children." Christy didn't know what to look at first as they wandered around.

"What kind of paintings do you like?" Ross asked as they reached the wide wooden staircase.

"More or less anything." Christy laughed. "If pushed, I'd confess to a special fondness for the Impressionists. I prefer that type of subtle light and shade to more garish colours. What about you?"

They were walking up the first flight of steps as they chatted and Ross paused at the top.

"I don't really have any favourites as such, but I like something different when I discover it. Come and see the famous Dali painting."

Intrigued, Christy followed him along to the end of the corridor. She couldn't miss it. Stretching almost the full length of the upper wall, Dali's huge painting of Christ of St John of the Cross looked down on all who passed by.

"That's simply stunning." Christy stared in awe at the surrealistic image of the elevated Christ on the cross surveying the world below.

"I never tire of looking at it," Ross said. "But there's a lot more to see. Have a look over the banister first."

Christy saw them at once. Huge white heads suspended from the ceiling right across one section of the gallery.

"Now that's amazing and weird!" she said. "I need to get a photo of those." Until she bought a better camera, her mobile would have to do.

"There's something else I'd like you to see, then you can choose where to go next," Ross suggested.

"Lead on. I don't think one day will be enough so we'll need to come back." It was only as she smiled up at Ross that she realised her assumption – that they would return together.

For answer, he took her hand as they wandered along the corridor. "It's a promise."

Christy was happy to be led along another corridor until they reached a doorway into one of the painting galleries. But instead of stopping, Ross continued through to a small alcove.

"Have a seat on the bench here and you'll hear a remarkable story about the Lafaruk Madonna."

"The what?" In answer, Ross smiled and sat beside her

From her seat, Christy could view what appeared to be an incomplete triptych of paintings in pride of place on the facing wall. The central painting depicted the Madonna gazing adoringly at the baby Jesus, an olive sprig in her hand, while an angel watched from the paintings on either side. Information was placed around the room but the voice-over claimed her complete attention when it began.

When it had finished, she was overwhelmed by the wartime story that had taken place in present day Somalia. How an artistic Italian prisoner of war, Giuseppe Baldan, had painted this actual triptych on the only available surface, discarded old flour sacks, so that it might be a focus for the prisoners in the little chapel where they worshipped. Even more remarkable was the unfolding tale of courtesy and subsequent friendship between the Italians and their kind British captors.

"What an amazing person this Captain Hawksworth must have been to appreciate how important the Italians' faith was to them," Christy said.

"And even more so that he rescued the damaged paintings from the Somali soldiers and kept them safe for the Italians. No wonder they became friends after the war."

"Thanks for showing me this, Ross. It's really special, isn't it?" Christy smiled at the man beside her, thankful that he seemed to appreciate the creative arts as much as she did.

He laced his fingers with hers. "I'm glad you enjoyed seeing and hearing it. It's a wonderful memorial to mutual respect at such a dreadful time. So, what about something lighter now. The Impressionists next?"

She nodded and kept her hand in his as they wandered past the more traditional art, stopping at any that caught Christy's attention. She took her time examining each of the French Impressionist paintings.

"Here's one of my favourites." She stopped to admire *The Sisters* by Mary Cassatt.

"Let me guess. Is it partly because it's one of the few by a woman?" Ross teased.

"Well that's certainly a plus, but I love this picture of sisterly love and innocence." She'd often wished she had a sister of her own, or even a brother, especially after her parents died. She would have felt even more alone without her dear Gran.

"Did you know they sell postcards of some of the paintings in the shop downstairs? Perhaps they'll have one of this."

She nodded as they wandered on through some of the Egyptian displays and an interesting one about Scotland through the various years.

"That was brilliant. Thanks so much for suggesting it," she said when they'd finally had enough for one day.

"It's a pleasure to see it all again through your eyes." Ross squeezed her hand.

As they were heading past the information desk towards the exit, Christy paused beside a poster.

"Look, they're advertising creative classes. Maybe that's something I could get involved in."

"Why don't you take a leaflet and maybe think about booking a place on one to see what it's like."

"Good idea" She could then investigate options for classes of her own.

"How about a walk before going back? Kelvingrove Park is just across the road."

"Why not?" She didn't want the day to end so was happy to prolong it with a walk.

It was a mild day for November, though it wouldn't be light for much longer. As they strolled hand in hand along the leaf-strewn paths, Ross suddenly stopped and turned to face her.

"Thanks for making today so enjoyable, Christy. I could get used to these outings with you. You've made a difference to my life already."

As he looked into her eyes, she had a sudden image of a future with this man by her side. But was it too soon to be thinking so far ahead?

"Me too," she finally replied. "You're introducing me to places I had long forgotten or never seen before, and there's no one I'd rather be with."

Under the tree dressed with the most leaves, Ross reached out and cupped her face. Then he lowered his head and his lips were warm on hers. He drew her closer as the kiss deepened and they were alone in their own private world.

When they eventually took breath, Ross tenderly held her against him as he smoothed her hair. "I seem to have fallen for you, Christy Morrison."

The words were those most women wanted to hear from the man she loved. And there was no use denying how she felt about him. But there was a hesitant note in his voice. Was either of them ready for any kind of promise or commitment? Perhaps it was better to give them both breathing space.

"I'm not sure what's happening between us, Ross, but I think I'm falling in love with you."

He held her at arm's length so he could look into her eyes. She kept her gaze on his and finally he kissed her again before letting her go.

"Then we'll see where it takes us," he said. "Be patient with me, Christy. I've only ever given my heart once before and that didn't work out well."

Now that he'd drawn back, she contrarily wished she was still in his arms.

"I know that, Ross, and I need to remember exactly what happened the night of my accident with Michael. Maybe we both need to lay our ghosts to rest before moving on. But there's no one I'd rather wait for."

He reached over and tenderly kissed her brow. "Me neither. Shall we go back to the car? Our parking time is almost up and it's getting a bit chilly now," Ross suggested.

She nodded, content to wander back through the park hand in hand, prolonging this perfect November afternoon for as long as possible.

There was a new understanding between them as Ross drove them back to Kilcraig and she remembered that first car journey when he'd picked her up at the station. Although they didn't chat much on this occasion either, their frequent glances at each other made her smile and she looked forward to their next outing. When they arrived at the cottage, he immediately turned to her.

"I'd better check on Darwin and see what's been happening at the house."

"Of course. You've given up enough of your time today."

He leaned across and kissed her lightly. "I enjoyed it very much, Christy."

She opened the door to save him getting out of the car and waved as he drew away. Where exactly was their relationship headed, such as it was? Yet she knew with certainty that she couldn't imagine her life without Ross McKinley by her side.

She had no sooner greeted Misty and made sure everything was secure when the phone rang. Her first thought was it might be Ross. But she almost dropped the receiver when the whispering voice began at once.

"Forget McKinley. You have only a few weeks left to go back to London."

Before she could respond, the line went dead. Hands shaking, she lifted Misty up beside her. Since she changed her number, the only people she had entrusted it to were Ross and Cameron. The idea that this was either of them was equally ridiculous. So who else had access to it?

Chapter Twenty-Nine

After a fitful sleep, Christy woke up with a headache and an even sorer heart. Since the incident at the bonfire, she had really hoped the person threatening her had given up. But was it an empty threat, just to scare her away? Or was she in real danger?

One person immediately came to mind, in light of the phone call to her new number: Fiona. It was time to go back to the antique shop and find out about the book in the glass-fronted case and hopefully chat to Fiona herself.

Since it wasn't a weekend this time, the food market stalls were gone, allowing Christy to appreciate the long view of Loch Lomond with its mist-covered distant hills and mountains. The antique shop was also quiet and she could understand the concern about the future of the business. Apart from during busy tourist periods, there wouldn't be much passing traffic on weekdays.

At first, she thought the shop was completely empty again and she was heading towards the cabinet when she heard her name called.

"Christy, darling! How lovely to see you."

Martin was walking towards her with outstretched arms, exuberant as always.

"Hi, Martin. How are you?"

Once the greetings were over, Christy told him the reason for her visit. "Last time I was here, I noticed a couple of interesting books in the glass-fronted cabinet. Could I have a proper look, please? Fiona didn't have the key that day."

"Of course – come and show me. Can't understand why Fi wouldn't have found the key in its usual place."

Christy didn't respond to that but it only increased her suspicion that Fiona had something to do with the missing *Rubaiyat*.

"This one, please." She showed Martin the cabinet.

Even before he opened it, she knew the distinctive red and gold book had gone. Maybe she had given Fiona a fright that day when she'd discovered these books.

"I'd like to see the book of Donne's poems, if I may." At least she could have a good look now in case the other book had slipped behind.

"Take your time, my darling. I've a phone call to make and no one else is about yet. See if there's anything else that takes your fancy."

"Perfect, thanks."

Once she had examined the Donne, which she did indeed want to buy, she had a browse through the other books. A few more caught her eye but she needed to check her finances before getting carried away. Carefully moving books aside and glancing behind each, it was soon evident that the other one had indeed gone. But was it sold or had Fiona removed it from that cabinet?

She had closed the door and held the Donne in her hand when Martin returned.

"Find anything?" he asked.

"This book of Donne poems – just what I wanted, thanks. Oh, and there's a Keats volume on another shelf. I might come back for something else another day."

"Any time, my lovely."

"Do you sell many from that cabinet?" She might as well ask.

"Now and then, but business is slow at the moment. Fiona usually looks after the books so she could answer that. I know the accounts, of course, but can't recall individual items without looking. Terrible memory."

"And Cameron? Does he have a specific job here? Sorry, I'm just being nosy about such an interesting business."

Thankfully, Martin seemed to have no suspicious bone in him.

"Ask what you like, darling. It's great to find someone so interested! Cameron helps out with the financial side as well as house clearances. And he adds the muscle, of course." Martin grinned.

So he would be looking out for anything that could be sold on. Unbidden, Christy remembered Cameron's interest in the cottage when she'd hardly arrived. But she wouldn't believe he had any ulterior motive. Not her dear childhood friend.

"Well, I'd better move on. Thanks again, Martin. I love this place."

"And it gladdens my heart to hear you say so. *Au revoir*, Christy darling. Come back any time."

Although delighted with the book of Keats and Donne poems, Christy was still puzzled about the missing *Rubaiyat*. Yet how could she come right out and accuse Fiona of taking it? It wasn't possible.

Throwing herself into the excitement and chaos around the pantomime rehearsals over the next couple of weeks, Christy put her misgivings aside. She was also looking forward to the ball. She still had no idea when, or if, she and Ross would ever progress their relationship to the next stage but her heart lifted whenever he managed along to give a hand with the pantomime music.

"I hope you're all set for the ball, Cinderella," he quipped one day.

"You've reminded me that I need a dress," she said, "or I'll be going nowhere." It was already the end of November and she hadn't been to the shops again.

She wanted to ask if he intended being her Prince Charming but the memory of his ex-girlfriend being invited prevented her from being so obvious.

"You'll look beautiful in whatever you wear," he said.

She was about to treat that as a gallant, flippant remark but the smile in his eyes meant for her alone made her serious.

"Much as I appreciate the compliment, I'm all too aware I don't have anything remotely suitable for so grand an affair and women notice such things, even if men don't! I definitely need a trip to the city."

"Want some company?" Ross asked.

"Not on this occasion, thanks. You'd be bored within ten minutes!" Besides, she wanted to find a dress to impress him with on the night and that required serious browsing.

"What about Fiona? You could have a girly day out together."

She could hardly admit her suspicions about Fiona and she certainly didn't think either of them would be happy to spend a day in each other's company.

"I don't think we have that kind of friendship. Honestly, this is the kind of shopping trip I'll enjoy by myself."

He nodded. "Have a look at George Square when you're there. It should be decked out for Christmas by the time you go and I'd love to take you to the outdoor skating rink one day."

"Now that I would love to try. I'll likely go in on Thursday as it's usually late opening that day. I'll park at the nearest station to here and get the train into Glasgow."

"A wise decision. I look forward to seeing the result of your shopping!"

On the Thursday morning, Christy rose with the wintry sun and dressed for a shopping day in the city. Maybe she'd been in the village too long after London, but she was filled with a definite sense of anticipation. No doubt it helped that she had someone to impress with a new dress. A sprinkling of frost already covered the roads and she was glad to be going by train most of the way.

When she arrived in Glasgow there was a definite Christmassy buzz in the air already, enhanced by the open-air ice rink on George Square that Ross had mentioned. Definitely worth a visit together. She remembered that the local loch beside Kilcraig often froze enough for skating for those brave enough to try. That might be fun if she persuaded Cameron and Martin to join them. She admired the wintery scene, with the big wheel and children's rides tempting passing families. When the lights came on later in the day, it would add to the magic.

But she was here with a purpose and after a quick coffee at the famous Willow Tearooms on Buchanan Street, she headed towards the main fashion stores. Although hoping to find a special enough dress for the ball, she didn't have unlimited funds so quickly discarded the possibility of expensive designer gowns in a couple of the big stores. Fortunately, she was a fairly standard size and only had to worry about the length and fit being comfortable enough.

She was about to enter a smaller dress shop when she paused. Walking along the street towards her was Fiona, and Nick Anderson was beside her. Should she pretend she hadn't seen them? The thought had no sooner formed when Nick glanced up and saw her.

"Well hello, Christy. Good to see you again," he said, offering his hand. "What brings you to the big city?"

Glad he hadn't tried to kiss her cheek, she returned his handshake and smiled at Fiona who nodded.

"I fancied a train ride to enjoy a good browse around the shops in Glasgow again." It was none of his business why she was there, although she wondered what *they* were doing here together.

"I might see you on the train then if we happen to go back at the same time," Fiona said.

"Yes, maybe." Christy had no idea when she would be returning and assumed Fiona was trying to be friendly.

"Well, have a good day." Nick obviously wasn't going to linger. As they moved away, Fiona threw Christy a strange half smile.

As she wandered around the next shop without really concentrating on the dresses, Christy realised she hadn't seen Fiona since the bonfire incident. What a puzzle the girl seemed to be. She shrugged her out of her mind and brought her attention back to the task in hand.

Half an hour later, Christy stood admiring a full-length gown in her favourite shade of olive green. On the mannequin at least, it draped in all the right places and the tiny cap sleeves stopped it being too bare, while the sweetheart neckline gave it an almost fifties feel.

"Would you like to try it on?" the girl asked.

"Yes, please." Christy couldn't resist it, even though it would be the second dress she'd bought since arriving in Scotland.

She knew it was going to be perfect before she stepped out of the dressing room to examine herself in the mirror.

"You really suit that colour," the girl said. "And it's not just sales talk. It could have been made for you."

Christy twirled and turned, loving the silky material against her legs. A dress made for dancing.

"Thanks. It feels wonderful but I need reassurance it fits okay."

"Perfectly. You suit that sort of vintage look. Even your eyes look greener."

Christy was sold on it, especially since she already had shoes and a bag that would go well enough with it.

"I'll take it, please." Blow the price tag. She might never find such a perfect gown again and this particular ball was likely to be the most important event of this or any other year.

The rest of the day rushed past as she browsed at the makeup counters in the department stores in search of subtle shades to tone with her dress. Noticing a hairdresser in one, and finding it quiet, she had half an inch off all over so that the natural wave stopped just above her shoulders.

She couldn't remember enjoying a shopping trip

so much for ages. To add to her pleasure, the rows of tiny white Christmas lights strung between two of the narrower streets at Royal Exchange Square were now lit up. In the late afternoon dusk, they sparkled like stars above the passers-by.

Returning to the station with a smile on her face, she relaxed into her train seat with a glossy magazine. Sheer indulgence. No matter what happened with Ross, her confidence had soared with the new dress and haircut. She was also ready to meet his ex-girlfriend if necessary and hopefully be reassured that he was well over her.

What a perfectly happy day. The joy of the approaching Christmas celebrations with the pantomime and ball made her glad to be alive. As her thoughts strayed to Gran and Michael, she concentrated instead on the magazine. No sadness for today at least.

When the train reached her destination, she hurried to retrieve the car. It was already fairly dark and she was glad to be on her way home to the cottage at last. She wrapped her warm scarf around her, shivering in the frosty December air. She had a feeling snow was on its way. The car had even started to freeze over, though thankfully not enough to stop her opening the doors. But she'd need to drive even more carefully on the country roads to Kilcraig.

Stowing her bags in the boot, she strapped herself into the driver's seat. It had been a long day and right now she longed for a light meal, a warm bath and reading by the fireside before bed. She also couldn't wait to try on her new dress again with the proper shoes and undies but that would keep until tomorrow.

She glanced at her hair in the mirror before pulling out onto the road home, pleased she had been so impulsive. There was time to get used to styling it before the evening of the ball and she was looking forward to the event even more now.

Christy was so lost in happy musing about dancing with Ross, while watching the country road ahead, that it was a while before she noticed the car in her rear-view mirror.

At first, she only supposed the driver was getting a bit close considering the road was fairly quiet. But as she maintained her speed, she was suddenly alarmed when the car following her began to edge even nearer. What on earth?

Remembering Michael's usual reaction to such tailgating, she pressed the break enough to warn the driver to pull back. It had no effect. In fact, the car seemed to be getting ever closer.

Heart beating faster, Christy was too aware of the empty country road and the increasing darkness, not to mention the frosty surface. Surely this was a deliberate attempt to scare her? Trying not to panic out of control, she increased her speed as much as she dared, hoping to shake the unwelcome tail. All the threats of the past few weeks crowded her mind to convince her that whoever was in the car was playing a dangerous game.

Pressing her foot harder on the accelerator, she swerved round the next bend. The wrong type of roads for speed but she was desperate to get away, driving on sheer adrenaline. Every time she increased the gap, the car behind caught her up again. She couldn't even see the make of car never mind any hope of identifying the driver.

Now she was really worried. Was the driver trying to cause an accident or only aiming to scare her? Either way, she had trouble controlling the car at this speed on such narrow winding roads. She was in real danger of skidding if any puddles of water had iced up.

When a car suddenly appeared going the other way, she eased her foot off the pedal a little until it was well past. But a terrified glance in the rear mirror showed her the threatening driver gaining on her again.

The realisation had hardly formed when the car came right up behind her leaving Christy little choice but to speed towards another oncoming bend. It was too fast. She struggled to hold the wheel straight but the car took on a life of its own. Next minute she was hurtling out of control towards the ditch at the side of the road. She was only vaguely aware of a car revving past as her own nosedived off the road and her seat belt jarred against her shoulder.

Then everything stopped and Christy slumped over the wheel.

Chapter Thirty

At first, Christy became aware of the silence as she tried to process what had happened. Then she gradually noticed the gnawing pain in her left shoulder and arm.

Michael! She moved her head carefully to glance at the driver's side. No, that wasn't right. She was in the driving seat. As realisation gradually returned, Christy rubbed her forehead. It wasn't that other accident. She hadn't been driving then; Michael had. He had crashed the car that killed him.

Head throbbing, she winced as the memories flooded back. She had tried to talk him into slowing down but he had ignored her pleas, angry from their last silly argument. Yes… she could picture them that evening, though the emotion of it had dulled. They had quarrelled before leaving for the party and she had made up her mind to end their relationship at the first opportunity after that night. She was tired of his need to control her which was getting worse. She hadn't even wanted to go to his friend's party but he'd insisted and she finally gave in as usual. It had been a dark evening then too and he'd been driving too fast.

The memories continued to crowd in… hitting the lamppost, panic and confusion… discovering Michael unconscious beside her. She covered her eyes and wept for the waste of a good life and the guilty burden she had carried around too long. There was nothing she could have done to prevent it in the end.

Christy rubbed her eyes, full realisation of her present situation suddenly hitting her. A car had driven her off the road deliberately. Who would carry out such a dangerous, idiotic action? Was the person waiting for her? Undoing her seat belt, she struggled to open the door. She needed to get out, find her mobile, call for help. But what if she was still in danger?

She couldn't just sit here, hoping to be rescued, or worrying about being attacked. Hadn't she heard a car driving right past after the crash? Opening the door, she climbed slowly out, making sure she wasn't stepping onto the road. Her light shoes weren't equipped for the thickening frost but at least the heels were low.

Her head still ached and the left shoulder and arm throbbed but at least she could stand. The country road was eerily silent, the dark sky heavy with the threat of snow. Where was the traffic when you needed it?

Glancing each way, she tried to breathe evenly. Her pursuer seemed to have gone. But the front of the car was well and truly stuck in the narrow ditch. Beyond it, a thick wood seemed more threatening than usual and Christy had never felt so alone. The only sound was a far-off hoot of an owl. But she couldn't lose it now. Surely someone would be passing soon.

Her phone! She could ring Ross and he might be able to get the car out of the ditch, otherwise she'd need a rescue service but hadn't got around to joining one yet.

Grabbing the mobile from her bag, she pressed his number. Nothing happened. Drat! No signal in this part with the woods on one side and stretches of hilly countryside on the other.

Now that she'd been standing for a few minutes, the dizziness began to recede though the aches had intensified and she longed for a couple of pain killers. She waited a little longer, scanning up and down the road. Still no car in sight. Only one thing for it – she'd have to start walking and hope some kind person pulled up soon.

Taking her bag and locking the car, she wound the scarf half round her head to keep the chill away. She started on the weary walk home, trying not to stumble or slip. Every nerve end was alert to any sign of danger and she listened for the first sound of a car engine. Maybe the driver would come back looking for her, maybe finish her off.

No, that was unlikely now that he'd gone. But she still didn't like how vulnerable she could be on this dark, lonely road. A little further on, she stopped. The sound of a car engine.

Standing as far back onto the verge as possible, she peered into the darkness. Impossible to tell if it was friend or foe but she could do with a lift, if she was visible enough in the dark. Maybe she should have stayed with her car and turned the lights on if they still worked.

She heard the car slowing down some distance away. Maybe the driver had caught sight of her abandoned car. Sure enough, it was a few minutes before the engine started up again as though the driver had checked for occupants. Now it drew nearer and she waited to see whether or not to step out.

The outline of the driver gradually became visible but Christy was suddenly caught in the headlight, unable to see who was behind the wheel. Too late to change her mind now.

The car stopped and Ross rushed to her side.

"Christy – thank heavens you're okay. What on earth happened?"

"I... I think someone ran me off the road and the car's stuck in the ditch. I couldn't get it out so I thought I'd better start walking..." her words caught in a sob as Ross pulled her into his arms.

"You're freezing. Get in my car and warm up. Here, take my jacket. I'll drive you home then Cameron and I can go back and check your car for damage."

Wishing he'd kept his arms around her to provide much needed heat, Christy slipped into the passenger seat, hugging his jacket around her, inhaling its reassuring scent.

"My shopping – it's in the back of my car." Even in the midst of the drama, she couldn't forget her new dress and it stopped her thinking what might have happened if the driver had come back.

"Don't worry, we'll rescue the contents even if we can't move the car ourselves. All you need to worry about for now is getting a hot drink and recovering from the shock."

He didn't speak again until they were almost at the cottage but she knew she would have to confront what had happened and why. All she could think about was a hot bath and a lie down.

When he stopped the car, Ross touched her cheek. "Will you be okay on your own for a while or would you prefer to go to the house?"

"I'd rather stay here, thanks. I'll be fine now I'm home and Misty will keep me company. Take back your jacket so *you* don't freeze out there. Thanks for its comfort."

He nodded. "I'll come back and check on you once we've had a look at the car. Fortunately, Cameron's up at the house and can go with me. Lock your doors and don't let anyone in but me."

Christy nodded, trying not to show her alarm, but of course he was right. Someone had endangered her life this evening and hadn't bothered to check if she was hurt, not to mention leaving her on a dark and lonely road by herself in the freezing cold.

As soon as Ross had gone, Christy lifted Misty into her arms for the reassuring contact as much as warmth. "I'm so glad you're here, little kitten," she said. Misty purred with pleasure and stayed close to Christy when she was set down again.

Once she had put the kettle on, she wearily dragged herself upstairs to run the bath, liberally adding her favourite scented oil. By the time she'd fetched a cup of strong tea upstairs and peeled off her clothes, the bath was full enough.

She sank back into the hot water immersing her body in the blessed cocoon. Pity she couldn't submerge her thoughts as easily. Who on earth had wanted to scare her so badly? She couldn't get the image of Fiona and Nick out of her head. Both of them knew she was heading home by train but she hadn't seen either of them again after that one meeting in town. It was easy to imagine Nick as the villain but surely Fiona didn't dislike her that much?

And in the midst of this new drama, the memories of her last evening with Michael refused to leave her in peace. At least now she knew what had happened and a little of her crushing guilt began to ebb away. She would always regret his death and the sad disintegration of their relationship, but she would try to remember instead the happier, early days of their first love when the future was before them.

When the water became too cool, she reluctantly climbed out and wrapped herself in a large towel. There was a dull ache in her neck, shoulder and arm, probably from the car's sudden halt but she was otherwise unhurt apart from budding blisters on her feet from the unexpected walk along the country road. Nothing that wouldn't heal, although she was annoyed it had made her arm throb again after all those weeks of improvement.

Once she had put on her pyjamas and dressing gown, she went back downstairs and opened an emergency tin of soup, pushed a slice of bread in the toaster and made sure the kitten had enough to eat. Half an hour later, she had started to relax, curled up on the sofa with Misty in her lap and a new novel to begin. But she couldn't concentrate on reading while the thoughts kept swirling. She felt safe enough in the cottage, but would never be safe in the village again until she knew who was behind this latest incident. Besides, she was alert for Ross coming back, hoping he had managed to rescue her car.

She had dozed off when the knock came at the door so it took her a few minutes to remember what had happened. About to open it, she paused. "Who's there?" she called, feeling slightly foolish but not taking any chances.

"Christy, it's me, Ross."

He was alone and she held open the door in invitation. Then she noticed the car back in its usual parking space.

"You've rescued it!"

He held up the bags she hadn't noticed him carrying. "Thought you might like these."

"Brilliant, thank you." Once he'd stepped inside,

she closed the door. "Cameron not with you?"

"He had to get back to whatever brought him to the house, but he added his much-needed strength to our rescue mission. I don't think the car has any lasting damage. What about you, Christy?"

Christy motioned for him to sit down. "I really am okay, thanks to you. A little pain from shoulder to wrist on one side but nothing that won't heal again."

He looked at her closely before speaking. "And I'm assuming it's the same arm that gave you problems before?"

She nodded. "You know, my memories all came rushing back when it happened, Ross, so I suppose I can be grateful for that."

"Do you want to talk about it?" he asked, beside her on the sofa.

"Not just now, but I feel a lot better knowing it wasn't all my fault that Michael died. Maybe I can move on at last." She glanced at the man beside her, wondering if he understood her unspoken message.

"That's good." But he looked away for a moment. "I couldn't believe that someone had tried to hurt you, Christy."

She heard the contained emotion in his voice but his words reminded her of something that had puzzled her.

"Ross – how did you know that I needed help?"

"I didn't. It was sheer luck that I was coming along that stretch at the right time. I'd been to see a potential client about helping him redesign his house."

"Lucky for me!" Yet something in his manner didn't add up. It was as though he was holding back, trying to think it through.

He looked into her eyes. "I'm just glad it didn't

turn out any worse. But I promise I'll find out who's behind this, Christy."

She couldn't doubt his sincerity or the anger darkening his eyes, and she touched his hand. "Thanks for being here, Ross."

He lifted a hand and touched her hair. "You've had it cut. I like it."

Unable to shift her gaze from his, she smiled. "I'd forgotten about that!"

They stared at each other for a moment longer then he leaned towards her and gently touched his lips to hers. Christy had no sooner relaxed into him when he drew her gently against him in a tender embrace.

"Christy…" he murmured against her lips before claiming them in a deep, lingering kiss.

She returned his kiss, passion stirring deep within, scaring her with its intensity. Even with Michael, she had never wanted to lose herself in love-making as much as she did now.

Pausing for breath, Ross stroked her hair before pushing it aside and leaving a gentle trail of kisses down her neck. She strained into him, willing his hands to explore further, glad the pyjama top had a low V-neck. Yet, even in the midst of need, she must have been aware of the ache in her arm and given some indication of it, as next minute Ross pulled back.

"Damn. I'm so sorry, Christy. I completely forgot about your arm and shoulder for a moment. You must be in pain."

Sitting up, suddenly embarrassed at her lack of inhibition, she tried to smile. "Don't worry, I forgot about it too. But you're right, it's beginning to make itself known. I should have taken a painkiller when I got home." Then who knew what might have happened.

"Come here." Ross held out his arms and cuddled her close. "That was unfair of me to take advantage after what you've been through, but I can't bear to think what might have happened. Forgive me, Christy."

Content in his arms, even so chastely, she glanced into his eyes. "You're being too tough on yourself. It was hardly one-sided."

He kissed her cheek. "I think before I get carried away again, you should get tucked up in bed for the night."

"Sounds like a good idea," she teased.

"And get a good sleep, after you've taken a painkiller," he added, kissing her again. "Now I'm going to leave before I change my mind. Sleep tight and we'll talk tomorrow."

Getting shakily to her feet, she stood in his arms reluctant to let him go until he moved away.

"Goodnight, Christy. Sleep well, my love."

Then he was gone and the room was suddenly so much bigger and colder, only those two added words alleviating the sudden emptiness.

Ross went straight home and without speaking to his mother or Cameron, he took Darwin out for a walk in the cool night air, avoiding going anywhere near the cottage.

He had not told Christy everything, which wasn't much yet, but he had badly wanted to stay the night with her and not just to keep her safe. She had well and truly cut through all the defences he had put in place after the betrayal by his ex and his business partner. But what part had Fiona played in the scare tactics against Christy?

He *had* been out on a visit, as he'd said, but had cut his appointment short when he received a worrying phone call from Cameron. He had trouble believing it when his brother told him to look out for Christy on her way back from the station. That he'd had a garbled text from Fiona about an accident but Cameron couldn't get hold of her when he had tried to call her back. And his brother still hadn't been any the wiser when he'd gone with Ross to rescue Christy's car.

By the time he had walked Darwin to the edge of countryside and back, both were tired and cold. He could even see his breath in front of him. Glancing at the eerily grey sky, he had a feeling they were in for snow. Tomorrow, he would find out exactly what had been going on before he went anywhere near the cottage. It was way beyond a joke since the bonfire incident. Being run off the road and left in the freezing night air could have endangered Christy even more and she might have been seriously hurt. Or she might decide she'd had enough of the village and he couldn't bear the thought of her going out of his life again.

When he let himself back into the house, all was quiet. Not the time for confrontation. He'd start with Cameron in the morning since he was staying there overnight and then they were going to talk to Fiona. Only when he had some answers would he go and see Christy.

Chapter Thirty-One

Surprised to find she had slept better than expected, Christy washed the sleep away and examined her arm and shoulder. Not too bad. If she was careful for the next couple of days, she should be fine for the ball. At that thought, she found the shopping bags where she had abandoned them the night before and after shaking the dress out, she chose a hanger for it. What an end to such a happy day in town. Yet it was Ross who had filled her dreams and banished any lingering nightmares about being run off the road.

When she opened the curtains, she wasn't surprised to see the first sprinkling of snow falling. The sky was white, promising more on top of the frost from the night before. While she ate a light breakfast, she tried to puzzle everything out and kept coming back to Fiona and Nick. But why? Anderson's client wanted the cottage and land to expand the house and estate but why would Fiona help him? Or was she working with Cameron to scare her away? No, that idea was even more ludicrous when she thought of her charming friend. He'd never agree to anything like that.

She was in danger of giving herself a headache by the time the morning was half over. She needed a walk before the snow increased yet didn't want to risk missing Ross. He'd promised they would talk and she wanted to hear what kind of future, if any, they might have together.

When the knock eventually came at the door, Christy hurried to open it, a smile on her face, forgetting to ask who was there. But it wasn't Ross. It was Fiona.

"Can I come in? I…need to talk to you," she said, hands nervously twisting together. Glancing behind her as though afraid of being followed.

Christy hesitated, but the girl was obviously distressed. Opening the door wider, she nodded. "I think it's time we talked."

But once inside, Fiona couldn't settle, looking about her, not meeting Christy's eyes.

"Do you want to sit down?" Christy offered.

"Okay… no! I can't. I don't know what to do. Didn't know he would take it so far. Thought you were hurt." She paced up and down, still wringing her hands.

Alarmed now by the girl's disjointed sentences and what she seemed to be implying, Christy tried to calm her down.

"Come and sit down, Fiona. Remember we used to be friends. Tell me what you mean. Who took what too far?"

At first, she thought she had succeeded when Fiona stopped pacing and stared straight at her. But the girl's eyes narrowed before she spat the words out.

"We've never been friends! It's all your fault for coming back here… he was mine!"

Even more alarmed and frightened at Fiona's increasing vehemence, Christy was conscious of being on her own with a girl who seemed too close to the edge. But she needed to remain calm.

"It's okay, Fiona. Please tell me what you mean so I can help you. Who are you talking about?"

Fiona glared at her. "Ross, of course. He's always been mine and you've come between us. I had to make you go away."

Christy tried to make sense of her words. "You made those phone calls? And the accidents?"

"Yes, of course. No, I mean I tried to scare you but he went too far."

Now the voice had become so reasonable that Christy wasn't sure if this was worse than the anger.

"Who did? Tell me, Fiona!"

Maybe the urgency in her voice alarmed the girl but she suddenly backed away until she was between Christy and the door.

"Cameron told me I had to apologise but I've said enough. I can't take any more of this…"

And before Christy could react, Fiona grabbed open the door and ran off towards the big house.

"What on earth?" Christy pulled her mobile out and dialled Ross's number. No answer. She was about to try Cameron when he came hurrying up the path.

"Christy! Are you okay?" He hugged her tight. "Thank heavens. What happened? What did Fiona tell you? She ran past me so fast, she was gone before I could catch her."

Bemused, Christy returned his hug before stepping back.

"You sent her here, knowing she's been threatening me since I arrived?"

"No, of course not. I think she's got a bit out of control."

"You *think*?" When she'd closed the door, Christy sat down. "Right, I want to know everything you know, Cameron McKinley." Fortunately, anger had taken over and she was determined to see an end to this. Starting with who Fiona was talking about and why Ross hadn't arrived yet.

"Ross sends his apologies. He has something important to do before coming to see you. I couldn't believe you'd been in such danger last night, Christy."

"As you can see, I'm very much alive, if a little sore and confused about what's going on."

Then she noticed something in his hand and a guilty frown on his face.

He didn't quite look her in the eye but held out his hand. "There's something else. I didn't want to wait any longer to give you this."

"*The Rubaiyat*? But how did you come by it... you didn't take it, did you?"

"No, of course I didn't. But I had my suspicions when Ross told me it was missing and I've only now found out that Fiona 'borrowed' it. She was going to get it valued but locked it in the cabinet and forgot about it. Then she was worried you'd seen it that day and didn't know what to do next. So, as Fiona does, she ignored it and hoped the problem would go away."

Christy shook her head. Unbelievable. "Obviously she hoped I would go away too?"

Cameron took her hands. "I swear I didn't know what was going on until last night. Fiona texted me in a panic. Something about an accident on the road home from the station." He pushed his hands through his already tousled hair, hardly able to look at her.

Christy stared in horror. "She didn't run me off the road, did she? She kept talking about 'he went too far' but who did she mean?"

He shook his head. "We can't believe she's so unhinged but somewhere inside she was beginning to feel bad about it. Especially after the incident at the bonfire."

"She was *beginning* to feel bad? So who *was* driving that car last night? Nick Anderson?"

"Anderson? What… no! He was interested in the cottage for development but nothing else, as far as I know."

"For goodness sake, tell me who it was, Cameron! Was it Fiona?"

"Well, no… not exactly. You know her cousin, Ewan. Mrs MacPherson's son?"

Christy nodded. "The big guy who runs the newsagents. What has he got to do with it?"

"Seems he was in trouble at one time and had big plans for the village if the development went ahead. He didn't take much persuading to help Fiona with the scare tactics. Except she didn't know he'd go so far as to cause you actual harm. He was the one who pushed you nearly into the bonfire and who ran you off the road. He'd picked Fiona up at the station and they noticed you getting off the same train so they followed. Then it got out of hand."

Christy shook her head in confusion. She hadn't even noticed Fiona on the train.

"Fiona freaked out when your car went in the ditch and that's why she texted me. I phoned Ross to look out for you on his way home. But she only confessed everything else to us this morning, before coming down here."

"Ewan MacPherson did all that?" Ross had been right about the man. Then a shiver went through her. "Cameron, where is Ross and why isn't *he* telling me all this?"

His guilty glance warned her in advance. "He's gone after MacPherson."

She jumped up, a sense of dread washing over her.

"We need to go and find them before Ross does something he'll regret. Or before he gets hurt."

As she grabbed a coat, she hoped they wouldn't be too late.

Chapter Thirty-Two

Ross didn't even stop to think it through once Fiona had confessed what they'd been doing to Christy. His only aim was to confront Ewan MacPherson and ensure that the threat of police would be enough to put a stop to it all. He had left Fiona to face her aunt while Cameron went to reassure Christy.

It was inconceivable that all this had been happening right under his nose and he wished he'd done more to find who was behind the scare tactics. Yet Christy herself had been unsure it was anything more than stupid pranks to make her think twice about settling in the cottage.

Until the bonfire incident, and now last night's dangerous stunt, both of which told him that MacPherson was getting out of control. He remembered the man been sent away when younger, so perhaps his efforts to change his life had not gone deep enough. As for Fiona – he had a feeling she had always been a little strange and easily led, though it sounded as though she was a good manipulator of other people when it suited her.

While the thoughts jumbled around and he tried to keep control of his rage, Ross drove straight to the newsagents but found it closed. He drove on to the house on the outskirts of the village where the man lived alone. No car in the drive. Had Fiona phoned to warn him?

Ross got out and had a look around, even knocked

on the door, but all was quiet with no sign of life. He was just turning away, when an elderly woman in the next-door house wandered out with rubbish for the bins.

She smiled across at Ross. "If you're looking for Ewan, he drove off not long ago. Seemed in a bit of a hurry. Didn't even stop to say hello."

"Did you happen to see which direction he took," Ross asked.

"Away from the town towards the loch, maybe. Is everything all right, young man? Aren't you young Ross from the big house?"

"Yes, that's right. Thank you. I'll see if I can find him later."

As he drove away, the woman stood and watched and he gave her a brief wave. No doubt nothing much happened around here and she was intrigued at the hint of urgency. He wasn't surprised she recognised him since she'd probably lived in the village since he was born.

Heading off in the direction of the loch, Ross fleetingly wondered where MacPherson was going. Snow was falling steadily now and the roads were already slippery in parts. It was only going to get worse when it iced up. Not the kind of weather to be careering about the twisting country roads.

Maybe he was worried about the police being after him, considering he'd probably had a record at one time, especially if Fiona warned him she'd confessed everything. Keeping a lookout as he drove, Ross wasn't sure what he'd do if he found him. Get some answers? Punch him for what he'd done to Christy? Maybe it would be better if he didn't find him and let the police deal with the road incident. He had a bad feeling about this and although the overnight frost topped with snow had made the narrow roads more dangerous, he sped as fast as he dared in hopefully the right direction.

He reached the edge of the loch and noticed a large vehicle parked on the grass verge near where the fireworks had been. Slowing down, he recognised the black Range Rover belonging to Ewan but there was no sign of him from the road. Only one way to find him. Parking off the road, Ross started down towards the loch.

The place was deserted which was hardly surprising. Definitely not fishing weather, and not exactly a day for a leisurely walk either. What had brought the big man down here?

A shout alerted him that Ewan Macpherson had seen him. "Stop where you are, McKinley. You're not taking me back to face the polis!"

"I only want to talk to you, Ewan. Why don't we chat over here," Ross called out, not liking the way the man was too near the edge of the icy loch.

"Aye, right. I'm sure a wee chat is all you want, is it? After what our Fiona must have told you."

"I only want to try and understand, Ewan. Why did you frighten Christy like that?"

"Because that cottage was stopping Anderson's plans for the village. I thought with the old woman finally gone, Anderson would sort it out. Then the lassie came back. And she stole you from our wee Fiona."

Ross didn't know which ridiculous accusation to address first. "The cottage doesn't even come into it, man. It's only leased to Christy and we won't be giving up that land any time soon. As for Fiona, I don't know what you're talking about. She's never been more than a friend."

He didn't even want to think about that comment about 'the old woman'. Surely Christy's grandmother had died of natural causes. Or had he hastened her death by scaring her? Before he could ask any questions, MacPherson was shouting again.

"You're lying. Fiona told me she was going to marry you after she helped Anderson steal that other woman from you. Then she knew you were falling for this one and we had to make her go back to London. But she's as stubborn as the old woman was."

Ross shook his head. How could Fiona be so delusional and he hadn't even noticed. Maybe he'd become so used to her following him around since childhood that he'd ceased to really see her as other than a semi-permanent fixture around the village and house, as well as being Cameron's assistant. But time enough to deal with Fiona later. What was he going to do about Ewan?

"I'm afraid Fiona is deluded or has been lying to you. I've never had those kinds of feelings for her or pretended we were anything but friends. Come back with me, Ewan, and we'll talk to her together." And he would find out what he meant by the comments about Christy's gran.

In the silence that followed, Ross really thought he'd got through to the man and he took a step forward. Then he heard another shout and Cameron was hurrying towards him, followed more slowly by Christy.

"Wait there," Ross called to them. But when he turned back to Ewan, the big man had already seen them and was running right on the edge of the icy water. Although not yet frozen over, it soon would be.

"Ewan!" Ross shouted. "Stay where you are! The ground's too frosty. Be careful of the loch, man."

His words were ignored as Ewan MacPherson lumbered further along the edge, glancing behind now and then. Then as Ross hurried after him as best he could on the uneven, frozen ground, he heard a splash.

Christy screamed and Cameron shouted, "Look out!"

Ross increased his speed, all the time aware of how cold and deep the water would be. "Call the police," he called back to Cameron. "Tell them someone has fallen in the loch. Get an ambulance too."

Scrambling over the final dip of grass, Ross was in time to see Ewan's head bob above the water before his large body and heavy jacket took him under. Pulling off his own jacket and shoes, Ross rushed to where he'd last seen him and waded into the freezing loch, breath catching at the shock until he was in deeper water. Ignoring the numbing cold, he struck out in a circle and even swam under a couple of times. But Ewan had disappeared into the loch's icy embrace.

"Ross. He's gone. Come out before you freeze!"

Christy's voice cut through the strange lassitude that numbed him all over and invited him to relax. Rousing himself enough to move, he pushed towards the side. Cameron hauled him out of the water and he collapsed on the snowy grass verge.

Christy put the jacket around him and held him close as she sobbed. "Please don't go to sleep, Ross. You have to stay with me!"

Cameron had been staring at the calmness of the dark, silent loch until Christy's voice reminded him his brother needed help.

"Here take my jacket as well," he told her. "Let's

get him back to the car. Maybe you can take his and I'll drive him to the house."

The far-off sound of a siren brought them up short. "Need to tell... the police what... happened," Ross said through chittering teeth.

Something else he needed to remember but he could hardly think for the numbness... oh, yes, why MacPherson had mentioned Christy's gran. But did it matter? The old lady had definitely died of pneumonia in hospital and it would only add to Christy's grief if he put any other thoughts into her head. Let the past go...

"We need to get you seen to first," Christy was saying, taking charge. "Cameron, you fill them in and tell them Ross and I will be at his house when they're ready to question us."

Cameron nodded and after retrieving the keys from his brother's jacket, he helped her to get Ross into the car. Then he waved them away while he waited for the police.

Christy could practically hear Ross shivering as she turned the engine on. Yet she knew he would rather get home than wait for an ambulance.

"Sorry... Ewan..." Ross said as he leaned back against the headrest.

"No talking," she ordered and swung the car onto the road and back towards the village.

Glancing at him now and then, she was worried at his pallor and the fact he didn't try to speak again. Drawing into the side of the road, she found her mobile and dialled the house, relieved to find a signal.

When Mrs McKinley answered, Christy told her to run a hot bath for Ross whom she was bringing home after an incident at the loch. "Should be okay, but he's chilled to the bone. I'll fill you in when I get there." She pushed the end button before she had questions she couldn't answer.

"Fiona. Mrs MacPherson... we need to tell them," Ross whispered.

"No doubt the police will soon be right behind us. We'll deal with it then," Christy said.

He didn't say another word and Christy didn't allow herself to think beyond making him safe and warm. She was not going to lose Ross McKinley now that they'd found each other. She would think about MacPherson later.

Mrs McKinley was even paler than Ross when she saw her son being supported to the door by Christy.

"Let's get him to his room. He needs to get out of these wet clothes," Christy said.

Give his mother her due, she didn't waste time asking questions. Thankfully, she had recovered well from her stroke though Christy couldn't expect her to help too much. There was no sign of Fiona or her aunt and Christy was grateful she didn't have to tell them the awful news just yet.

Ross was aware enough to keep himself upright as they climbed the stairs to his rooms and she was glad of his determination to help.

"The hot bath is ready," his mother said, the practicalities softening her obvious distress.

"Perfect," Christy said, just as the doorbell rang. "That might be the police, and Cameron should be right behind them."

I'll go and let them in." Mrs McKinley turned away. "Will you manage here yourself?"

Christy glanced at the older woman and nodded. "Keep them busy for a while until Ross is more human again before they try to question him."

She was thankful that Mrs McKinley was happy to let her take charge, even though her curiosity was as great as her anxiety for her son.

Once alone with Ross, she was pleased to see some colour coming back to his face. "We need to get you out of these wet clothes, Ross. Can you help?"

Nodding, he tried to unbutton his shirt but Christy saw at once that his fingers were so numb they were virtually useless.

"Let me." She didn't look at him as she quickly got him out of his shirt. This was *not* how she had ever pictured this scene. "Trousers next."

As she hesitated, Ross touched her hand. "It's okay, I know you're not trying… to ravish me," he quipped in a hoarse, stuttering voice. "I'll help as much as I can."

"Glad to see you're still compos mentis enough to care." Christy smiled in relief that he could joke. "I'll preserve your modesty and let you remove the boxers before you get into the bath."

The sight of his naked torso was having quite enough of an effect on her senses, though he was still too chilled to the touch for her liking and they were both trying not to dwell on what had happened to Ewan.

"Right – into the hot bath when you're ready."

"Yes, nurse. But I might need some help to warm me up first so I don't get chilblains with the extreme temperatures."

She hadn't thought of that. "Well they do say the quickest way to heat up is body contact, if you're okay with that," she suggested.

"Fine by me. Come here, Christy." He opened his arms and she snuggled against his chilled body, wrapping her arms around him and laying her hair against his cold chest.

She expected it was as much for comfort from the shock as for the heat, then he started to sound more like his usual self.

"Mm, I'm getting warmer already," Ross murmured against her ear. "I can feel the blood beginning to course again."

"I can tell," she whispered, as another part of his body reacted to the warmth and her nearness. She was glad he'd kept his boxers on for both their sakes.

"Time for that bath," he said. "You can watch if you like but I'm about to get completely naked."

"Much as I would enjoy that in other circumstances, I think I'll get you some warm clothes and find out who was at the door. I'll be back in a few minutes."

Leaving the door of his bathroom slightly ajar, Christy ran downstairs and found two policemen drinking tea in the kitchen with Mrs McKinley and Cameron.

"Ah, here's Christina now. How is Ross, my dear?"

"He's thawing out now and should be ready for your questions very soon. I'm just about to get him some warm clothes, Mrs McKinley."

"Good. I'll show you where they are." She turned to the policemen. "Finish your tea, officers, and I'll tell my eldest son to join us when he's ready."

"Is he all right?" Mrs McKinley asked as they went upstairs. "I can't believe what Cameron was telling us, and *he* evidently only arrived at the loch when you did. I'm afraid the police are going to need the details from Ross."

Tentatively, Christy touched the older woman's hand. "He's fine, really, and he did nothing wrong. It was all Ewan's fault, and Ross even tried to save him. But Fiona might have questions to answer."

"We can't find her or Effie, her aunt. I don't even know if they've heard what has happened to Ewan. What a terrible mess."

"We'll tell you as much as we know. Perhaps Fiona is at her aunt's house after her confession earlier."

"Why am I always the last person to know anything around here?"

The petulant, imperious tone was back but Christy wasn't fazed by the woman any longer. "I expect your sons don't like to worry you," she said. "I think Ross should be about ready to get dressed."

Mrs McKinley put a hand on Christy's arm, making her pause. "You're very like your grandmother, Christina. And I don't wonder that my son thinks he's in love with you. At least he is free, unlike my father."

Christy stood at the top of the stairs, shocked by the suddenness of the older woman's revelations. "So they did love each other? Your father and my grandmother?"

"Oh, I'm quite sure they did in their own way. But my father did the honourable thing and stayed with my mother and me. We were happy enough but mother always suspected she didn't have all of my father's heart. Unfortunately, *my* husband followed his own selfish desires."

Christy could imagine the years of hurt and suspicion this woman must have suffered and she briefly touched her hand. "Thank you for telling me. I never knew any of this."

"It's all in the past, but I know about the book you found in the cottage. Fiona told me. Please keep it between you and Ross now, if you will."

"Of course. It's no one else's business," Christy said. Fiona had still been trying to cause more mischief.

"Now I think we'd better make sure Ross is ready to face the policemen," Mrs McKinley said in her usual business-like manner. "Thank you for bringing him home."

Christy nodded. What a strange conversation to have in the middle of such a traumatic day, yet she appreciated the woman's honesty at last.

When she knocked on the bathroom door, Ross called out at once. "Come in if you dare, Christy. But I hope you've brought some clothes for me."

Her face heating by the second, Christy didn't dare look at Mrs McKinley. But she was surprised to hear the woman's chuckle beside her.

"I don't think he wants to see me, my dear. You take his clothes in and tell him he'd better get dressed right away as the policemen are getting impatient."

As she entered the bathroom, Christy knew from Ross's expression that he'd heard his mother's words.

"Ouch, hope you weren't too embarrassed just now," he said from the deep bathtub.

"I think your mother is more a woman of the world than we give her credit for. But she's very worried about you, Ross, and bewildered at what's been going on."

As she spoke, Christy handed the large towel to Ross and averted her eyes as he stood. This was neither the time nor place to appreciate his finer qualities.

"I'll leave the clothes on this chair and wait in the other room to make sure you can walk downstairs unaided."

"Of course I can, but your moral support would be welcome. I'm not looking forward to going over those last minutes at the loch and I expect they'll haunt me for some time."

She knew this short respite from thinking about Ewan MacPherson and all that had happened was over for a while. Ross was indeed back to normal, on the outside at least, and he took her hand as they went down to face the endless questions and piece together the answers between them.

Chapter Thirty-Three

Two weeks later, Christy stood in front of her full-length mirror and surveyed her new gown with the high heels. Not bad, considering the traumatic events since the happy day in town when she had bought it, full of anticipation for the Winter Ball.

And now it was here and everything had changed. The villagers had rallied round Mrs McKinley once news of Ewan's death had filtered through. No doubt the story had been embellished and exaggerated in the manner of Chinese Whispers, with only a certain few knowing the whole story. She had been grateful for the minister and his wife; never had she needed a friend in Eileen so much as now.

She had hated seeing Mrs MacPherson so inconsolable at her son's drowning yet the elderly woman ensured that no blame attached to Ross once she had heard the truth. Since the revelations about Fiona, she had decided to move to her sister's home in Inverness and take the girl with her.

Mrs MacPherson had insisted on speaking to Christy first.

"I canna tell you how sorry I am that my family made your time here so frightening and I can assure you I had no inkling of what they were up to, Christy dear. I hope you find lasting happiness here as your granny wanted for you."

Christy had cried as the housekeeper hugged her, before reassuring her.

"Please don't feel guilty about any of it, Mrs MacPherson. You have always been one of the kindest people I know and you gave me the warmest welcome when I returned. I hope you'll settle in Inverness. The big house won't be the same without you. And I hope Fiona finds a happy new life there."

It was true the housekeeper would be missed, but it was for the best all round. Already, Mrs McKinley had interviewed three people for the role and the villagers would soon find something else to gossip about. Besides, Christmas was almost upon them and the first performance of the pantomime would be a highlight for Kilcraig. The festive celebrations and all the preparations of the season would soon brighten everyone's lives, for a few weeks at least.

She hadn't seen Fiona again and knew her cousin's death had been enough punishment for the girl who had always felt an outsider. At least Christy wouldn't have to pretend to like her now, or worry about seeing her around the village. She truly wished for a better future for her, and at least the girl's conscience had wakened in time to stop her cousin causing any more harm.

Once she was completely dressed in her finery, Christy sat on the edge of the sofa and opened the treasured *Rubaiyat of Omar Khayyam*, glad to have it restored to her since it had been so meaningful to her gran. It was good to know that the two grandparents had formed such a strong connection yet had been strong enough to prevent their love from ruining a family.

She turned to one of the more poignant verses to read again:

One thing is certain, and the Rest is Lies;
The flower that once has blown for ever dies.

Death was one of the few certainties of life, though she would never have wished such an end for Ewan MacPherson. Whether or not he had drowned on purpose, they would never know. Then there was her beloved Gran and Michael who had both touched her life in different ways. At least she was now learning to let go of the crushing guilt she had carried around too long.

Her own future lay ahead and she hoped it might include the heir to the big house. Although they had been getting ever closer and she at least knew her heart belonged to Ross, even now she wasn't so sure about his. And tonight she would finally get to meet Moira, his ex, at last.

When the knock sounded, she put the book down before going to open the door. Cameron and Martin stood resplendent in kilts and both bowed with a lavish flourish.

"Your escorts await, my lady." Cameron grinned and kissed her on the cheek. "You look stunning, Christy, love."

"May I kiss the other cheek?" Martin asked, but didn't wait for an answer before giving her a quick kiss and a hearty hug.

"Careful, Marty," Cameron said, "don't crush the lovely dress.

"Course I won't, Cam, you know how careful I am of fashion."

Christy smiled at them both. She couldn't have asked for more delightful escorts and guessed it was as much for Martin's sake as hers when he was about to be introduced to the family and village as Cameron's loving partner. She had got over her disappointment that Ross had to stay at the house but knew it was inevitable. His mother had been immovably insistent that he must welcome the guests as the official host to Mrs McKinley's hostess while he was still single. At least she wouldn't be arriving alone and Martin should be distraction enough.

She couldn't believe how formal and festive the old house looked in its winter decking of holly and ivy and mistletoe, much as it must surely have appeared centuries ago. Fortunately, the guests were not formally announced and she was able to gaze at Ross from a distance as a few people before them stopped to shake hands.

Although she had never doubted he would suit a kilt, the full formal highland attire took her breath away. His tall stature was enhanced by the knee-length kilt in green and blue tartan with a thin red stripe running through it, presumably his family colours. One of the thick knee-high socks held a *skein dhu*, the obligatory small dagger, peeking out at the side, while the fitted black jacket moulded to his strong physique over a snowy white shirt with lace jabot at the neck and edge of the sleeves. With his dark brown hair just touching his collar at the back, he too could have graced any century from the past.

Then he looked up and their eyes locked across the short space between them. His smile widened as he held out his hand to welcome her.

"Beautiful," he whispered, as he leaned in to kiss her cheek. "I'll seek you out as soon as I can get away from my duties."

A slight cough from his mother reminded him he hadn't greeted his brother and Martin.

"Cameron, and Martin, it's great to see you both looking so happy and well. I look forward to seeing you dance later."

"You can count on it," Martin said, grinning at

such a warm welcome.

"May I present my mother, our hostess. Mother, this is Cameron's partner, Martin, and a lovelier man I have yet to meet."

"I can see where your sons get their looks," Martin said at once and Christy smiled at Mrs McKinley's expression.

Then the older woman held out her hand. "I am pleased to finally meet you at last. Perhaps you will save me a dance?"

As Martin agreed at once, Cameron raised his eyebrow at Christy while Ross winked at them both. Evidently Mrs McKinley had joined the twenty first century after all. Christy had no sooner begun to like the woman even more when a stunningly beautiful young woman arrived with an older lady.

"Ah, Moira, how lovely to see you again. Let me introduce you to Christina and Martin," Mrs McKinley said, making it sound as though they were a couple.

"This is Moira, a good friend of Ross," she said, "and her mother, Elizabeth."

Christy shook hands, as did Martin, then she watched with interest as Ross greeted the girl with a peck on the cheek. But Moira surprised her by turning back at once to Christy and taking her arm.

"You must come and tell me what it's like being back in the village after London. I don't know how you can stand it here without the city buzz."

Casting a glance at Ross and the others, Christy allowed herself to be led away. Not that she minded, since Moira was not quite what she had expected, apart from her looks.

"Mummy insisted I come with her this evening but it's horridly embarrassing for Ross since we used to be an item. It would never have worked, you know. I need the bright lights of a city while he seems content to remain in this place."

"I suppose it's just as well we're all different and eventually find the right person to suit," Christy said when she could get a word in.

"Oh, absolutely. I hear you and Ross are becoming great friends." When Christy stopped and looked at her, Moira grinned. "My mother keeps me up to date and she gets her info from the matriarch of the big house."

Christy couldn't help smiling at Moira's honesty and openness. She was the kind of woman who would always know her own mind and let no one stand in the way. She wasn't surprised she had soon seen through Nick Anderson.

"Are you staying in Kilcraig for long?" Christy asked.

"Heavens, no. I only came for a couple of days because I was in Edinburgh and Mummy was keen for me to get to the ball and to see everyone again. I'm off to Paris in a few days for a fashion shoot. I'm a make-up artist and occasional model."

Christy could believe it as she glanced at Moira's immaculate face and hair. But she liked her, much to her surprise, and was pretty sure the girl had no designs on Ross, whatever they'd had in the past.

"Here's Cameron and Martin. I'll leave you in their hands while I go and rescue whichever man Mummy has nabbed. See you later."

That set the friendly tone for the evening and Christy couldn't believe how quickly time passed by to the skirl of the pipes and twirling of kilts in one dance after another. Martin proved an excellent and boisterous dancer and he wouldn't let her sit out more than one dance at a time. Yet she had eyes only for one person. Ross seemed to have danced with every female in the room apart from her. She shouldn't complain since he was more or less like a laird of the country village and must be in high demand.

By the time supper was served in an adjoining room, Christy was dying to sit down for a good rest and a much-needed long cold drink.

"At last!" Ross sat in the vacant seat on her right and all at once the evening was complete. "Thought I'd never get the chance for a dance with you, so please keep the first for me when the band comes back."

"Of course. I'm glad to see you're so popular."

He gazed into her eyes before speaking. "Are you, Christy? I'd hoped you were pining for me by now."

"I haven't had time. I like Moira, by the way."

He raised his eyebrows. "She's a very likeable girl and I'm glad you got the chance to meet her. I think my mother has finally accepted that Moira would never have suited country life, or me. Besides, I have my eye on someone else entirely."

Christy sipped her drink, aware of his intense masculinity and the light in his grey eyes as he continued to regard her.

"Do I know her?" she asked at last.

"I think you might have met now and then. She's beautiful, intelligent, creative and brave."

"She sounds like too much of an unlikely paragon to me. Are you sure this is not a fantasy person?"

"I'll introduce you when the music starts." Ross grinned then turned to speak to the woman on his right while Christy was engaged in conversation with a shy man on her left, all the time aware of the proximity of the man she loved.

By the time the meal ended and the first notes of an Eightsome Reel sounded, most people had gravitated towards the dance floor leaving Ross and Christy together.

"Shall we dance?" Ross said standing up and holding out his hand.

Christy put her hand in his and they headed out to the ballroom. Before they reached it, Ross suddenly stopped.

"There's something I need to do first. Will you come with me? Better bring your wrap."

Intrigued, Christy nodded and was surprised when they ended up outside in the large lawns. The Scottish ceilidh music floated out to mingle with the chilly but dry night air and the stars sparkled in the black sky. Although the previous fall of snow had melted away, there was talk of it returning before Christmas and Christy looked forward to it.

Ross put his arm around her and held her close as he turned her to look back at the house and its grounds, the rest of the estate stretching almost into the hills.

"This is all I have to offer one day, my darling Christy, but there is no one I would rather share it with than you. Do you think you could imagine a life here with me and hopefully our children?"

This was not what she had expected. Turning in his arms, she gazed up into his dark eyes seeing his unreserved love expressed at last. She hugged him tight before replying. "I can't imagine a more perfect future but I would live with you anywhere, even in the cottage. Unless the development is going ahead?"

He cupped her face in his hands and kissed her deeply, awakening her own need of him. Then he finally drew back to smile at her. "You might prefer it to begin with until you get used to Mother's interference. And no, the cottage is safe. Anderson has moved on to his next scheme."

"You might find your mother has mellowed since your dramatic rescue so she may even welcome me now," Christy said. She would surprise him with his mother's revelations about the *Rubaiyat* tomorrow.

"I love you and your optimism, Christy Morrison, but nothing matters at the moment except that we are together. I can't bear the thought of losing you. Besides, I want to see our children running through these old corridors one day."

Christy could think of nothing she would love more than raising a family with Ross in Kilcraig, whether it was in a cottage or a castle. As he pulled her to him again in a lingering kiss, the door opened, letting light flood outside.

Cameron called to them. "Hey you two, enough snogging. We need you for the next Dashing White Sergeant."

"Be there in a minute, brother," Ross replied, his arms still around Christy. "I suppose we must join them or Mother will have a fit," he said when Cameron had gone.

"We have tomorrow. Right now, you are the host of the biggest ball in the county and we don't want to fuel any gossip about us," Christy said.

"Give us time, my love, and they won't be talking about anything else." Ross dropped a kiss on the back of her hands. "Let's go and face them. But we'll continue this later and I'll tell and show you all the reasons why I love you."

She could wait that long. Smiling in anticipation of loving this man in every possible way, Christy took his hand and they entered the ballroom together. The first dance of the rest of her life was about to begin and she was ready for the challenge with the man she loved by her side.

Acknowledgements and Author's Note

Huge thanks to Catriona Gordon-McMillan and Victoria Gemmell for their excellent content editing, proof-reading and suggestions.

The village of Kilcraig is entirely fictitious, as are the characters in the novel, but the setting is inspired by the lovely country villages around Renfrewshire near where I used to live. Loch Lomond, Conic Hill and Kelvingrove are real places, of course!

The Rubaiyat of Omar Khayyam, which is quoted in the novel, was translated from the original by Edward Fitzgerald and is available in many editions, including a first version of the text similar to the one I own.

Published Books

Highcrag
The Highland Lass
Return to Kilcraig
Dangerous Deceit
Midwinter Masquerade
Mischief at Mulberry Manor
Christmas Charade
Pride & Progress
Venetian Interlude

Aphrodite & Adonis Novellas
The Aphrodite Touch
The Adonis Touch
The Aphrodite Assignment

Short Story Collections
Beneath the Treetops
End of the Road
Two of a Kind

Non-Fiction Articles
Scottish People and Places

Middle Grade Children's Fiction
Summer of the Eagles
The Jigsaw Puzzle
The Pharaoh's Gold

About the Author

Rosemary Gemmell lives in central Scotland and is the author of historical and contemporary novels and tween books. She is also a prize-winning freelance writer of short stories, articles and poetry, many published in UK magazines, the USA, and online.

Rosemary is a member of the Society of Authors, the Romantic Novelists' Association and the Scottish Association of Writers. She has a Masters in Literature and History, and Diploma in European Humanities.

You can subscribe to her newsletter on the website or blog for up to date news and occasional special offers and competitions.

Printed in Great Britain
by Amazon

56467682R00163